THE GOOD SAMARITANS

Robert Banfelder

BB

~

BROADWATER BOOKS
Riverhead, New York

Broadwater Books
141 Riverside Drive
Riverhead, NY 11901
Email: broadwaterbooksinfo@gmail.com
www.robertbanfelder.com

The Library of Congress Cataloging-in-Publication Data is available on file.

ISBN: 978-09859486-6-5

Printed in the United States of America
10 9 8 7 6 5 4 3 2 1

For Donna

AUTHOR'S NOTE

The prestigious Bohemian Club, located in San Francisco, California, boasts members who are among the country's elite in the world of politics, corporate business, industry, finance and entertainment. Its annual gathering has been dubbed "The greatest men's party on the face of the earth." Every Republican president since Hoover, who in fact coined the phrase, has been a member. I have taken literary license in this fictional work to include the Bohemian Club's annual meeting as the setting for my antagonist's keynote speech.

Robert Banfelder

ACKNOWLEDGEMENT

Heartfelt thanks to Paul M. La Grasse, Corrections Office Sergeant, Firearms Training Supervisor, Suffolk County Sheriff's Department Academy Bureau (retired) for so generously spending the time answering questions regarding firearms for this work.

ALSO BY ROBERT BANFELDER

Fiction

Knots (A Justin Barnes Novel)

Trace Evidence

The Author (A Justin Barnes Novel)
"Best Suspense Novel 2007" - NewBookReviews

The Teacher (A Justin Barnes Novel)
"Best Suspense Novel 2006" - NewBookReviews

No Stranger Than I

Nonfiction

The Fishing Smart <u>Anywhere</u> Handbook for Salt Water & Fresh Water

Chapter One

Robert Redler briskly entered the corner delicatessen, stooped and grabbed a copy of *Newsday* and *Riverhead News-Review*. Marching up to the self-service counter, the writer doffed and put away his gloves, setting aside the newspapers before dispensing a squeaky Styrofoam container. Simultaneously, he tore open two small sugar packets, chuting the tiny brown crystals into the cup. Another customer entered the store, breaching its inner warmth with an icy stillness that pervaded the bitter cold, dark March morning. He grabbed and paid for a paper, placing change upon the front counter.

Adding a splash of half-and-half then filling the rest of the container from a freshly brewed pot of rich Columbian coffee, Redler whirred the piping hot liquid with a wooden stirrer before affixing a lid securely, stepping across the aisle with Monday's papers.

"Good morning, Rob," the store owner greeted the man warmly. "Cold enough for you?"

"Morning, Steve."

"You're up very early."

"Liza and I are going to try for some flounder over at Shinnecock in a little while."

"Well, good luck. Better bundle up, though. That be it?"

"Nope. You can fix us up a Shelly's Deli Super-Duper Italian Hero; nice and wet with extra oil and vinegar, sweet peppers; please and thank you. Cut and wrap me up the largest half," he half-kidded, lifting the plastic tab and taking a sip of coffee.

Steve grinned. "How's she enjoying retirement?"

"Don't know. Sleeps too late to assess the situation," Robert answered jokingly through a yawn.

"Well, I think she's entitled," the man said decidedly, walking over to the cold cuts section and placing a log of Genoa salami upon one slicer, a block of cheese on another.

Two men entered the store.

Robert Redler reached into his jacket pocket and withdrew a crumpled twenty.

"You can hand that over," one of the men demanded, snatching the bill from Redler's hand. "Wallet too, chump."

The other man leveled a pistol at Steve's face. "Move fool," the gunman raved, gesturing toward the rear of the store. Steve scooted clumsily along the counter, heading for the kitchen.

"I *said* the wallet, asshole," the thickset, muscular man commanded, sticking his face before Redler's. "Give it up."

Robert reached into his right front pants pocket and gave his wallet to the man.

The gunman, tall and willowy, passed behind his partner and met Steve at the far end of the counter. "Stand right there, chump," the robber ordered, stepping around and behind the counter, opening the register, grabbing the cash before grabbing Steve and pushing him into the kitchen, out of Robert Redler's sight.

"Please, tell him not to hurt him—please," Robert pleaded.

"Shut your face," the stocky man snapped. "My man's jus' gonna help hisself to the weekend's *re·ceipts* that Mr. Deli-man had no time to deposit and keeps stowed in back and better find fucking fast, 'cause if he don't—"

A moment later, Steve and the robber returned from the kitchen, the latter bearing a wide grin and carrying a five-pound coffee can, mumbling excitedly and jokingly . . . something about Prince Albert in a can.

In the next instant, the solidly built buck wore the entire contents of Redler's own container, hot liquid scalding the shocked black man's face. Over his broad shoulder a shot sounded, and the wiry soul fell back hard against a wall, the noise of the coffee can bouncing then rolling in a semi-circle along the green tile floor as a second bullet caught the well-built bull in the throat.

Steve trembled and watched in amazement as Robert Redler retired his weapon, donned his gloves, retrieved the twenty from the floor along with his wallet and two spent cartridges. He then went back over to the self-service counter and, with a damp napkin, wiped the handle of the coffee pot from which he had poured. Next, he draped a scarf about his head like a hood, simulating the dark hooded sweatshirt worn beneath the bloody brown leather bomber jacket that the man lying nearest him sported, raising the collar of his own coat like the bandits'.

"Listen to me, Steve," Robert said quickly but calmly, reaching down and stuffing the empty Styrofoam cup and its lid into his coat pocket. "Their getaway car is waiting just outside the door to the right. If I get away, you tell the police what happened here—less the fact of who you saw. All right? And put those newspapers back for me—middle of the pile." The good Samaritan was already at the threshold.

Standing trance-like, Steve Quick suddenly nodded, then immediately shook his head. "Don't go out there, Rob! Don't—"

Robert Redler stepped out into the darkness and disappeared, swallowed up by the inky predawn.

Headlights lit and hit the parking area adjacent to the building along East Main Street. The vehicle flew forward toward the stooped figure rushing toward the car.

"Where's Moses?" the driver demanded as Redler pulled open the passenger door and jumped onto the front seat. "What happened to Moses, man?"

Robert Redler pulled away the scarf. "Moses, just like you, is dead along with his accomplice," he answered straightaway.

The stunned wheelman hit the accelerator before two bullets cracked open the right side of his cranium.

Within sixty some seconds of the first shot fired at Shelly's Deli in Riverhead, gateway to the North Fork of Long Island, three pieces of garbage lay ready for Monday morning's pickup, Robert Redler thought rather satisfactorily as he fled the scene in his car.

Chapter Two

It was a good hour and a half before Robert Redler returned home. Liza Downs greeted him anxiously at the back door. The look on her domestic partner's face alerted Liza as to the gravity of the situation.

"What happened, Rob?"

"Guess I'm going to have to find another place to pick up coffee and the morning papers for a while," he offered, forcing a smile.

"I heard sirens down the block."

Robert nodded. "The deli was almost robbed."

"Oh, my God. Steve and Shelly all right?"

"Shelly wasn't working. Steve's fine. Shook up is all, I guess."

"You guess?"

"I didn't hang around to ask questions."

Liza collected her thoughts. "So then where were you? I've been up for the past hour."

"Cleaning up."

"Cleaning up what? Where?"

"The gun club. Clothes. The car. The—"

"What are you talking about?"

"I took them out at close range."

Liza stood transfixed.

"Two guys came into the store while I was getting the papers and coffee. One pulled a gun."

"Jesus Christ, Rob!"

"He took Steve in the back—"

"You shot them both?" Liza asked incredulously.

"Yes."

"Dead?"

"As in coffin nails."

"But . . . I don't understand. It was self-defense, yes?" Liza closed and locked the back door off the vestibule. "No? Well, what? Why did you have to go to the club to clean up?"

"We have sportsman pistol licenses, Liza," he hedged.

"Yes, to carry. They're *carry* types."

"To the range and back."

Liza was shaking her head emphatically. "We've been through this with the sheriff's office, Rob. We've researched this thoroughly. You can carry on your person to protect the other handguns we take to the range for target practice. You can't go out to dinner with your piece, but you can certainly carry into Shelly's Deli to grab a cup of coffee on the way there or back, or even a 7-Eleven for crying out loud."

"But we were on our way to go flounder fishing whenever you decided to get up, goddamn it! Not the range, which doesn't even open till nine. I can also carry a weapon to hunt in the woods upstate, not the third piece of garbage who was sitting behind the wheel of the getaway car," Robert came clean.

"You shot another person, too?!"

Robert nodded.

"Was he armed?"

"Don't know."

"What do you mean you don't know?"

"Just what I said. I went outside and the car pulled up. I opened the passenger door and got in and put two bullets in his brain."

"Good God, Rob! Why?"

"Why? Because Monday is garbage pick-up day, and I thought I'd do the town and county a favor!" he blew. "Besides, the Suffolk County lab boys, not unlike sanitation, won't have to go much further than the curb. As a matter of fact, the driver of the car *is* curbside."

Liza's mind was reeling. "What's Steve going to tell the police, pray tell?"

"Exactly what happened, omitting the fact that I was the customer who opened fire."

"You hope."

"He's cool."

"We're talking murder here, Rob."

"I don't exactly see it that way."

"It really doesn't matter what you *see*, you well know. It's what the law of the land *is*," she gave back. "Who knows that any better than you, Rob? Tell me."

"What would you have done? You tell me."

"I probably would have taken out the one with the gun who robbed the deli."

"Tried to rob the deli," Robert made clear.

"Provided I had the perfect opportunity and didn't put Steve or anyone else in harm's way. I would *not* have gone outside the store and taken out the driver. But if I had, I'd have shot him through the window—not gotten into the goddamn car."

Robert Redler nodded numbly.

"So why did you, Rob?"

"I guess because I had the perfect opportunity," Robert stated flatly.

Chapter Three

Robert Redler and Liza Downs sat beside one another in the living room. Although still cold outside, the temperature was climbing steadily. Blue porcelain coffee cups inscribed with the name of their boat, *Write On*, rested on decorative napkins along the edge of an Old Salem design cocktail table in American cherry. It was used for and lent itself perfectly as the couple's chart table. Partially open blinds facing east let in the first rays of Monday morning's sunlight.

"Let me see if I understand this CoDIS business," Liza brayed. "The police can't—"

"Not CoDIS. CoBIS: Combined Ballistics Identification System," Robert corrected. "They can't check ballistics because I first ordered the frame and then the barrels for the gun. Got it?"

"Not entirely, but—"

"But what?" Robert barked.

"You yourself said—"

"Said what?" he snapped.

"Said that other marks such as the firing pin make—"

"I don't know exactly. All right?"

"No, it's not all right."

"Look. What I do know is that they can't match the bullets to the barrel unless the barrel was CoBISed, which it wasn't."

"But they can match other markings to the frame if they have an empty cartridge. Correct?"

"But they have to have the gun. Okay?"

"Nothing's okay. Did you collect *all* the cartridges? No. You told me you took two off the floor in the deli. Not the other two in the car."

Robert Banfelder

"It was dark. There wasn't time."

"So if Steve gives you up, they've as good as got the gun unless you dump it."

"He won't say anything. And if I dump it, I'd be wise to report it as stolen."

"Now there's an idea, Sherlock."

"If I report the gun stolen, especially now, it's a red flag. And if Steve does roll over on me, what's the fucking difference?"

"Maybe if you tell the truth, now, it'll make a difference."

"Yeah, maybe the difference between twenty years and ten. No thank you."

"Then you tell the truth up until the point you left the store. Steve didn't see anything after that, you said. As you went out, the driver pulled up and put a gun to your head, or what you thought was a gun, and demanded that you get in."

"Why would he do that?"

"Then you shot him in self-defense."

"I said why would he do that?"

"Do what?"

"Tell me to get in the car."

"I don't know. A hostage!" the retired school teacher blurted out excitedly. "He needed you as a hostage. What the hell does it matter anyhow? He's dead. They can't get into his head to contradict your story seeing as how you blew his skull wide open," she snipped ruefully. "Why didn't you just grab those two casings or go back into the store and wait for the police? They wouldn't have made a federal case out of it."

"Maybe yes, and maybe no. You never really know. I told you, I don't know whether or not he had a gun."

"He had a goddamn finger in his pocket, you tell them. A ballpoint pen for all anyone would care. Your life was threatened and you had the means to take him down and you did. End of story. But as the police investigate and time goes by, you'll only make things worse for yourself. They have those two shell casings from the car, and that's going to come back and bite you in the ass, Rob. Mark my words."

"Once again, Ms. Omniscience, they can't match the casings or the bullets to a gun they don't have. The barrel was never CoBISed. There's no record. So there's no reason for the police to come looking

16

here to match any other markings that may or may not be forged on the frame."

"Not unless Steve points them in this direction."

"There's no reason for him to do that."

"Maybe not intentionally. But just suppose he tells someone he trusts who tells someone else and the police eventually do find out. It's a small world out here on the East End."

"Who's he going to tell?"

"Shelly, for one. Perhaps in confidence. I'd give that a week before the whole town knows."

"I thought you like Shelly?"

"I love Shelly. And Shelly loves her boyfriend. And her boyfriend loves to drink. Wake up, Rob."

Robert was staring blankly out the back window at the Peconic River.

"Hellooo," Liza said with a leer.

"Tell you what."

"Tell me."

"We'll dump the barrel in the Sound. When we're at the gun show, we'll pick up and replace the firing pin and maybe another part or two. How does that sound to you?"

"Like an accessory after the fact."

"I'm serious."

"This *is* serious."

"We'll go through Plum Gut and drop the barrel in a hundred sixty-five feet of water, halfway across the Sound. That's three and a half nautical miles out."

"Well, there may not be a ballistics record, Rob. But what about a purchase order for that barrel? Did you stop to think about that?"

"That's the one I picked up at a yard sale in Vermont. No purchase record, period. All the other interchangeable barrels are legal and listed collectively as MULTI on my pistol license. But not the one I paid cash for in the backwoods of the White Mountains. As a matter of fact, none of those barrels are CoBISed."

"You're kidding."

"Not a single one. Makes little sense, I know. But when you buy the frame and barrels separately, that's how it works. At least it is with my weapon. But when you buy the entire piece, the frame is registered, and the barrel is CoBISed."

"You would think law enforcement would want a ballistics record of every single barrel manufactured."

"They probably would."

"Then why don't they?"

"Matter of practicality. You have to understand that some owners, especially collectors, purchase numerous barrels in a variety of calibers for each of the scores of handguns they own. Do the math. The numbers are staggering. Instead of a person carrying a license in their wallet, they'd need a billboard on their back. It's simpler just to list MULTI on the license in lieu of the sheriff's office having to log each and every barrel for each and every handgun. Saves the hunter in the field a headache, too."

"How do you mean?"

"Well, picture this scenario. A guy starts out by buying one complete target handgun in a small caliber and later decides to purchase additional barrels in larger calibers: one for varmint, and still a larger caliber for deer hunting. Keep in mind that the frame and barrel for the initial purchase is on his license, not those additional barrels. Now, say one day he decides to go deer hunting upstate. He removes his small caliber barrel and replaces it with the largest of the three for big game, as all the barrels are interchangeable. With me so far?"

"Yep."

"He's in the woods and is approached by a conservation officer who asks to see his pistol license. The recorded caliber on his license does not, of course, match the high caliber barrel he's carrying. Guess what? It's been known to happen that hunters such as these have been hauled off to the hoosegow and worse. Same thing can happen if a state trooper pulls you over and discovers that you have a different caliber barrel than what's on your license. So the way around this problem is that folks first buy and have only the frame of the weapon registered, and then go out and purchase all the additional barrels they want for that one particular handgun. The barrels are recorded but not CoBISed. MULTI goes on their license, covering the first barrel to the last."

"That's nuts. It leaves all sorts of wiggle room for all kinds of shenanigans, which you don't have to be a genius to figure out."

"And that's what I'm trying to do at this precise moment—wiggle out of this mess as best I can."

"Why did you have to shoot the driver, Rob?"

"I told you. He was garbage like the other two. And to tell you the truth, I'd have still left the scene if the driver had simply sped away."

"But why?"

Robert looked at Liza for a long moment before he answered. "After what we've been through with the law, Liza, I'm surprised you can even ask me that."

"Exactly my point: the law, defense attorneys, prosecutors, judges, the police, the cult, the whole damn lot of them. I don't want any more trouble, Rob. I'm tired."

"I don't go out looking for trouble, Liza. Trouble has a way of finding me. And I'm tired of that. Hear what I'm saying?"

Liza stared down at the carpeting, not knowing what else to say to him.

Chapter Four

Steve Quick quickly made a three-foot-long Italian hero for the homicide detectives as well as the forensic team that filled his store. Nervous by nature, Steve was still petrified by what had happened six hours earlier. Lengths of yellow tape cordoned off a perimeter from curbside to the entrance leading to the building. All three bodies had been removed, but surely not the vivid memory of early morning, which played like continuous footage of some B-movie thriller in Steve's mind. Over and over it ran. Steve concentrated mightily on the description and details of the shooter he had created and given to the police.

"Let's go over a few things that I'm having a little trouble understanding," Detective Victor Posteraro pressed the deli owner.

"Yes, sir," Steve said anxiously.

"You described the shooter's handgun as having pearl handles or grips."

"Yes, sir. Something like on those six-shooters you see in Westerns."

"And you told Detective Archer that the shooter's hands were rather large."

"Yes, sir. Fat fingers with a series of silver rings."

"And that at no time did you see the shooter actually draw his weapon or put it away."

"Yes, sir. I mean, no sir. I did not. Everything happened so fast."

"You said he held the gun with two hands. The left hand wrapped around the grip like this." Detective Posteraro simulated a handgun in his left hand. "The right hand supporting the base of the gun, like so.”

“Yes, sir. In a classic combat shooting stance.”

“And even when he walked out of your store, he was holding the gun like this.”

“But down.”

“Like this?”

“Yes.”

“You told the responding police officer that the gun practically fit into the palm of the shooter’s hand.”

“Yes, sir.”

“And you’re sure the gun was in his left hand.”

“Yes.”

Victor glanced over at his partner. Brian Archer raised his eyes in doubt toward the ceiling and shook his head.

“What?” Steve swallowed hard.

“Well, to tell you the truth, Steve— Oh, by the way, you are telling us the truth; am I right on that count?”

“Of course. Why wouldn’t I be?”

“Oh, for a myriad of reasons, I suppose. Like trying to protect someone.”

“I told you guys. I never saw the guy before. I’d remember him. Believe me. He had these distinguishing features.”

“Yeah, that would fit a rather large yet somehow frail, loudmouthed, soft-spoken gentleman truck driver,” Detective Gary York snapped and laughed truculently. “You’re a man of many contradictions, Steve Quick. Quick is what you are behind the counter, I’m told. Quick is what you were at your deli in Arizona before you came to Riverhead. A man of above average IQ. Well above. Not too intelligent today, though, I’m afraid, Steve. Today you’re acting stupid with the emphasis on the word acting. Let’s see here.” Gary pulled a sheet of paper from his coat pocket. “Speedo’s Deli before you changed the name to Shelly’s Deli. Nice ring to it. Good for business, I suppose. Everybody loves Shelly. That’s good, because she may have to run things here for you for a spell.”

“What are you talking about?”

“Making false statements, which translates into perjury in a court of law.”

“What is he talking about?” the owner asked defensively of

Detectives Posteraro and Archer.

Detective Posteraro took Steve Quick aside.

"Look, not much of what you're telling us adds up, Steve. Not when it comes to the shooter. For openers, we believe the man was right handed."

"All right, I could have been mistaken. Okay? Everything happened so fast."

"Including putting together your flimsy story. It just doesn't wash, Steve. For instance, how could you see the pearl handles of a small caliber handgun you described in great detail while wrapped the whole time in the shooter's fists, from the time you were led out of the kitchen until the time your customer left the store?"

Steve flinched. "He's not my customer."

"You see how defensive you are about that word, *customer*? Of course he was your customer. The question is was he a *regular* customer that you recognized, Steve? You said he poured himself a cup of coffee over there, which you forgot to tell us about until you were reminded of another mess besides the bloody one. And where'd that Styrofoam cup and lid disappear to? Huh? Poured himself a second cup before he left?" Posteraro questioned with a smirk. "And how come there are no fingerprints whatsoever on any of those coffeepot handles? Not even yours."

"I don't know. I guess he had his gloves on at that point. Maybe he wiped them clean. And maybe he filled his own cup or thermos. I keep telling you, everything happened so fast."

"Steve. You either did or didn't see those handgun grips. The question is did you physically see the handles in his hands or in your head?" he asked patiently. "At first you said 'a rather long barrel gun with mother-of-pearl grips wrapped tightly in two fists.' How could you see those handles?"

"Wait. I just remembered something."

Victor Posteraro waited.

"He pulled a scarf from around his neck and put it over his head before he ran out. That's when I must have seen the pearl handled revolver."

Detective Posteraro smiled. "A revolver is it now?"

"I think so. Everything—"

"I know. Everything happened so fast."

"Well, it did."

Detective York stepped from behind the counter with a section of hero sandwich and a lump of potato salad on a paper plate.

"Why do you suppose he did that, Steve? Put a scarf over his head?" York chewed upon the question.

Steve shrugged.

"Wouldn't be because it resembled a hooded sweatshirt like the one the guy this side of the counter wore, would it?"

Steve realized his mistake. "Cold outside," he said sillily. "Maybe he didn't want to be recognized by anyone," he recouped.

"Like the driver of the getaway car," Detective Archer postulated. "We know the creep was shot at point-blank range. Maybe it was self-defense. The customer exited your store. You said the car roared up."

"Was he armed?" Steve asked then waited for their silence to end.

"Look at me, Steve," Posteraro bade. "I said look at me."

Steve looked.

"We're not out to persecute this guy. He probably did us all a favor. But we do have a job to do. I'm sure you understand that."

Steve nodded.

"Anything you can tell us to help us help him?"

Steve shook his head. "I told you everything. I never saw the guy before. Never saw any of them."

Detective Gary York walked up to the deli owner. The cop chomped on his sandwich as he spoke. "Anything further you care to tell us to help us help *you*?"

Steve choked. "I told you everything there is to tell."

"Not everything. What color was the scarf? Let's see how you're gonna twist this one around."

"Brown."

"Solid or plaid?"

"Solid."

"Shade?"

"Light brown. Camel."

"One hump or two?" York said with a sneer.

"Very funny."

"Fabric?"

"Soft, like cashmere."

"Fringe or clean edge?"

"Fringes. Definitely fringes."

"Know what I think?"

Steve shook his head and really didn't care.

"Damn good sandwich and potato salad," the detective declared, reaching inside his coat pocket and withdrawing a clear plastic evidence bag.

Steve stared blankly at the checkered gray-black silk scarf displayed within the transparent window.

"We found it on the ground near the victim's vehicle. Note the machine-sewn edge. You even called that one wrong for us, buddy. At this point, I'd have to say that you're deliberately trying to impede our investigation. What would you say, Steve?"

Steve said nothing.

"Vic?"

"That's the way I see it."

"Brian?"

"Ditto, I'm afraid."

"Shelly has keys to this place, you said?"

Steve nodded.

"Good. No reason why she can't open up for you tomorrow. You guys done?" York called over to a member of the forensic team.

"Done with everything here but lunch," the man answered with a mouthful.

"I want to call a lawyer," Steve decided out of desperation.

"You can do that from Yaphank," Detective Archer said coldly.

"Oh, by the way, Steve. You said earlier that the shooter had dark, wavy hair. We found strands of straight dirty-blond hair on the scarf that doesn't match the victim's in the car. Just thought I'd mention that," Detective York added for good measure.

"I think if we just inverted everything Steve told us, we'd have a pretty good description of our mystery shooter," Posteraro offered. "What do you think, Brian?"

"I'd say so."

"Gary?"

"What was that?" Gary York asked, stepping back up to the counter.

24

"I said, what do you think?" Vic repeated.

"Said it before. Great cold cuts and salad." He turned abruptly to the owner. "Think we can get some of this grub to go, Steve? Might want to take something for yourself, too. Not that we wouldn't feed you tonight. It's just that this stuff doesn't compare to the crap we order in," the lanky detective said decidedly with a wide grin.

Chapter Five

"**D**id you see my scarf?" Robert asked Liza.

"The silk one?"

"Yes, the silk one. The only one."

"That's not true. You have several in a box at the top of the closet last I looked."

"It's the only one I wear."

"Then say what you mean, grouchy."

"Fuck!"

"What's your problem?"

"My problem is I think I lost my scarf."

"When?"

"Yesterday."

"Yesterday, when?"

"When I came home from the club."

"Christ, did you leave it there?"

Robert pawed his face with one hand and pulled at the back of his neck with the other, passing along the hallway toward the front closet. "Did you wash the coat like I asked?"

"Of course I washed the coat."

"Anything in the sleeves?"

"No."

"How do you know?"

"Because I turned the coat inside out to wash it twice. That's how I know. Next question," she snapped with a scowl, firmly folding her arms across her chest.

Robert rummaged through the closet. "Damn."

"Did you leave it in the car?"

"No, I just looked."

"In the trunk?"

He shook his head.

"You probably left it at the club."

"I don't think so."

"Well, I think you better go check."

"No, I'm positive." Robert raked a set of impatient fingers through his hair. "Shit."

"What?"

"I think I left it in the car."

"I just asked you that."

"Not *our* fucking car. *The* fucking car," he quailed, roughly sliding a row of winter coats on plastic hangers along a horizontal pole. "The getaway driver's car."

"Mother of God!"

"Did you ever wash or iron that scarf?"

"Not that one."

"Why?"

"Why? Because there is silk you can wash and silk that has to be dry-cleaned. That's why."

"Did we ever have it dry-cleaned?"

"Not that I recall. No. I'm almost positive."

"How about a label? Recall what it says?"

"Probably, '100% silk. Dry Clean Only.' Otherwise I would have washed it by now. The others are a hundred percent wool but can be washed in Woolite. They're all cleaned and ironed, but you never wear them like you had said."

"Where did I get it? I can't recall."

"Flea market, I think. Yes. Back in Queens. Roosevelt Field. You know how your throat closes up when you hit the cold. You wanted something super warm around your neck for when it's really frigid, always complaining that the wool scarves itch your neck. I guess you grabbed it yesterday because you insist on wearing something light like your field coat I just washed. If you're questioning whether or not they can trace it back to you, I don't think so. But you better start being careful. I'd double-check the club if I were you. And I'd do it now."

Robert grabbed a warm coat out of the closet then headed back down the hallway to the kitchen. He took his keys off a counter and opened the back door leading to the vestibule.

"Want me to come with you?"

"Maybe you'd better. You can look around inconspicuously while I shoot the breeze with some of the other members. Better you find it than they see me hunting high and low."

Rob and Liza drove to the Peconic River Sportsman's Club in Manorville, having returned empty-handed.

Chapter Six

Sam Carper kissed his pretty wife good-bye and headed out the front door of their split-level home in East Marion, Long Island. He would be gone for at least a fortnight, promoting a new product line for his hidden interest in a company headquartered in Maryland.

Sam walked briskly backwards toward his vehicle parked in the driveway, blowing and throwing Karen and their two young daughters a series of kisses as he made his way agilely toward the van, the four of them exchanging tiny to exuberant waves and affections.

Karen pushed open the storm door and immediately pulled up the collar of her housecoat, stepping out and onto the stoop.

Sam made a semicircle with an index finger, ordering her back inside. "Too cold out here," he said and shivered with exaggeration. "You'll catch your death. Go on now. I'll be back before you know it," he assured her with a tentative smile.

Karen stayed put while his younger daughter wiped away a tear or two then blew her father a final kiss from behind the closing glass door.

Sam wasn't thirty minutes south of Philadelphia when he abruptly pulled off Interstate 95 and quickly set up shop.

Janet Phillips and her nine-year-old son, Billy, were coming out of a shopping center and heading toward their car when a bullet from a .22-250 Remington cartridge stopped the boy dead in his tracks.

At first the mother thought a firecracker had sounded and frightened her son as he suddenly jerked sideways and out of her grip. As she turned toward him, a pool of blood was streaming down the side of his face. Before Janet could bring a hand to her mouth and the other to her child, the boy slumped upon the pavement in the parking lot.

Sam Carper quickly reloaded his single shot, variable scoped Thompson/Center Encore pistol with another round. Benching the weapon for support on a wooden platform at the rear of the van, he meticulously set the cross hairs upon the woman's head as she knelt screaming beside her boy. The gunman touched off a second round with the sound of breath leaving his body and that of the woman's some thirty yards away. Janet Phillips dropped atop her son.

Closing the back doors to the van from within, Sam ducked and scuttled forward toward the driver's seat.

A couple entering the parking lot from the north stopped their vehicle several yards short of the bodies, staring down in disbelief at the surrealistic noonday scene. Neither of them saw the blue van exit quietly to the south, behind a narrow boundary of barren hedges.

"I know I've got a long way to go to play catch-up, M&M," the serial killer said with a chuckle at the irony, popping several of the multicolored candies into his mouth. "But I can assure you both that I'll far surpass your numbers, guys," Sam assured himself rather satisfactorily, adjusting the rearview mirror a fraction of an inch. "Mohammad and Malvo. Malvo and Mohammad. Had to go and get yourselves caught, fellas. Well, it was a good run while it lasted, but you got careless. Me? I'm gonna live to a ripe old age and take scores of secrets to the grave. Just wait and see. Yeah. Just you wait and see. Sammy's a very bad dude, boys. B-A-D," he spelled deliberately.

The man let the spent cartridges rest precisely where they lay.

Chapter Seven

Steve Quick raised then quickly lowered his head the moment Robert Redler entered the deli. Robert picked up a copy of *Newsday*, opened it, and sadly shook his head.

"Sick bastard or bastards out there, Steve. Mother and son shot to death like that. And now a mail person."

"I didn't give you up," Steve whispered, even though there was no one present in the store. "It wasn't easy, and they know I'm lying through my teeth. But I'll tell you one thing. Good customer or not. If I had a family, I might have told the police it was you. They're in here every few days with another question. I had to go with them to headquarters in Yaphank after you left. Know what that was like? I got home at midnight."

"They say anything about a scarf?"

"Of course they said something about your scarf. You dropped it by the car. I didn't catch on at first what you were doing when you went out of here, draping it over your head like a babushka. I thought you didn't want to be recognized by anyone is all. Not that you were masquerading as one of the thugs you shot. Why did you do that, Rob?"

"Suppose he blamed *you* for the death of his two accomplices, Steve? Suppose he came back into this store one day and put a gun in your face and blew you away? Suppose he went to another deli with other friends someday and robbed and hurt someone? Well, now you don't have to suppose. The hoodlum's where he belongs."

"You should have waited for the police. I don't really know what happened out there, and I don't want to know."

"That's right, you don't."

"You just should have waited for the police," he repeated. "Even if you don't have a pistol permit."

"License," Robert said.

"Even if you don't have a license."

"But I do, Steve." Robert opened his trifold and displayed his pistol license. "See? Make you feel any better?"

"No," the deli man stated flatly. "It's even more reason why you should have let the police handle this whole business. Not go out there looking for trouble."

"Is that what you think, Steve?"

Steve raised his eyes to the ceiling. "I don't know what to think anymore. All I know is that I've got a business to run. All right?"

"Maybe I shouldn't have shot those other two creeps either. Yes? No? Maybe? Maybe I should have let them take the money and go. Is that what you've been saying to yourself for the past week?"

"Maybe. I don't know. I'm insured, Rob. How much did you have on *you*? Fifty or hundred dollars tops? Was it worth it? You tell me."

"Well, maybe I can get you to rethink that scenario, and then you decide. I've been doing a little research on those three creeps. A description of the first two I sent south fits the description of two men who shot to death a gas station attendant in Queens last month, who incidentally turned over the money to them without a question or an argument. A customer hiding in a backroom saw and heard everything. The getaway car fits the description of the car used in last week's attempt. Police share any of that with you, Steve? Of course they didn't."

"How do you know that?"

"How do I know that? I'm an investigative reporter/freelance writer. That's how. I research crime stories and write about our criminal justice system, most often in a very negative vein."

"I thought you wrote novels."

"I do. My nonfiction becomes fodder for those books."

"Did you know about those two—that it was them—I mean before they came in here? I'll bet not."

Robert smiled sadly. "Let me ask you something, Steve. Does it really matter? Two guys came in here and one of them stuck a gun in our faces. We didn't have crystal balls to peer into to know their full intent. I looked into their eyes, along with the driver's. All three pairs of eyes. And I made a snap decision, if you'll pardon the awful pun."

Steve thought for a moment then nodded, and Robert had the feeling that the owner perhaps now understood.

A heavyset black woman walked into the store, and the two men went about their business. Robert went over to the coffee counter with his newspaper and fixed himself a fresh cup of Columbian. Steve made small talk with the lady before taking her breakfast order.

Chapter Eight

Mac Pace, a.k.a Sam Carper, put his newspaper down alongside his coffee cup. His happy wife smiled across the kitchen table with loving lovely eyes. He reached out and took her delicate hands into his.

"Good to have you back for a while," she sighed contentedly. "How long can you stay?"

"Couple of weeks. Month at the most. But believe you me, Rebecca, we're going to make the most of it. We're going to eat out every night. Fancy and plain. Maryland crab cakes for openers, which I positively miss as much as you, my darling," he both swore and winked. "I don't want you lifting a finger. We're going to movies and shows. Walks on the beach. That is, if it ever warms up around here," he promised her.

Rebecca was slowly shaking her head and smiling. "No we're not. We're eating in. I've been planning meals that are going to bowl you over. Just you wait and see, dear. And we're going to watch movies and shows at home on our new big screen TV. You haven't even seen one single program yet. I know how you love *The Sopranos*. Well, I have a little surprise for you. We have all of last season on tape. Nancy brought them over when she heard you might be coming home. And with our new system, we can tape our own shows; that is, once I learn how to work the program when you're gone again," she added with a heavy sigh. "And as far as walks on the beach go, I think we'll save that for late spring or early summer if you're around. No, Mr. Pace. You're not going anywhere for a while except right here with me. I won't share you for a second with a waitress, waiter, maître d' or a ticket taker. Not even a single seagull for that matter. Selfish is what

I am."

Mac couldn't help but smile. "Well, the name Rebecca does mean binding," he surrendered merrily.

Rebecca giggled like a schoolgirl. "Yes it does, Mac. Indeed it does, my dear."

Mac raised his cup of coffee to her then lowered his eyes to the paper.

Rebecca suddenly turned quite serious. "Mac?"

Mac looked up.

"Is this terrorist business ever going to go away?"

The forty-three-year old shook his head. "I'm afraid it's going to get a lot worse before it ever gets better, Rebecca."

"That's what I thought," she said so sadly. "Can you tell me anything at all about Long Island? Was it or is it a potential target?"

The gainly figure summoned his attractive wife forward with a crooked finger.

Rebecca went to him as he shifted his chair back and to the side. He had her sit upon his lap.

"You know I can't talk about these things. True?"

Rebecca nodded.

"But I don't want you ever to worry your pretty little head. You're safe here in this house. You're safe here in this town. If I didn't think so, I'd have us relocated in a heartbeat. Hear what I'm saying?"

Rebecca moved her head up and down a millimeter.

"I don't think you are," he concluded, gently bouncing her on his knee.

"I worry about you out there, Mac. I really and truly do. I don't want to lose you. I wouldn't be able to stand it if anything happened to you."

"Nothing is going to happen to me. Know why?"

Rebecca shook her head of curls.

"Because I'm going to live to a ripe old age. Know how I know?"

Rebecca shook her head again.

"Because I see you standing next to me in long white hair and a hobbling cane, handing out orders."

"Hobbling cane? Long white hair?" she tittered.

Her husband nodded firmly.

"How horrible! And *what* orders?"

"Marching orders."

"Marching orders?"

"Yep."

"What marching orders?"

"Your marching orders. Telling me to retire. To leave the congregation once and for all. To come home to stay. Permanently. To lie and die in my own bed. Explaining to me, for the hundredth time, that I had paid my dues."

"Pretty morose picture you're painting there, Mac Pace."

"It's how I envision it."

"Really?"

"Really."

"And what will we be doing, exactly, in the autumn of our years?"

"Finally eating out in fine and ordinary restaurants, going to movies and shows, and taking long walks on the beach."

"Long walks with a hobbling cane?"

"I'm going to carry you across the sand and along the stretch of beach, your long white hair flowing and blowing in the wind."

"And what about *The Sopranos*?"

"Be serious, Rebecca. They'll all be dead," he said so seriously

"Then we'll watch reruns," she decided merrily, kissing him fondly upon an unshaven cheek, gently scratching and stroking the other affectionately. "Homebody that I know you truly are."

"Are you calling me a closet stay-at-home?"

"A classic case of a shut-in."

"Oh, yeah?"

"Yeah, an old stick-in-the-mud. That is, whenever you're home long enough to call you that."

"An old fogy before my time."

"I know you love staying home once you are home, Mac. So we don't have to paint the town fantastic. It's all right, really. I told you a moment ago, and I mean it. I don't want to share you with anyone."

"How about Nancy and Danny?"

"Those two know we need our space, but we do have to have them over for dinner at least once, you know. And they'll want to reciprocate."

"How are they doing?"

"Great. They try to be a big help when you're away."

"They're nosy."

"I know. But they're okay."

"They still ask a lot of questions?"

"Not since I told them you worked for the government. We just left it at that. They never bought the traveling salesman story. Danny said he knew early on that you couldn't sell a life preserver to a drowning man."

The two laughed hysterically.

"Is that what he said?"

"That's what he said. Should I shoot him now or simply suffocate him after you leave?" Her laughter degenerated to a giggle then finally a prolonged sigh.

"But I am a salesman," the man protested with a presumed pout.

"Oh, yeah?"

"Yeah. Sold you a bill of goods the day we met to the day I married you."

"And I haven't had a single regret, I want you to know."

"Not one?"

"Not one."

"Sure?"

"I'm sure."

Suddenly the doorbell rang.

"Guess who?" she said and smiled.

"Give me two. Nancy and Danny."

"Well, your vehicle *has* been parked outside for hours, you know."

"I'm going to have a garage built and sneak in during the wee hours, draw all the blinds and shades, maybe even put a SOLD sign on the front lawn."

"Be nice, now," Rebecca coaxed, sliding off his lap and heading for the front door.

Mac stood up and went over to a corner window, staring at his neighbor Danny staring at the blue van parked in the driveway.

Nancy was coming through the door but stopped abruptly.

"Will you come on, Dan? The Paces are not heating the outside. Jesus." The overweight woman reached out and put her arms around Rebecca as though she hadn't seen her next-door neighbor in eons. Releasing a bear hug about Rebecca's thin-framed body, she turned and faced Mac. "And you? You the man my bosom buddy calls her 'mystery guest?'"

"That's me. How are you, Nancy?"

"Fat. How do you think I am? How do you stay in such great shape, Macky? I hate you."

"Macky!" Dan Wheeler chimed in, pecking Rebecca on the cheek and firmly taking Mac Pace's hand.

"Hi, Danny."

"How do you keep that van of yours so shiny with all that traveling around you do?"

"The company takes care of it. I just put gas in and go."

"The company or the Bureau?" Dan asked and winked slyly.

"Coffee?"

"Sure, why not?"

Chapter Nine

Sam Carper got off at Exit 71 on the Long Island Expressway just as the heavy downpour relented and a bright orange ball became visible in the east. The driver switched his wipers from a fast to intermittent setting. After two brutal winters in a row, the month of April was a welcome break for everyone, in spite of the heavy rains.

"I want you to know that I really appreciate this," the college student said sincerely, sitting comfortably in the front seat, resting a shoulder against the door. "You don't have to go out of your way. Honestly."

"No sweat. I'm going to drop you off at a phone booth and wait while you call your folks. Then I'll swing over to Home Depot and pick up some paneling I need to finish off a room."

"They open this early?"

"Very early. Especially for contractors. I'll just grab a painting cap from back and stroll right on in," he kidded.

"Well, I know you're still going out of your way. You could have continued straight to the last exit and onto route fifty-eight."

"And let you off in the pouring rain? What kind of guy do you think I am?" Sam said and smiled pleasantly.

"Hell, you gave me a ride all the way from Delaware. I could have been standing out in this weather for hours. Besides, I'm making the trip in record time. My parents don't expect me home until tomorrow or the next day. Boy, are they ever going to be surprised."

Sam grinned from ear to ear. "Happy to oblige."

"How long have you lived out east, Sam?"

"Fifteen years."

"My parents bought out here in eighty-seven."

"Couple of years before me. That's when I started boating and found the place."

"East Marion, you said."

Sam nodded.

"On the water?"

"A block away. Got me a place in Maryland, too."

"These days it's tough to find a place on or near the water out here. And if you do, you're going to pay beaucoup bucks. Real estate's gone wacko from Riverhead on out. The North Fork of the Island is like the Gold Coast back west, or the Hamptons on the South Fork. My dad says Flanders is the next hot spot. Speculators are buying up properties like there's no tomorrow. And they're not cheap. No bargains over there today."

"Your dad in real estate?"

Michael hesitated. "Insurance, but he dabbles."

"What kind of insurance? Home?"

Michael Matuco shook his head. "Life."

"Life?" Sam roared.

"What's so funny?"

"It's just that the people I've been running into lately could certainly use the coverage. Look. Over there." Sam pointed to the phone booth across the narrow, deserted road. "You go make your call while I wait. You tell them exactly where you are. Once I know your mom or dad's coming for you, I'll take off."

Sam parked across the road, parallel to the booth, and Michael stepped out then pulled his bag from the back. With his free hand, he gratefully shook the driver's. "Thanks a million, Sam. I really appreciate." The young man closed the door and trotted across the wet pavement.

"Got change?" Sam called out cordially after sending down the window.

Michael stopped and whipped out his phone card. "Plastic, man. Never ever leave home without it."

"Plastic," Sam repeated with a big grin, giving the lad a thumbs-up.

Sam waited patiently as Michael pulled open the phone booth door and punched in a set of numbers. A moment later, the young man smiled warmly and waved good-bye.

Sam waved back, waited, and the boy faced away. Reaching behind the backseat beneath a pile of clothing, the marksman withdrew his Thompson/Center handgun and aligned the cross hairs of the 1X fixed power scope just slightly left of center of Michael's back. A heavier round from a heftier barrel but from the same gun used to terminate a mother and son in Pennsylvania, as well as a mailman in Maryland, was employed to pierce the heart of the hitchhiker. The .207 Winchester cartridge and bullet did its intended damage.

Chapter Ten

Detectives Brian Archer and Gary York shook their heads in sheer disgust. Detective Victor Posteraro did his best to console the grieving parents who had arrived minutes after Riverhead Police responded to the scene. Mrs. Matuco bit the knuckle of a forefinger. Mr. Matuco smashed a fist into the fender of his Lincoln Town Car.

"He wa- was co- coming home for Easter," the boy's mother stammered through a mournful cry. "I couldn't believe he was already here. In Riverhead! He called me from *that* phone," the women declared and pointed with a shaky hand. "Fifteen minutes from home. FIFTEEN MINUTES!" she screamed hysterically. "Fifteen fucking minutes . . . and now my boy is dead," Mrs. Rosina Matuco swore then sobbed bitterly, pulling insanely at her hair.

Mr. Matuco went from punching a fender to kicking the car doors. "When you get him, and you better get him before I do, you give me five minutes alone. Five–fucking–minutes–is–all–I–ask," he insisted, putting five good-sized dents into two door panels along the passenger side of the shiny black Lincoln.

Brian and Gary left Vic to deal with the wrathful souls whose son lay beneath a shroud not fifty feet away.

"Man's got issues above and beyond the norm here, Bri. Better that Vic handles him."

"Let him vent. I got a feeling, though, that this is just the tip of the iceberg. So. What do you think we got here?"

Gary shrugged. "Rule out robbery for starters."

"Just because the guy's wallet's intact? Somebody driving by might have spooked the prick."

"At six thirty a.m. or thereabouts, in this neck of the woods?"

"Is deserted. I'll give you that."

"Why the fuck even *have* a phone booth out here?"

"Remember that big drug bust back in the late eighties?"

"Sure I remember. That Columbian warlord, I forget his name, used to drive down here or over to that pay phone in Manorville to conduct his drug business, figuring the feds bugged his hacienda. Figuring right. But not figuring they'd bug those booths. Last I heard he's doing two dimes up in Attica. So why still have this pay phone here?"

"You'd have to ask some of our local boys and girls, having only to *threaten* torture to get it out of them," he began to explain with a grin. "Troopers, Riverhead P.D., Sheriff's Office. The stuff they eavesdrop on keeps them busy twenty-four-seven."

"Feds never lifted it?"

Brian shook his head. "As a favor to some undercover talent, they never removed the tap, leaving both booths as is instead of converting over to those partitioned or open stalls, offering instead, a false sense of security to a few shitheads. You'd be surprised who uses those booths, seeing as how they provide both privacy and protection from the weather. Interestingly, those calls and cryptic conversations are recorded and channeled elsewhere today, but with the promise of a heads-up to the feds should anything fall into their jurisdiction. It's probably sometimes tempting not to share, I'm sure, but those involved know it would prove unwise to fuck the feds, so everyone out here capitulates."

Gary laughed. "Capitulates? You sound like Vic with his five-dollar words."

"Something's got to rub off," Brian agreed with a grin.

"Anyhow. Back to basics, buddy. What do *you* think we got here?"

"Maybe a random drive-by. Maybe a hit."

"Maybe a drive-by, but a hit on a college kid?" Gary shook his head skeptically. "I don't think so, Bri. I think they knew one another."

Brian thought for a considerable moment. "Care to share?"

"For openers, ask yourself why just a single shot? Drive-by guys and dolls just love to drill their victims silly and senseless. And if it was a hit for hire, why screw around with a Lexan phone booth?"

"The door was wide open. But let's say for the sake of

43

argument it was closed for privacy. Even bullets fired from a large caliber would have deflected or had one hell of a job trying to penetrate shatterproof polycarbonate resin."

"You're helping me prove my point, Bri. We're talking a single round that just happens to smack the kid in the back for a perfect kill shot."

"Seemingly at close range. No great feat, partner."

"Still, all too perfect. Too pat."

"Listen. The first words out of the kid's mouth, according to his mother, are— Brian flipped a page of his notepad and read—'Hi, Mom. I'm here at a phone booth in Calverton,' and he gives her this exact location. Next, he tells her, 'I got a ride practically all the way home from this great guy.' Probably meaning a ride from the Delaware State University area to here, which could have been with anyone heading anywhere north, say from as far away as Florida. Wish us both lots of luck with this one, pal."

"Or maybe the Maryland-Delaware line," Gary posited, leaning against their sedan.

"Maryland-Delaware line? How'd you come up with that?"

"Recall last month around the Philly area when that mother and son were shot? Less than a week later, an M.E.'s doing a postmortem on some postman in Ocean City, Maryland."

"So?"

"Mother and her child—both single shots to the head; .22-250 round. Bet the mailman bought the farm with the same caliber bullet."

"But it looks like we got ourselves a caliber here that could take down a deer. You're not seriously suggesting a connection?"

"First, two fatal head shots fired from around thirty yards to bring down a mother and son. Then another well-placed shot to the head of a mail carrier making his rounds, fired from approximately the same distance."

"Yeah, thirty yards, not thirty feet. And back to why you think they knew one another."

"Listen to me."

"I'm listening."

"Michael Matuco was facing the field when he was hit."

"Right."

"His back to the shooter."

"Obviously."

"Around six-thirty this morning."

"Go on."

"What would you do if you heard a car approaching at that hour in this godforsaken location? Especially if it slowed down or stopped."

"I get your point."

"No, I want to hear it."

"I'd turn around and keep a watchful eye . . . unless I didn't hear anything because I was so engrossed in talking to my mom," Brian added to the mix, playing devil's advocate, presenting a thorough examination of the possibilities in lieu of any argument.

"An approaching car or not, I'd have my eyes working the area like a fucking periscope. No, Bri. The car was already there, waiting for the kid to place the call, I'd wager."

"It was raining lightly but pretty steadily. Maybe the guy was waiting to drop the kid someplace else after he made the call."

"Where? He told his mother to pick him up *here*."

"So maybe another car or person came by after the guy left. The mother was getting a pencil and paper. Michael gave her the crossroads and told her he was a quarter mile north when she heard the shot ring out."

Again, Gary shook his head. "There's no sign of any other footprints or tire tracks off the road but the victim's and one vehicle. And with this rain, there certainly would be in all this soggy ground around. No, I think the guy wanted to be sure the kid touched base with his family before leaving him here alone."

"Why would he do that if he was hell-bent on killing him?"

"I meant *pretending* to show some concern, all right? Michael trusted this person. They probably built a rapport on the drive up. That's why the kid's guard was down. That's why he was facing the fields when the bastard shot him in the back."

"Then why not two shots, or three or four for insurance? Why not one in the head like the others, making certain the kid was dead?"

"He didn't need two shots, Bri."

"Why?"

"Because I think the perp's a professional, but this was not necessarily a professional hit."

"Why, because he shoots and kills the kid from thirty feet away makes him a professional? Okay, probably through the heart or lungs from all the blood we got. Probably just a lucky shot; unlucky for the kid."

"I'm telling you he knew the kid was dead or he *would* have put a second bullet in his brain," Gary said agitatedly. "He's a fucking sharpshooter, I'd bet. Maybe military because—"

"Zip it up. Here comes double trouble on a pair of patent leather pumps."

Mrs. Matuco marched right up to Detective Archer, her hands placed rigidly on her hips, her hair a mess.

"I understand you're the lead investigator in this case. Is that right, Detective?"

"Yes, I am, ma'am," Archer answered up smartly and politely. "And I can assure you—"

"You can assure me nothing. Can you understand that? But I can assure you that the head of homicide will have *your* head, like I will have *his* if any one of you fuck this up. Do you hear me, Detective Brian Archer?"

"I hear you loud and clear, Mrs. Matuco."

Mr. Matuco stepped forward and took his wife firmly by the arm, moving her aside. "You let me handle this, Rosina." Sergio Matuco put his face inches from Brian's. "Man to man. I'm gonna tell you who did this to my boy. It was some fucking Riverhead nigger. A fucking *melanzana*. Eggplant. *Capisce?* And I want to know right now what you're going to do about it. And if I don't like what I hear, I'm personally gonna start kicking some black asses all over West Main Street until I get some fucking answers. We clear?"

It took every ounce of restraint to resist cold-cocking the tendentious tormentor exactly where he stood. But Archer kept his cool. Although his face was red with anger, the detective promised to send two of his best people, within the hour, to the Matuco home to take further statements and assure the couple a thorough investigation.

Sergio collected his wife and walked steadily back to Posteraro, the pair cursing "this nigger neighborhood" and all its kind.

Brian and Gary exchanged knowing looks. The latter, smiling sardonically; the former did nothing but let the color crimson drain completely from his face and neck before telling his partner to play his hunch.

"Your theory's a long shot, Gary."

"First to admit it, good buddy."

"I'll pass along the info to Kim; see what she can dig up. You never know. But not before she and Justin pay a visit to our grieving bigots in Remsenburg."

"You bet, partner."

Chapter Eleven

Justin Barnes and Detective Kim Archer parked in the circular driveway behind Sergio Matuco's Lincoln Town Car. Rosina Matuco's Mercedes Benz faced forward before their oversized four-car garage. Justin and Kim stepped out of an unmarked Plymouth sedan, the clunk of the closing car doors resounding simultaneously.

Sergio Matuco was in earshot and turned around suddenly, staring out from behind the prodigious bay window to the walkway upon which the pair approached. "Jesus."

Rosina walked in from the kitchen. "What now?"

"Seventh-Day Adventists, or something."

"At this fucking hour? Tell them to take a fucking hike."

Sergio opened wide the front door before Kim Archer ever reached the doorbell. "Yeah?" the homeowner growled, his body language telling Justin that the man was loaded for bear or better.

Justin stepped forward of Kim, folder in hand. "We're here to —"

"To turn yourselves right around and head the hell back out of here," Sergio stated. "We don't want or need no Bible-touting brothers or sisters spoutin' the gospel. Now, beat it!" he demanded, staring fully into the two nonplused black faces standing below him on the steps.

Kim had her badge out, but Justin's shoulder blocked it.

"You don't understand," Justin said. "We're here to—"

Rosina shot around her husband. "You two better get the hell out of here this minute," she said threateningly, "or Jehovah, or whoever the hell you worship, will witness the beating of your lives, and only then will I call the police. And if I find any oil spill on my driveway—"

At that point, Kim shoved her gold shield past Justin's body and in the Matucos' faces.

Rosina looked dumbfounded.

Sergio's features turned from anger to hatred in a fraction of a second. "What is this? Some sort of sick joke?" he demanded to know.

"Only if the murder of your son is a joke to you, Mr. Matuco," Justin answered challengingly, stepping up and past the woman of the house while waiting for the next response from Sergio.

"Are you going to invite us in, Mrs. Matuco?" Kim asked with an edge to her voice. "Or should we just locate and leave you with a couple of copies of *The Watchtower*, with which to wipe your driveway clean should we have defiled it with our presence?"

"I don't believe this shit," Sergio said, staring up menacingly at the towering figure. "Detective Archer promised to send over two of his best."

"And you were expecting two white knights, I'll bet," Justin offered, smiling broadly and exhibiting his pearly whites for all they were worth.

"Let me ask you something, mister," Sergio smirked.

"Ask."

"Do you know who the fuck I am and the influence I have around here? Do you?"

"Sure I do. That's why Detective Archer and I were able to check you out and still be over here within the hour," Justin stated. "You're a low-level mafia figure operating an insurance company as a front for a group in Brooklyn that the feds have all but devoured. And as far as influence around here goes, I'd say it's limited to a several block area."

"Is that so?" was all that Sergio could manage for the moment.

Rosina glared. "Did he say, 'Detective Archer'?" Rosina asked the woman detective, a hint of confusion written upon the housewife's flushed face.

"Yes," Kim answered matter-of-factly. "Detective Brian Archer sent us over to take additional statements and investigate the—"

"And I take it that you coincidentally have the same last name as—"

"As my husband's?" the pretty black woman asked and answered. "No, no coincidence at all. Detective Archer sent Mr.

Barnes and me over to do a job. Now, are you going to invite us in, or are we going to conduct an interview on the stoop if at all? Tell us."

"Wait, wait, wait, wait, wait," Sergio Matuco interrupted. "Let me see if I got this business straight. You're the wife of the lead detective on our son's case; and you," he turned back to Justin, "you're a mister? No rank? Not even a detective?" he asked in disbelief.

"Like you, Serge, I freelance. Let's just leave it at that. We're gonna find your boy's murderer with or without your help and in spite of your prejudice." Justin paused just long enough to include Rosina Matuco into his sights. "Now, the fact that we don't like one another for starters, and probably never will, doesn't mean we can't or won't do our job. Just makes it a little awkward is all."

"What kind of experience do you have in these matters, Barnes?" Sergio asked sarcastically.

Justin looked at Kim and laughed. "He wants my fucking résumé."

"Last chance, Mr. and Mrs. Matuco," Detective Archer stated emphatically. "Tell us now before we take a permanent hike. My husband promised you the best shot. We're standing right before your disbelieving and discriminating eyes."

Rosina looked at her husband for a moment, turned her back then waved for everyone to follow her inside.

In crossing the threshold, Sergio stopped the pair in their tracks. "I have another question for you, Mister Barnes."

Justin was just about out of patience. "It's your last one, Serge. You see, the way this works is that we ask the questions. Then you answer them. Then we ask some more. But I know you know all this because that's the same way it worked when the cops had you at the station house in the Graves End section of Brooklyn, some years ago. Nothing's really changed except the color of the *in·ter·view·ers*, which make you and yours the *in·ter·view·ees*. Ya dig? That's the equivalent of *capisce*?" he clarified, the tips of Justin's stout black fingers bunched beneath Matuco's nose. "So, what's your final question?"

"How are you connected?"

Justin smirked. "I'm not *connected*," Barnes toyed. "*You're connected*. I just connect the dots and unravel puzzles," the maverick answered ambiguously. He looked over at Rosina. "Now, where do we sit?"

"On your ass, Mr. Barnes," was the woman's reply.

Justin turned to Kim. "You know, I think I could get to like her," he reflected aloud, strolling over to a huge wraparound leather couch then taking a seat.

The slightest trace of a smile, sad but discernible, crossed Rosina's mask of dissemblance before she broke down and wept bitterly over the hours-old murder of their beloved son, Michael.

Chapter Twelve

Robert Redler couldn't sleep and decided to get up and write. The LED on the clock/radio read 3:10 a.m. Careful not to wake Liza, he quietly got out of bed and made his way in the dark to the bathroom. After urinating, washing his hands then brushing his teeth, he headed downstairs to the kitchen; a dim glow from the night-light at the base of the staircase illuminated the way.

Robert opened the refrigerator and discovered that they were out of both milk and half-and-half. The fact that there was a sufficient amount of coffee in the cupboard was moot, for although the insomniac had to have his octane brewed fresh and rich, he also had to have milk or cream with one level teaspoon of raw sugar, times however many cups necessary, in order to make it through the morning. Usually four cups would do it. Decaf was out of the question.

Steve Quick would arrive and open Shelly's Deli at 3:30 a.m. but wouldn't open for business for another hour and a half, so Robert fixed himself tea and did some research for an article he was writing. At 4:50 a.m., he headed out the back door, securing both top and bottom locks, walking briskly to the garage.

Shelly was already cutting cold cuts and putting together ready-to-go sandwiches and salads for her regular early morning crowd as Robert pulled into the parking lot just west of the building. It annoyed him when customers parked directly in front of the store, blocking the narrow entranceway, jamming up the area. It always amazed him that people found it bothersome to park and have to walk from Town Hall's parking area adjacent to the deli. And even though there wasn't a soul around at that hour, he still parked in the lot.

"Hey, Rob," Shelly greeted her customer enthusiastically.

"Hi, Shell."

"Long time no see. Busy as a bee, I'll bet."

"Pretty much. Where's Steve?"

"Under the weather. Got a bad cold along with an intestinal virus or something. Got a call late last night."

"Something's going around. Liza wasn't feeling well herself about a week ago."

"Crazy weather the past month. Down into the thirties at night. Up into the forties and fifties during the day. Then we get hit with snow again. Then sleet and freezing rain. Who can keep up? I don't know what to pull out of the closet next," she went on as Robert fixed himself coffee. "How's she feeling now?"

"Back to normal."

"Enjoying retirement, I'll bet."

"For sure."

"Need anything to go with that coffee? Those blueberry muffins just came in. To die for," she promised, smiled and brushed her ponytail aside.

"Wrap one up, and I'll just grab a quart of milk and half-and-half."

"That be it?"

"*Newsday*'s not here yet, right?"

"Saw the truck go by only a few minutes ago. So I'd be surprised if 7-Eleven even had it this early. Figure another half hour. Wait! Today's the day he collects, stands around and bullshits with anyone and everyone. Better make that more like an hour and a half."

"You know what astounds me, Shell? *The Daily News* and the *The Post* are here when you open, or maybe a little bit after that. But *Newsday* rarely ever gets here before six or seven."

"Tell me about it. Guy's a creep. Steve argues with him all the time about that. And talk about creeps, here comes another. Joe Cool."

"Liza and I see that guy all over town, without fail, no matter what time of day or night we go out. It's uncanny."

"And if you see him three times in the course of the same day —" She let her words hang for Robert to finish her thought.

"He'll have changed his outfit three times," Robert completed the picture perfectly.

The two of them laughed lightly as the man in his mid-fifties crossed the street and headed toward the entrance.

"He's harmless, but he's still a creep. He owes Steve over twenty dollars for coffee. We had to tell him, 'No more credit, Joe.'"

Joe Cool, as Shelly nicknamed him, ambled into the deli wearing an open raincoat and a freshly pressed suit with trouser creases that could cut butter.

"Hi, Joe," Shelly said pleasantly.

"Uh," Joe uttered, heading for the coffee machines.

"No credit, Joe," Shelly warned. "Steve's orders. Cash on the barrelhead," she added firmly.

Joe did an about-face and walked briskly from the store without a word.

"Sometimes when we're busy, he sneaks by me with coffee in hand but no money in his pockets. Well, what am I going to do?" Shelly smiled. "So I take it out of my own money and feed the register."

"What's his story, Shell? I've heard different versions."

"The official version, and believe me we've checked him out especially after what happened here last month, is that he was shell-shocked during the Vietnam War. He has a good check coming in monthly from Uncle Sam, but spends most of it on his wardrobe and dry-cleaning."

Robert smiled and shook his head. "Never saw him looking shabby, that's for sure."

"Never ever," Shelly agreed.

"Steve okay? I mean other than the flu or whatever?" Robert Redler poked for information. "That had to have been some experience, I'll bet."

"A bit spooked as you can well imagine. Especially when he pulls in here at three-thirty in the morning to open up. I'll tell you, Rob, I'm glad I wasn't here that morning or I'd have freaked."

"You and me both," he tested, studying Shelly's sea-green eyes for the slightest hint of deception, convinced that Steve had said nothing to her.

"Strange, though," she added.

"What's that?"

"The description of the guy Steve gave the police, saying he

54

had all these silver rings on one hand. I know someone like that. Not a regular here, for sure, but somewhere I've seen those rings. I just can't place them."

"Maybe it was Liberace," Robert teased.

"That's very funny, Rob."

"I'm surprised you even get it. He's way before your time."

"Oh, I'm not as young as you think I am."

"No?"

Shelly emphatically shook her pretty head, the long brown pony tail flying in opposite directions. "As a matter-of-fact, I can remember my parents couldn't wait for his weekly show, just to see his outrageous outfits. Liberace and Lawrence Welk, too. Of course, I was only a little girl, but I do remember them."

"You mean you could view the tube from your crib?" he kidded.

She blushed. "You're much too kind."

"How much do I owe you, youngster?"

Shelly went over to the register. "Half-and-half. Quart of milk. Large coffee. That's four eighty-three. Muffin's on me and keep your mouth shut."

"Keep the change, kid. And thanks."

"Thank you," she said and curtsied from behind the counter. "I'll put it toward Joe Cool's coffee next time he rips me off, but I'll give you all the credit. He'll never leave you alone after that."

"No thank you, lady."

"Uh-oh, here come the troops."

Seconds later, day laborers from Hunter Insulation lined the aisle from the front door right up to the coffee machines. Directly in back of them came the men from LIPA and Verizon.

Everyone and his brother was up and milling about; everyone, that is, except the *Newsday* delivery man, Redler thought with irritation.

Spanish and English brought the quiet morning to life, with Shelly speaking both languages while taking orders for containers of soups poured steaming hot into workers' thermoses or to be heated up on hot plates later in the day.

Like magic, a young man appeared from the kitchen and wrapped a clean white apron about his waist, immediately going to work helping Shelly fill the orders as the men joked and filled their own thermoses and containers with hot, rich coffee.

"Hi and bye, Rob," Albert acknowledged.

"Bye, Albert. Bye, Shelly."

"Bye, Rob. Best to Liza."

It was not until Robert Redler stepped outside that he recalled one of the would-be robbers from the previous month muttering something about Prince Albert in a can.

An old joke, to be sure, Robert entertained. *Maybe even older than Liberace or Lawrence Welk. Older than dirt*, he ruminated. The gunman had held Steve's proceeds, contained in a large coffee can. *Was it mere banter . . . or some sort of strange connection?* The writer weighed the possibility, wondering as he walked back toward his car.

Chapter Thirteen

Sitting down to a late-night dinner, Detective Kim Archer started telling her husband a piece of intriguing news, passing a bowl of creamy homemade mashed potatoes across the table.

"Gary's theory on the Philly and Ocean City murders?" she began. "He's right on target. No pun intended."

"Really?" Brian responded with little surprise, spooning out a generous portion of spuds before reaching for the mushroom onion gravy. "They got a match?"

"Yep. Mother and son as well as the mailman. Remington .22-250s. Perfect match." She took the gravy boat and passed a plate of meat.

"So Pennsy and Maryland have themselves an area sniper."

"We might, too, Brian."

He stared quizzically at his wife. "Is this a test?" he pressed.

"Carrots?"

"I hate carrots."

"You do not. You ate them at my mother's."

"I'm afraid of your mother."

"Will you be serious?"

"All right, so how might we have a problem like Pennsylvania and Maryland? The victims were hit with .22-250 Remingtons. The Matuco boy was hit with a .270 Winchester round. Cartridges don't match. Neither does the M.O. Mother, son, mailman—all frontal lobe head shots. Matuco boy—shot through the back," he said, touching his head with one hand and his back with the other to indicate the difference. "Mother, son, mailman, all shot in the head from a distance. Michael Matuco was shot in the back at close range, and several states away I might add. Where are you and Gary going with this thing, Kim? Tell me."

"Firearms Identification," she said while smiling cagily. "Been there and back," the computer maven/detective added for the intrigue, tapping her polished fingernails upon an imaginary keyboard. "Big Sister and I have been pre-tty busy communicating with Bulletproof and Drugfire databases. Also, with a firearms training supervisor at the Academy Bureau in Westhampton."

"Grasso?"

"The one and only," she affirmed with a grin.

"Be serious. You're not trying to tell me there's a match here," he stated through a laugh.

"Well, not exactly."

"And what exactly does 'not exactly' mean, if I might ask?"

"You like the steak?"

"I'm losing patience quicker than my appetite," he warned. "Give."

"Barrel length."

"What?"

"Same type of weapon as well as barrel length was more than likely used in all four murders. Don't you find that just a little bit odd?" she baited.

"No," he answered flatly. "Generally, barrel lengths really don't vary that greatly. Twenty-six, twenty-seven, twenty-eight inches or thereabouts," he threw out as an example. "And what the hell does that have to do with the price of eggs?"

"Try fifteen inches."

"What?"

"Fifteen-inch pistol barrels, or thereabouts," Kim offered, "give or take an inch," she added, "may have been employed to waste all four victims, Mike thinks. Not the *same* barrel or caliber in the case of Matuco, of course, but the same gun was definitely used to terminate the mother and son just outside of Philly, as was used to murder the mailman in Ocean City. Got it? Now, get this. The firing pin indentations found on the three .22-250 Remington casings recovered at those two crime scenes *are* consistent with the mark on the .270 Winchester casing at ours."

"Yeah, consistent but not conclusive," Brian snipped. "I just love hearing that word *consistent*, especially in a courtroom. Makes me want to vomit. Steak is delicious by the way."

"Not proof positive, yet, my doubting Thomas. But striations made by the breechblock are being compared with striae recorded on the base of those shells as we dine, my dear. What's with the negative expression? Don't get as thick on me as my gravy, hear? Listen up. Four center-fire cartridges were discharged to kill four people. Two barrels, as determined by those bullets, are left-hand twist. And think about where the boy was probably picked up. Pretty much in the middle of that madness. We'll have our hands on the audiotape from that phone booth in Riverhead sometime tomorrow and may learn something further, although I think Rosina Matuco, bless her little black heart, was pretty thorough in our interview. Justin and I grilled her pretty good. Anyway, there are just too many coincidences here. I really think Gary and Mike are onto something."

"You do, do you?"

"Yes, I do."

"You know what galls me?"

"My carrots."

"The fact that those Matuco folks have more money than God, but their kid hitchhikes home. Why? To save a few dollars? And where's the kid's cell phone? Why make a call from a pay phone?"

"Well, you know I'm not a fan of those two, but in defense of the parents, they were sending him a weekly allowance that would boggle the mind. They even bought him a new car, but he lost his license because of a chronic drinking problem. Anyhow, maybe he hocked the cell for booze. Who knows? Seems he was spending his parent's money like there was no tomorrow, but not very wisely."

"Got that right, girl," were Brian's last words on the matter as he delved deep into thought before pushing back his chair and heading for the den to call his partner.

"What about your dinner?" Kim brayed.

"Save it."

"No dessert for you, mister," she swore.

Chapter Fourteen

Marc Espe, a.k.a. Sam Carper and Mac Pace, drove north along the coast and loved it. A week away from all his wives and businesses. He opened the glove compartment and reached for the bag of M&Ms, popping several into his mouth like pills. He turned on the radio at six precisely and listened to the news. "Boring," he lamented. All about Bush and Kerry.

"Time to make my own headlines," he decided, consulting his watch, a surge of excitement filling his brain and body simultaneously, a rush as real as any athlete running a marathon would experience.

In a sense, Marc Espe felt as though he were, indeed, an athlete. Did he not out fish some of the most consummate sport fishermen in the country if not the world? Did he not take huge striped bass over the gunnels at a staggering rate through an entire evening and then head for the tuna grounds that very morning, finishing up the day with fifteen-pound bluefish just as the sun was about to set? *Who could keep pace? Who could go that distance?* He smirked satisfactorily.

The serial killer turned off the highway and headed for the overlook. He parked the van, marveling at the vista that afforded a breathtaking view of miles and miles of sea . . . a sea as blue and soothing a color as his precious vehicle. His excitement was mounting by the minute.

To his left sat a late model sports car. Low to the ground and sleek. He could clearly see that no one was in it. Marc Espe slowly turned his vehicle around, its tail end facing the sloping terrain. He shut the engine and climbed into the back, opening the rear doors wide before donning a pair of nitrile gloves.

From sixty yards away, a seventy-something-year-old-man stood with his dog.

Marc Espe raised and deliberately ran the cross hairs along the leash and up the arm of the owner, resting the alignment on the bridge of the old man's glasses. After finessing the scope's variable power to nearly 5X, the killer gripped the handgun solidly in both hands, steadied the weapon, then evenly applied pressure to the trigger until the .308 Winchester bullet left the chamber at 2800 feet per second, tunneling through the man's forehead and blowing out the back of the septuagenarian's skull on a cool late morning in early May.

Apart from the barking terrier that disturbed an otherwise still and silent early Sunday morning, all was dead quiet. Even the wind out of the south lay down and remained motionless. Espe withdrew the cartridge and annoyingly threw it down the slope toward the puppy.

"Let the authorities work for that one," he decided.

The animal glared and growled up at killer.

"How rude, you little mongrel" the madman grunted through tight and angry lips.

Chapter Fifteen

Massachusetts State Police cooperated fully and completely with Long Island Suffolk County Homicide. And why wouldn't they? They had found absolutely nothing. No bullet. No spent round. No witnesses, except for the victim's dog that the troopers temporarily adopted and tried in earnest to find a good home, with the emphasis on *good* and which seemed to supersede the investigation itself. The poor dog had lain around the barracks for two full days with its bottom jaw fixed atop its front paws. The terrier would not eat or drink anything and had to be pulled or carried outside in order to do its business. It shivered while it slept, which was most of the time.

Justin Barnes entered the Danvers Barracks on the morning of the third day following the homicide and strode immediately over to the pooch, picking him up and holding him out at arm's length.

"Who the hell are you?" the duty officer asked, coming around a partition with the tops of his thumbs planted solidly behind his belt.

"Justin Barnes, Suffolk County," Justin answered politely, fumbling with a free hand for I.D. "Detective Lieutenant Ethan Powell gave your commander a holler earlier; said that I'd be coming up for the Everett file."

"Right, right. Said that you were driving. What did you do, fly here instead?"

"In a matter of speaking, I guess."

"What do you mean, you guess? And put that dog down."

"Sorry. Flew up here doing ninety plus on open stretches. Not much traffic during the wee hours of morning," he explained. "Didn't want to get stuck in rush hour."

"And no one pulled you over? Come on. You had to be stopped

at least three times in this state alone."

"You mean by Smokey?" Justin laughed. "I had the highway boys chase me down once in Connecticut and once again in Rhode Island. Flashed my dash-dome and radioed those guys. It was smooth sailin' from there on up. Breezed right by you fellas catchin' some shuteye off I-95," he let it be known.

"You're so full of shit it's coming out your ears," the trooper challenged.

"Well, maybe Rhode Island called ahead and clued you fellas in that I was comin'. Who knows?"

"Tell me what the hell you want."

"Copy of the file, which should be ready, that there dog, and good directions to the crime scene."

"You're not going to find a damn thing out there. We've been over that place with a fine-tooth comb. We didn't miss a thing, hot-shot. And the dog stays right where he is. He's our mascot for the time being."

"Number one, the dog's a she," Justin fabricated. "That's not a pecker; that's a tumor . . . Donahue," Justin read aloud off the trooper's nametag.

"What?"

"Number two, it's got an infectious disease."

"What!?" The cop took one step back.

"Poor appetite, right?"

The man nodded.

"Pissin' and shittin' all over the place, I suspect."

The state trooper nodded quite emphatically.

"You saw all those black and brown spots around the privates when I lifted her up?"

The man just stood there quietly.

"I didn't think so."

"What's she got?"

Justin shook his head sadly. "Acute Monocotyledon."

"Mono what?"

"An endogenous growth. Irreversible and quite fatal I'm afraid."

"What do we do? The guys all love this little dog."

"Nothing *to* do 'cept put 'er down."

The duty officer was beside himself.

"Is there a vet nearby?" Justin asked gravely. "Listen, you can jot down those directions as well. Sorry, I really didn't want to tell you like this, but when you told me the dog stays, well . . . ."

"What do I tell the men who handled him, I mean her?"

"You mean within the past forty-eight hours?"

"I guess so."

"To wash their hands thoroughly and to see a doctor at the first sign."

"First sign of what?"

"Drowsiness. Depression. Fatigue," Justin listed, pushing the envelope. "Maybe that's why your boys were dozin' off along the Interstate as I blew by,"

"Let me ask you something, Barnes," the cop said suspiciously.

"Ask away."

"How come you know so much about dogs and diseases?"

"Well, my father was a vet." Justin didn't lie in the informal sense of the word. "My mother was into animal husbandry," he mocked, taking the liberty of twisting the figurative truth to the nth degree. "And my stepsister was a breeder," he concluded with a straight face.

"I see," Donahue said unsurely.

"Hey, I'd really like to stay and shoot the shit and all, but I gotta get a move on."

The officer went back behind the petition to get a copy of the file and then wrote down two sets of directions. "You're really not going to find anything out there. And good luck with the dog," he added, handing over the papers along with a leash. "Make a right when you go out of here, around the circle and pick up 128 East to Gloucester. You'll see the overlook. Vet doesn't open till nine o'clock."

"You've been a trooper, Donahue." Justin smiled broadly, flaunting his pearly-white, perfectly framed set of teeth.

On his way out, Justin passed two uniforms.

"Hey, where's he going with Pug?" a young recruit asked.

"I guess Donahue found him a good home," the senior man answered.

"I sure hope so," the bleary-eyed rookie said with a heavy

heart. "I sure as hell hope so."

Chapter Sixteen

It was daybreak when Marc Espe arrived home in the middle of Maine with fish and more fish. Coolers filled with ice lined the back of the van. He stepped from the vehicle and was immediately showered with kisses from his adoring and expecting wife, expecting that he should have been home days ago, expecting their second child within the next few weeks.

"It's going to be a boy," she whispered, although no one for miles around would ever hear a shout, a scream or a cry for bloody mercy if one's life depended on it.

"I thought you didn't want to know," he said with a queer smile. "I thought you wanted it to be a surprise."

"I did, but then I didn't," she explained. "You're not angry, are you? I couldn't stand it if you were ever angry with me," she declared, affecting a plausible pout.

"Not in a million years," he swore. "Not in a zillion centuries," he hyperbolized then laughed, holding Sharon in his arms and returning her affections ten-fold.

"You be careful, you crazy man," she warned then giggled delightfully. "I'm very delicate these days."

"Then you turn right around and head straight on back to that house." He gestured with a forefinger. "And don't lift or touch a thing because I'm going to do everything. I want you in bed and doing nothing. Understand?"

"Marc?"

"Yes, love."

"How long can you stay this time?" she asked rather nervously, no pretense in her tone or facial expression.

Marc began slowly counting on his fingers. Silently. The saddened look on her lovely face truly moved him. He began the count again. Aloud. "Let's see, now. One." A thumb shot out like a hitchhiker's. "Two." The thumb and forefinger formed a gun-finger. "Three." He added another digit. "That's three full months, not days or weeks," he outright lied with a great big grin.

Sharon's jaw dropped. "Are you serious?" she beamed, radiating beauty beyond his imagination.

He nodded excitedly. "The committee gave me three months off, for good behavior," he teased. "And, of course, for bringing to the forefront new policy that will help reelect the president of the United States come November."

"Oh, my God, you're serious!" she exclaimed, bringing the tips of her fingers to her lively, lovely lips. "Oh, my God, he's serious," she screamed to no one save her fetus and the wildlife. "Three full months."

She turned and started heading for the house just as quickly as she could move.

"Where are you going, Sharon?" he called after her.

"To bed. To do absolutely nothing like you said, except have this baby in three weeks," she announced so happily then laughed.

"But don't you want to see the fish first?" he teased.

"I don't want to see them, or touch them, or cook them," she answered decidedly. "That's your department." Sharon was on cloud nine and returned after a few minutes with a fillet knife, a sharpening stone and a box of freezer bags.

"I thought you weren't interested."

"I'm not. I just came to cut your heart out for not telling me sooner."

"Oh."

Chapter Seventeen

Justin Barnes and Pug were at the overlook for a good forty-five minutes before the maverick found the spent .308 Winchester cartridge beneath the hollow of a fallen tree along the edge of the ravine. Nevertheless, he continued searching for anything that the area police might have . . . well . . . overlooked . . . anything that might further lead Justin to the killer. Anything . . . including a proverbial needle in a haystack.

Initially, the puppy refused to go anywhere near the crime scene, let alone the spot where the victim had crashed back into the bushes and lay dead for hours before someone eventually came along and heard the barking, discovering both the body and the distraught animal that simply would not leave its owner's side.

Justin hadn't gotten off his knees for the next half hour, literally scouring the area inch by inch with a fine-tooth comb and his fingertips. The dog lay some fifty yards to the east, its pug-face resting squarely on its paws, its ears erect and alert.

As the sun rose steadily above the horizon, the dog gradually became interested and edged its way toward the strange, swarthy creature that crawled about on all fours, not unlike the large black Labrador that Pug had played with for an entire summer on Cape Cod Bay some seasons ago. Back then, the tiny terrier had been terribly frightened by the big, dark, powerful male dog that stood nearly thrice as high as he. But in time, Pug learned that the prodigious beast was as gentle and as playful as the next-door neighbor's kitten. Therefore, curiosity, combined with a bit of trust, now had the short-haired canine venturing a little closer to the human who presently stooped no higher than Ranger had stood; that was until Pug's summer companion upped upon its hind quarters to beg for food or attention, which Ranger usually did around the family of laughing children that he towered over. Still and all, this odd being crouched before him turned even frightfully taller than the retriever ever had, especially when the black man suddenly rose and stood fully erect.

"Hey there, Pug," Justin said invitingly, grinning and displaying his teeth like a hound. "Decided to take a gamble, did you, fella?"

Pug did not chance crossing over and into Justin's immediate territory. Instead, he merely sniffed the surrounding area where his master had lain.

"It's called 'returning to the scene of the crime,' Pug. Sorry to do this to you, pal. You see, I had this weird feeling that you might somehow be able to help me out here."

Pug looked over at Justin like he had two heads.

"I'm gonna take a look at your owner's sports car perhaps a little later, although I don't think it's gonna tell me very much, according to the police report anyhow. Viewing the body firsthand might however, even though I saw enough pictures from every conceivable angle to get the general idea. Not a very pretty sight, I know. I'm sure you'll never forget it as long as you live. So believe me when I tell you I understand your reluctance to even be here, Pug."

Making very little eye contact with the pup, Justin busied himself while he talked, not really paying the dog much mind—apart from a rather nonsensical one-sided conversation.

Pug busied himself, too, running his snout along the ground in ever-widening circles.

Every so often, Justin would stand and complain miserably, massaging his kidneys beneath his outer clothing with a pair of dirt embedded thumbs. He'd read and reread the report, study the drawings, once again measure the trajectory with a long tape, from the top of the overlook from where the fatal shot was fired to point of impact. Covering one square foot section at a time, the maverick worked his way further and further back from where Ellis Everett had fallen.

It was midday when Justin broadened his scope, strategically placing sticks and stones to mark off the expanded area thoroughly covered with *his* (both metaphorically and literally speaking) fine-tooth comb. Whenever he stood and stretched his aching back and legs, Pug would move into the space as if not having wanted to interfere while the man was busy working on all fours. Justin looked down and around and smiled enviously, wishing he could cover as much ground and at the speed the hound was swiftly moving about.

Justin finally broke for a late lunch, removing a sandwich from a brown paper bag. He continued watching as the dog moved from the spot where his master had expired to an area set well beyond a tree line.

"Hey, Pug. Want half a liverwurst and cheese—hold the rye?"

Pug looked up and over with interest but then returned to sniffing the ground and pawing at it.

"Last call, fella."

Pug seemed to sense the finality in Justin's tone.

"With a nose like yours, I just know you gotta get a whiff of this wurst."

Not sixty seconds later, Pug stood several yards from Justin's work boots . . . then several feet. A good moment passed between them before Pug was sniffing and eating out of Justin's hand.

After a ten-minute break, the two went back about their business. Pug: shifting around like radar on four short swift legs; Justin: down on all fours again and moving slowly forward toward the tree line with his rattail comb in hand, probing the ground with one end, then raking through it with the other.

It was as the sun was going down that Pug returned to a neutral corner; not distanced from the total stranger, having inched itself closer to the man as dusk was settling in upon them.

"Well, I think we're going to call it a day, dog," Justin said with a considerable degree of exasperation, standing and stretching, arching his aching back. "Tell you what, pooch. If those bozos back at the barracks really and truly cared an ounce about your well-being, someone with half a brain would have insisted on a second opinion, especially after that cockamamie story I handed Donahue about your sex and health. I'm sure he clued someone in as to our whereabouts, so at least one of them could have come by here looking for you. What do you have to say on the matter? Huh?"

Pug raised his small body and went over to an area not very far from where his master was murdered. More to the south but just to the right of a big boulder, big by Pug's standard anyway, he sniffed and whiffed and turned about in tight little circles before relieving himself.

"Good idea, Pug. But I think I'll hold my bladder and bowels till we hit the diner I saw back there earlier. Then I'll take you back to the boys at the barracks and tell 'em the vet in town informed me that I made a terrible diagnosis. It's not like I got a degree in medicine or something. Right?"

Pug looked up and nonchalantly headed toward Justin, when suddenly the pup stopped dead in his tracks, sniffed about, then started digging. A moment later the dog returned with something in its mouth.

"Whattaya got there, Pug? Huh?" Justin asked with little interest.

Pug dropped the tiny dark object at the man's feet.

In the dim light that they were quickly losing, the uncredentialed detective almost missed it. What appeared to be an irregular shaped small stone or piece of broken rock was one of the things Justin had been searching for during the past eleven hours.

"Jumpin' Jesus," Justin said quietly, picking up and examining the fragmented hunk of lead between his fingertips.

Chapter Eighteen

Sergeant Mike M. Grasso wore three hats: armorer for the Suffolk County Sheriff's Department at the Academy Bureau in Westhampton, corrections officer sergeant, firearms training supervisor. He had carefully studied a report and photographs before voicing his opinion to detectives from homicide squad's Team Three out of Yaphank.

"It's my belief that all five rounds were discharged from a Thompson/Center Arms, single shot, Encore pistol with interchangeable barrels. Meaning the three .22-250 Remington cartridges, the one .270 Winchester cartridge, and the .308 Winchester cartridge, the last of which Justin found. Not to mention the bullet."

"How sure are you, Mike?" Detective Brian Archer asked in earnest.

"I'd have to answer you like this, Brian. Several of the breech-face markings *appear* to correspond with striae found on the base of all five casings. But I wouldn't stake my reputation and certainly not my life on it," the stocky man stated. "I'll leave that business to the lab boys and girls. Instead, I'd put my money on the indentations made by the firing pins." Mike spread the first three photographs next to one another across his desk. ".22-250, .22-250, .22-250. Note the distinctive crater formed within each primer. Now, note the mark or blemish just to the right of center. Tell me what you think."

"I'd say they're identical markings," Detective Gary York answered up smartly.

"Brian?" Mike asked.

The lead detective nodded his head in acceptance.

"Would you bet Kim's life on it?" the firearms expert tested with a grin.

"Not in her presence, I wouldn't."

"Vic?"

"I'd bet mine," Vic Posteraro replied.

"Meaning your wife's or yours?" the armorer bantered playfully.

Vic smiled. "Both."

"Good answer. And you'd both probably hang onto your lives. By the way, say hello for me. Lorna? Justin? What do you two think?"

The detective and Justin nodded in agreement.

"Great. We're all on the same page so far. Now, let's examine this one." Mike placed a fourth photograph below the row of three. "Anyone?"

Justin stooped and carefully studied the array. "I'd bet Brian's, Gary's, Vic's and your life on it," he said in deadpan.

"That's taken from the .270 Winchester cartridge. And I'd comfortably join you in that bet. Brian, what do you have to say?"

"Certainly looks the same," Brian agreed.

"Ah, but would you bet your partner's life on it?" Both eyes gleamed.

"Which partner, Mike?" Brian played the firearm expert's game. "The one at home or the troublemaker standing next to me?"

"Put your money where your mouth is," Mike retorted. "Why not both," he challenged boldly.

"Fine, Mike. I'll roll the dice," the detective acquiesced.

"And now for the .308." Mike laid the blowup of the base of the cartridge below the others. "Anybody? Lorna? Take a shot," he insisted gallantly.

Detective Lorna Hanover nodded with assurance. "So what you're saying here, Mike, is that the same handgun *frame* was used with interchangeable barrels."

"You got it, girl. Now, whether or not the bullets were fired from those respective barrels belonging to a Thompson/Center single shot Encore pistol of a certain length is the arena we'll enter next. But as an aside, if I had some extra *dinero* lying around I'd buy some stock in that company," Mike Grasso affirmed. "They make one of the most accurate handguns going; additionally, they have the most versatile shooting system in the world. From a caliber for just plain plinking, to a mother lode with custom barrels tooled to do some very serious damage. From a round for varmint, right on up to taking down a pachyderm."

Once you got Mike Grasso talking about firearms, there was no letting go. He was an *Encyclopedia Britannica* and a *Shooter's Bible* packed into one prodigious volume. He could talk with authority about the .44 caliber Derringer with which John Wilkes Booth assassinated President Lincoln, then take you through the Roaring Twenties and the .32 Colt automatic used in the famous Sacco and Vanzetti case. Next, he'd cover, if you let him, every single aspect of the Kennedy assassination, right up to and including the so-called 'magic bullet' that appeared on the stretcher at Parkland Hospital in Dallas, Texas. And Grasso was on a roll, having segued into the never-ending JFK conspiracy theories.

". . . Of course, that mystery bullet was remarkably intact, although I prefer the word, suspicious," he nodded knowingly. "It was found in perfect contour. Not flattened out. Not even fragmented. Yet, it was supposed to have done all that damage to both President Kennedy and Governor Connally. All fucking bullshit if you want to know the plain truth of it. It should have been demolished like the bullet Justin found up north."

"Can you tell us anything about that piece of lead, Mike?" Vic asked.

"From the picture Kim brought over yesterday, very little. Without holding it in my hot little hands, even less. But coupled with the report, you'd have to be a complete idiot not to realize it came from a .308. Sorry I can't take it any further than that for you guys and gal," he said and winked rather fatherly at Detective Lorna Hanover, whom he thought of as his own daughter.

"What about this business with respect to barrels belonging to a Thompson/Center Arms, single shot Encore pistol of a certain length?" Brian questioned rather skeptically but respectfully. "How can you determine type and model, et cetera?"

"Again, I don't have the actual bullets *or* the cartridges before me for examination—just those pix. So you'll have to yield to forensics in the final analysis," Grasso punned and grinned. "However, the signature markings I showed you on the primer struck by the plunger are telltale, which you all agree. The firing pin indentation of a Glock, striking the base of a cartridge, I'm sure you're all well aware, is rectangular rather than round." He tossed a fired aluminum casing from a 9mm shell to Lorna, who snatched it from the air like a bird upon a bug. "Yes?"

Lorna nodded and passed along the item.

"Well, unfortunately, not all signatures are that distinguishable or discernible: breechlock markings, extractor, ejector, cartridge, bullet and so forth. In the case of Justin's recovered hunk of lead, fuhgettaboutit. The only lands and grooves forensics will find are those which landed and grooved its way in and out the back of the victim's skull, then glanced off a good size boulder, ricocheting and burying itself in the ground. The fact that you even found it, Justin, is amazing."

The maverick smiled. "I had a little help."

"You're still not telling us how you came up with Thompson/Center Arms', single shot Encore pistol barrels, Mike," Vic said politely, noting that Brian was losing patience by the minute. "Fifteen inches—no more, no less."

"Is that a pun?" Mike invited. "Because I could round up or down if you like," the armorer toyed playfully.

"No pun intended," Vic swore.

"Didn't think so. But fifteen inches is what I believe your killer used. All three barrels' twist ratios: 1 in 12 for the .22-250; 1 in 10 for the .270; and 1 in 10 as well for the .308. All left-hand twist barrels."

"Mike."

"Yes, Brian."

"This Thompson/Center Encore. Why a single shot?"

"Because that's all they manufacture," Mike Grasso explained, grinning from ear to ear.

Vic and Gary couldn't help but smile. Lorna kept a straight face. Brian strained to keep his temper in check.

"Mike."

"Yes, Brian?" Mike was beaming mischievously.

"What I meant was, why do you believe a single shot Thompson/Center Encore pistol was used in the commission of five murders? How could you possibly know with any degree of certainty the type of handgun and model?" he asked rather testily.

"Because I just happen to own all three models along with many interchangeable barrels the company offers: the older Contender in twelve- and fourteen-inch barrels, also a couple of sixteen and a quarter-inch beauties; the newer G2 Contender, twelve- and fourteen-inch barrels; and the unparalleled Encore, accepting twelve- and fifteen-inch barrels. I own all sixteen barrels for those two particular lengths. Some with blue finish, walnut grips and forends. Others in stainless steel and rubber grips and forends. Sixteen calibers ranging from 17 HMR to a 500 S&W."

Brian slowly shook his head and smiled. "Is this a full confession, Mike, or are you going to tell us something further?"

"He scopes them."

"He scopes them," Brian repeated in a daze.

"Meaning his handgun barrels are mounted with pistol scopes."

"You got some kind of crystal ball, Mike?" Vic asked the firearms specialist.

"Why does it have to be a pistol and not a rifle?" Brian pressed. "Just because the killer wasted the kid from a vehicle several yards away?"

"Well, in a sense it is a rifle, Brian. A compact rifle at that. Then again, he could be switching back and forth, smacking a rifle barrel onto the same frame, which I tend to doubt. In any event, it has to be an Encore because the Contender doesn't offer barrels for calibers in .22-250, .270, and the .308. The Encore does. My guess is that when he becomes a bit bored, he'll go up in caliber, not barrel length."

"Why, Mike?" Lorna questioned.

"Simply because he enjoys the challenge of a handgun. And not just any killer with a handgun, but the *same* serial killer sporting a single-shot pistol with a scope. That's his game."

"Gary feels he's a professional," Brian said.

"Oh, indeed he is."

"Why do you say that?"

"Why do I say that?" Mike pushed back his chair and pulled open the top desk drawer then closed it. "Here's why I say that," he declared, withdrawing several graphic photocopies in living color although all five victims were surely as dead as presidents on greenbacks. "Billy Phillips," the big, baldheaded man began, "shot through the right temple just as clean as a whistle," he declared. "Several seconds passed as the serial killer reloaded his weapon, according to earwitness reports. Next came Janet Phillips; the shooter's bullet scoring a bulls-eye, dead center at the very top of his target as the mother bent over her boy's bloody body. Brad Madison, mailman. Left temple drilled as deftly as the eight-year-old boy's. Michael Matuco, hit in the heart of the heart through the back of the teenager's body. Ellis Everett, shot in the forehead through the very center of his brain. Next question."

Everyone stood silent before Brian finally spoke. "Where did you get those photos, Mike?"

"Where do you think I got them?"

"You know you're not supposed to have them."

"You know, you're an arrogant prick. You want my help, and then you hand me a ration of shit. Go find this fuck yourself. And go fuck yourself while you're at it." He pushed the photographs across his desk toward Brian.

Brian gestured. "You got copies of the reports in your drawer, too?"

"Oh, you mean these," he snapped, reopening his drawer and removing a file folder. "Here."

"They're classified, Mike."

"They're copies, and they're under lock and key whenever I leave this office."

"*You're* going to be under lock and key if you're not careful," Brian warned.

"Yeah, you're just upset because your own wife and your partner put your shit out on the street. Better listen to them carefully next time, hotshot. Their instincts are second to none."

"Have a nice day, Mike," the lead detective concluded.

"I was even gonna show you an Encore, for an encore, dickweed. Maybe you better *back* the hell out of here."

"Is that a threat, Mike?" Detective Brian Archer retorted and smirked as he turned around and headed for the door. "Listen up, troops," he added good-naturedly. "Better cover my back."

"And why not? You've got your wife to cover your ass," Mike Grasso rejoined and laughed heartily. "And close the fucking door behind you."

Lorna and Mike exchanged glances before she furtively and fondly blew the man a kiss, followed by the forming of words silently shaped and set upon her lips . . . *Johnny Chih's*.

Two o'clock, he signaled with two fingers raised before his face.

Detective Lorna Hanover nodded and quietly closed the office door. She loved that Chinese restaurant.

Chapter Nineteen

Johnny Chih's Chinese Restaurant sat near the southwest corner of Montauk Highway in Westhampton. Sergeant Mike Grasso was already seated when Detective Lorna Hanover appeared at 2:15 p.m. The young woman wended her way past several seated customers engaged in banal conversations as she approached Mike's table in the rear of the establishment. He stood and cordially pulled out a chair for her.

"Uh-uh," the detective waved a finger in mild protest. "Not there. I can't sit with my back to the door either. Sorry I'm late," she said and sighed heavily, leaning over the table and giving him a peck upon the cheek, moving her place setting and chair next to his. "Couldn't get away so fast. Sit, sit."

"Glad you could get away at all," the armorer said fondly. "This case keeping you pretty busy, I suspect."

"What case? I can't talk about any cases," the comely homicide detective chided coltishly.

"Bet your pretty little bottom you can and will with me," he challenged. "Unless you wanna pay for lunch," the big man threatened with a smile and a twinkle in his eye.

"What are you so upbeat about? Brian wants to ring your neck and probably mine if he knew I was sitting here with you."

"Jealous you think? If he saw the way we're sitting, that might cause him pause."

"If my fiancé saw the way we're sitting, he might pause just long enough to pull his piece and put a bullet between your eyes," she considered through a giggle.

"That supposed to be funny? You're the one who rearranged

the furniture and utensils."

"Shut up and order me a Tsingtao."

"Only if you're officially off duty," Mike put forth and made her swear.

"I swear," she promised.

"Good, now you can talk about the case," he decided, winked and nodded.

"Nothing to talk about, Mike," she said quite seriously. "We really got little to go on."

"Oh, really?" The man was miffed. "I just gave you dicks the lead of your life and the lead detective sticks it up my ass. That's some gratitude, Lorna. No?"

Lorna lowered her eyes to the tablecloth.

"What? You don't agree?"

"Mike. You've got to look at it from Brian's perspective."

"Really?"

"Yes, really. Look. There's little doubt that the same frame was used in all five homicides. All right?"

"Little doubt?" he grumbled.

"All right. No doubt as far as the frame goes. Okay?"

"And if you agree the same frame was used, then it stands to reason the perp is using interchangeable barrels. So what's Brian's fucking problem?"

"Come on, Mike. You know what the problem is here. None of us know with any certainty that the frame is from a Thompson/Center Encore handgun, with a fifteen-inch barrel no less. Why not an Encore rifle with a twenty-four or twenty-six inch barrel? Why not a Marlin or a Ruger pistol or rifle. But no. You have to narrow the weapon down to an Encore pistol with nothing to go on except a hunch."

"Well, excuse me for living and breathing. What the fuck do *you* people do for openers when there's little or nothing to go on? Huh? The lab folks won't be able to tell you the length of the barrel with relationship to rate of twist. They'll sure as shit tell you, though, that the same frame was used with interchangeable barrels. I'm just taking it to the next level for you doubters based on what's available out there in the finest of firearms. Understand?"

What Lorna was about to say next, she realized, was going to hurt. But she felt she had to say it regardless.

80

"You're taking it to the next level based on *your* familiarity and love of that handgun. It's what *you* would have used if *you* were this madman. Okay? But it's not necessarily real world, Mike. All right?"

"Why?"

"Essentially because a serial killer doesn't go around shooting people with a single shot pistol. That's why. Can you see where Brian's coming from?"

"I thought I explained all that. This nutcase is looking for a challenge. What I didn't get a chance to explain is that unless a person purchases a complete handgun, frame and barrel together, the barrel or barrels one acquires aren't fucking CoBISed! Get it?"

Robert Redler sitting with Liza Downs at a distant table got it immediately, their ears ringing with alarm.

"The guy's a fucking sicko, Lorna, but a smart one."

"Keep your voice down. You're attracting attention," Hanover ordered.

Mike expelled an angry column of air. "Sorry. But that's what this nut is counting on," he said in exasperation, lowering his voice to a whisper. "Those barrels are untraceable because he probably bought or acquired the frame and barrels separately, I'd bet good money. At best, the frame alone is registered on his pistol license, if he even has one."

"Along with the word, MULTI, which means he can interchange and legally carry. I know the deal, Mike," she assured him with a smile.

"Excuse me. Would you folks like something to drink?" Mickey Chih, the owner's son, inquired politely.

"Tsingtao for the lady. Dewar's and water, neat, for *moi*."

"Coming right up, Mike."

Tea, noodles and duck sauce were immediately brought to their table by a middle-aged server wearing a black and white uniform and a big bowtie. "You ready order?" he asked without expression.

"Later, waiter," Mike snapped with some annoyance, launching back into their conversation.

Robert and Liza were eating quietly. Not a word had passed between them for twenty minutes while they tried in vain to pick up and put together further bits and pieces of the couple's disturbing conversation from more than halfway across the room, convinced that the talk at the back table revolved around the disposal of a pistol barrel lying on the bottom of Long Island Sound in 165 feet of corrosive seawater.

"So, to summarize," Mike persisted, "your first step to finding the guy sooner than later is in trying to trace that frame," he said to Lorna in a hushed tone after the server took their order for a second round of drinks along with spareribs and steamed dumplings for appetizers. "Secondly, get a profile on this guy. I'd examine military records and gun clubs in looking for a match. Thirdly, like I already said, I'd anticipate him going up the scale in handgun caliber."

Redler passed by the couple on his way to the men's room.

"It's still all supposition at this point, Mike. Plain and simple."

"Will you do me a favor and at least have Kim look into this a little further?"

"Believe me, she is."

"I'm talking about an *Encore* pistol frame. Please."

"I'm sure she'll explore all avenues, Mike. You know that."

The firearms training supervisor nodded then shook his head in disappointment.

"What? Not good enough? We can't put all our efforts into a *single* direction, my good and dear friend. Not yet. Not with what we have to go on. Can't I get through to you on that? If we had something concrete, you know damn well that Kim and Big Sister would go to any length, including fifteen inches," she toyed with a winsome grin. "CoBISed or not, you know better than most what a farce and fallacy that program has become. A politician's platform come voting time. Ain't worth a pound of spent brass for reloading," she quipped, trying to assuage matters and bridge the divide.

"Right. But the frame. It's worth a shot. Just try."

"You know that Gary and Kim's in your corner. But she lives with and has to listen to the man who's running this show. Your pal, Brian. And there is such a thing as police procedure. And Brian has a boss, too. Detective Lieutenant Ethan Powell, head of homicide. Remember him? Kim's already stuck her neck out. Big time. Yes? And tonight when Brian comes home, he may chop it off for her. I know you know what I'm talking about."

"I didn't deny it, did I? Nor did I confirm where I got the pix and reports."

"But now you want her to stick her neck out again."

"Lorna. Look into these baby browns," he pleaded. "What I want more than anything is for the team to nail this guy. More than you can ever imagine," he stated as he actually started to tear.

"What is it, Mike?"

Mike was shaking his head slowly, doing everything within his power to keep from blubbering.

"Tell me," she commanded.

"Neph-nephew through my first marriage. I loved that kid and couldn't even go to the fu-funeral without there being a full-blown scene. Told to keep away."

"What are you talking about?"

"Michael Matuco."

"Oh, no, Mike. I'm so sorry," she responded, moving the chair closer to her companion and wiping away his tears with a linen napkin.

"You know something?" he threw out bravely and jokingly to conceal both his embarrassment and grief.

"What Mike?" She took and held his hand.

"I hope your fucking fiancé *does* come by and find us like this," the man swore, trying to cover both his tears and grief with humor.

It took everything inside of Lorna to repress both a sob and a little laugh.

It took everything within Mike to keep from bawling in a public place.

Ironically, in the very next instant, Lorna was quietly wiping away her own tears as Mike coughed and choked while trying to suppress a nervous giggle.

"I'll push Kim along on this, Mike. I promise."

Mike nodded appreciatively. "Let me tell you how sure I am about this Encore pistol, Detective Lorna Hanover."

"Tell me Sergeant Grasso."

"I told you dicks back there, and I'm telling you once again, that the guy's going to go up in caliber."

Lorna nodded.

".45-70 Hornady Government cartridge would be *my* call. He's experimenting."

".45-70 Government," Lorna repeated and committed to

memory.

Mike nodded. "He could jump to a .450 Marlin cartridge, or even a .45 Colt/410 gauge. But my guess is he'll go with the .45-70 Gov for now."

"How do you figure?"

"There's a pattern emerging here. He likes to skip one or two barrel selections, moving into the next group or class of caliber: small, moderate, large. If he chooses that old favorite U.S. military round next time out, I'll be able to tell you a bit more about this fuck."

"Give me something to go on now."

"Just did."

"You mean military?" she asked rhetorically.

"You got it, girl."

"Tell me more."

"First, I'll have to do a little more research myself."

"Don't know it all, big guy?" she needled playfully.

"Not by a long shot, pretty lady. Not by a long shot."

Chapter Twenty

Liza and Robert hardly touched their food, waiting for the couple at the back table to finish theirs. The writer and his soul mate dawdled over tea and then more tea, waiting for the man and his companion to pay the check and leave.

Robert wanted to ask Mickey Chih about the pair but then decided against it. Liza agreed. Instead, they watched from a window as the two got into their respective vehicles. Robert jotted down the license plate numbers.

"You can't have your friend Dennis run their plates without creating suspicion," Liza cautioned. "The last thing you want to do is draw attention to yourself."

"Dennis is retired from the force."

"Then what are you going to do, Mister Civilian? Huh?"

"Not sure."

"That's what I thought. I think they're detectives, Rob."

Robert shook his head. "The guy's a range instructor or something."

"How do you know?"

"Shoulder patches on his jacket. I think he's with the Sheriff's Department."

"How could you see anything with the coat under his arm?"

"He had it on the back of his chair when I went to the bathroom. Almost pissed in my pants *before* I hit the head."

"Very funny. Seriously, what are we going to do?"

"Have the waiter wrap everything except the broccoli."

Liza gave him a cold stare that could kill.

"Listen. The barrel is in the middle of the Sound. The signature parts of the frame have been changed. So let's just relax. I'm sure they were talking shop regarding some other case. Not the deli scene. Let's not run paranoid. Just relax."

"Paranoid? Relax? Who was it who hardly touched his plate?"

"Well, neither did you."

"Who was it who just admitted he practically pissed in his pants?"

"Not that you didn't shit a brick back there at the mere mention of CoBIS."

"Mere mention . . . ." her voice trailed off. "Strange how shit just happens to follow us around like a swarm of flies. I have a bad feeling about all this."

Robert didn't like it when Liza had one of her unfavorable feelings.

"You know what I think this is all about?" he tried to reassure her.

She didn't answer.

"I think that business had to do with the missing twenty-three-year-old woman from Westhampton Beach."

"Vinessa somebody." Liza shook her head. "I think not."

"Why not?"

"Because there's no mention in the press of any weapon. Her car and a coworker's were found set on fire. There's obviously foul play, but I doubt that a gun calling for CoBIS-ing enters into it."

"Well, maybe it does now, and we just happened to stumble in on and overhear part of an ongoing investigation."

"Maybe it has to do with the shooting in Riverhead. That college kid they found in a phone booth."

"Then why a meeting in Westhampton? I'm sure it has something to do with that missing woman. And why was the guy so personally upset?"

"Maybe a friend or a relative. It's a small world out here."

"We're probably just making a mountain out of a mole hill."

"I sure as hell hope you're right."

Chapter Twenty-One

It was twilight. Albert Simone trembled as two young thugs stood blocking his path at the back of Shelly's Deli in Riverhead. The older youth brandished a four-inch blade.

The younger boy threatened the deli employee with a string of profanity. "My stepfather and uncle are dead because of you," the stocky teenager accused the man.

"That's not true," Albert pleaded.

"Shut your hole," the taller, older, knife wielding felon barked. "My brother-in-law never hurt anyone in his entire life. He was just the fucking driver. He wasn't even armed." The black buck ran the back of his blade menacingly across Albert's throat.

"I—"

"I said shut the fuck up!"

Albert stood shivering in his shoes.

"Now, here's what you're gonna do, honky motherfucker. You're gonna tell us where your boss *now* stashes the cash. Just like before. *Déjà vu*, dirtbag cocksucker."

Albert was shaking his head and sobbing as he tried to speak.

"You saying no to me, motherfucker?" the twenty-two-year-old snapped as he slashed at Albert's apron with the sharp edge of the blade.

Albert fell backward then scrambled for the back door, but the teenager stopped him abruptly with a steel-toed boot to the side of the deli worker's ribcage.

"He doesn't keep money around here anymore," Albert screamed. "Shelly makes the deposits. I swear it!"

"I told you to shut the fuck up," the older thug forewarned.

"You wanna disturb the neighbors? You wanna bring down the police? Because if they come, Prince Albert, we're gonna tell them how you helped plan that fuckin' job. You understand what I'm sayin' here, scumbag?"

The boy who booted Albert was smiling gleefully as he helped the frightened figure to his feet, brushing him off neatly with hands the size of catchers' mitts.

"Now ya can't go in there waitin' on customers lookin' like this when you open up," the older punk decided. "So, listen up. After Friday's three o'clock deposits, the fucking bank is closed. That's still three more hours till closin' time that y'all rakin' in the green. And since this ain't no bakery, bro, there ain't no other place the dough gonna go," he jived and giggled insanely, "'cause we know fo' a fact he don't take home no cash, no how. Next day's Saturday, and Washington Mutual got no business hours; but Steve, Shelly and you got ten o' them. Sunday, six more. That's nineteen motherfuckin' hours from Friday afternoon till the close of business on Sunday, sucker. Nineteen motherfuckin' hours of cash flooow, flunky. And I'm gonna be the monkey on yo' back if we don't have it all by Sunday evenin'. Ya dig?

"Ya see, I look at it this way," the older hoodlum went on, tilting his head bizarrely at a forty-five degree angle while studying Albert like he was some sort of strange bug. "This place is a cash cow but with no cream in the kitty whenever my *compadres* came by in the past and hit the cash box. That's because your boss hid the bulk of big bills in a big tin coffee can as we both know. So, where does he hide it now, Fat Albert? That's all we gotta know for now."

"I don't know," Albert lied.

Barret Dexter glanced at his older cousin.

Terrance Lincoln licked the blade of his knife before plunging its tip into Albert's outstretched palm that Barret had grabbed and was holding in a vise-like grip. Albert instinctively closed his bloody hand before Terrance repeatedly ran the blade between three knuckles of the deli man's flabby fist.

"What the fuck did we just tell you about that screaming?" Terrance warned. "Come back—hold still here . . . you bloody fat fuck!"

The three struggled furiously, clumsily climbing the steps

88

leading to the top of a gated wooden platform, level with an open rusty Dumpster set behind the building. The two cousins roughly lifted Albert and dropped him into the bin. Peering down at the helpless wounded employee lying in a pile of fetid garbage, crates and cut up cardboard boxes, Terrance unzipped his fly and withdrew his penis.

Barret removed a book of matches from his coveralls along with a good-sized can of lighter fluid.

Albert was quietly sobbing and shaking his head.

"I wanna help you out, Al-ol-pal," Terrance swore. "I really and truly do. But you gotta understand that *we* have a business to run, too. It's a cash-and-carry kind," he explained and nodded brightly. "And as you well know, we had some recent unforeseen expenses like burying my brother-in-law along with Barret's uncle and stepfather. So sorry your funeral has to be an open casket for the viewing, Al . . . for Steve and Shelly to personally weep above your ashes, not to mention your poor sister who we know you love and cherish and will surely die on the spot when we pay her a little visit and tell her the sad, sad news. 'It was so tragic, Gretchen. Al's entire blob of a body was a ball of fucking flames as he raced around and through the garbage like a great big fucking rat with no place to run or hide.'"

Barret Dexter was busy squirting Albert and the interior of the Dumpster with lighter fluid, finally emptying the contents of the can.

"Of course, I'll do my best to extinguish the flames should you change your mind midstream," Terrance Lincoln declared and giggled hysterically after realizing his own sense of serendipitous humor. "Midstream, get it?" he roared, shaking his penis at Albert.

Barret struck and cupped a match, about to drop it into the flammable, rank container.

"ALL RIGHT!" Albert screamed at the top of his lungs. "All right," he yielded in an incoherent whisper.

"What was that, Albert?"

"I said, all right."

"All right, what?"

"I'll tell you his new hiding place."

Barret extinguished the flame.

"Are you sure, Al? It's not like you're gonna get nineteen more chances," Terrance, assured the employee before snatching the book of matches from his cousin's hand, ripping all but one from the tiny package, tossing them one by one in the still, stale air as if they were petals being offered from a single deadly flower. "That's one for every hour of booming business we better collect on," he declared with a sly wink. "Ten percent to you as always as promised, sport."

"I don't want any money. Just get me the hell out of here," Albert begged.

But both men shook their heads.

"First you tell us where the money's stashed so we don't have to do a song and a dance with your boss when we walk the fuck in on him." Terrance readied the head of the last match in one hand—the striker in his other. "Where?"

"In the second oven in back of the kitchen. The one that doesn't work. Below the broiler plate. That's where he keeps it. Wrapped in aluminum foil. Now get me the hell out of here."

"You sure you ain't got keys to this place, Albert?" Barret questioned. "Make things real easy for everyone."

"Would I be out here in the cold—trying to clean up in the dark — waiting on one or the other of them to open up? Would I?"

"Could light and warm up this place for you in a heartbeat, Albert," Terrance assured him. "Better be levelin' with us, whitey."

Albert Simone wept bitterly. "I am. Ple-please believe me. I am."

Chapter Twenty-Two

Justin Barnes and his new partner were returning from a whirlwind tour of several cities and suburbs: where Janet Phillips and her five-year-old son were murdered; where a mail carrier had been found shot to death along a quiet residential street; where Michael Matuco attended college; and where Pug's 'parents on premises' had lived for many years with a breeder, Ellis Everett's brother, before Ellis moved north to Massachusetts.

"Well, partner. We're batting a fat zero. The only thing we learned is that you're a purebred and with papers to prove it. Big shot with a pedigree. Registered with the A.K.C. Me? In my heyday, and according to records, I had a.k.a. fixed to my surnames. A long list of them in fact. My favorite was Justice B. When a magistrate once asked me what the scrawled B stood for, I told him the truth. Barnes. So he said, 'Then why didn't you sign the sheet like that?' I explained that I didn't know how to write. So then he asked me, 'Who wrote the name Justice on the sheet?' I said the deputy did. So he called the deputy over and had him write my last name on the paper, having me put an X next to it, but with a little help," Justin jawed. "When we got to trial, my court appointed attorney argued that I never admitted to the charges. 'But we have his signed confession,' the judge remarked. My lawyer insisted that the court did not, that the document was a forgery, crafted by the deputy who had it in for me. 'Is that your X next to your name?' the judge asked me. ' No, dat be da Sheriff's deputy mark dat he made wif his hand on top o' mine, yo honor. I don't know how to write no letters, no how. Never did learn my X Y Z's,' I explained, showing him a perfect set of teeth. 'Can count, though,' I added, tapping my middle finger to all thirty-two ivories long after he announced, 'Case dismissed.'"

Pug moved from the center of the front seat on over to Justin's side, nestling his small face against the driver's leg.

"You liked that story, didn't you? Got a score or more like that one. Of course, not all of them turned out so well. Not so funny when a judge says 'two to five' and no one laughs as you lift your head and stare blankly at the clock on the wall while scratching your head."

The dog stretched, yawned and rearranged its body, climbing up and onto Justin's lap, nuzzling a warm head in a fold of the man's tan cloth coat. Justin drove and stroked the brindled, short-haired pup.

"We'll be home in a bit, Pug. Just don't piss or poop on my pants or I'll have a sissy fit."

Chapter Twenty-Three

Case Reece, a.k.a. Sam Carper, Mac Pace, and Marc Espe, drove his blue van with the AM station blasting his ears. It wasn't that he enjoyed the song, the soloist, or even the station; it was simply that the afternoon bluegrass music helped keep him awake. It had been a long ride down the coast from Maine to Virginia, and there was really no point in stopping now, Case considered through a yawn. He was so close, and the man yearned for his old Kentucky home set in the foothills of Black Mountain in Harlan County. A couple of catnaps had sufficed along the way, but the man was in need of a decent night's sleep. Still, even more immediate was his insatiable desire for bloodshed.

"Better to commit sin in Old Dominion than my beloved Bluegrass State," he talked and tittered through still another deeper, longer, wider gape, leaving Highway 58 on his way to Big Stone Gap, Virginia. "Hold off on the snooze until after the snuff," he said decidedly and excitedly, the adrenaline already coursing through his veins.

It wasn't ten minutes before he spotted her in the distance, plodding along with a walking stick, heading in his immediate direction, crossing the field of knee-high dried grass. Case moved casually out of his seat although his heart was racing. "Calm down," he told himself aloud. "Just calm the hell down." He crouched in back and withdrew his handgun, passing a forefinger lovingly forward along the length of cold blued steel, up and back atop the matte-black optical tube, then down and around each side of the semicircular Weaver-style rings that wedded the telescopic sight to the barrel. *A precision weapon personified*, he mused. And in the hands of a master, of which there was no doubt, he'd deliver tack-driving accuracy of the most deadly sort, he promised himself through still another, but muffled, yawn.

She wore dark glasses and was a good eighty yards away when Case stepped from the vehicle and raised his weapon, running the cross hairs along the loose cloth knot just below her bosom that closed the garment's belt like a big buckle. He remained synchronized with her laggard but steady gait.

Up.

Down.

Cross wires centering within the focal plane.

Circling its target . . .

Right ~ three o'clock

Low ~ six o'clock

Left ~ nine o'clock

High ~ twelve o'clock

Little higher still.

The killer flawlessly kept pace with his moving target . . . the very center of her swollen belly . . . which he'd surely deliver back into oblivion.

Standing with his arms extended fully, the base of the pistol butt planted solidly upon a palm, he slowly exerted a rearward pressure upon the trigger, controlling his breathing, deftly tracking the tiny black bulls-eye centered between the vertical row of fifteen plastic buttons.

Button number 7.

The round from the 45-70 Government spiraled counterclockwise as it left its chamber. The pregnant woman, along with her eight-month-old fetus, flew backward like a delicate young bird thrown clear of its late spring nest.

"Bet you never knew what hit you," Case Reece said and smiled in jubilation. "Now, maybe I can get some rest."

Slipping on a pair of lightly lined linen gloves before opening the action by pulling back on the trigger guard spur, the serial killer manually removed the spent cartridge and purposely dropped it precisely where he stood.

"Wow! That has got to be a sixty-five yard shot," Case calculated excitedly. "If I wasn't so damn spent, I'd pace it off. But

I'm quite sure the media will oblige me with a full report," he muttered quietly with a sense of serenity and total satisfaction written across his handsome face.

Chapter Twenty-Four

Detective Gary York stood before the head of homicide, directing the man's attention to the open travel atlas on the boss's desk. From a seated position, Detective Lieutenant Ethan Powell slowly and deliberately shook his head.

"No, no, no; and above all, *no*. I can't spare you. We've got too much crap going on right here, right now."

"One week, Lieutenant."

"What part of no don't you understand? How many more times do I have to say it?"

"I'll book a flight and be back long before the Cameron case goes to trial, so not to worry."

"I'm not worried about the Cameron case. I'm worried about two unsolved cases we've got right here."

"One of which is Matuco, connected to another five."

"Yeah, with all but *that* one being out of jurisdiction. The others might as well be measured in stellar distances as far as you're concerned. Get the picture? " he growled. "Let Virginia and the rest of the other states handle theirs. We'll handle ours. I'm not going to have you travel eight hundred miles and back. And let me clue you in on something further. It may be the Appalachia area and all, but they've got good people down there on that case. Unlike you, I let my fingers do the walking, my mouth do the talking, and I get things done."

"Fine!" Gary was fuming. "Just great. Tell you what. Meet me halfway."

The lieutenant looked down at the map and grinned. "Let's see here. Meet you halfway, you say. That would be somewhere around Aberdeen or Baltimore, but quite frankly, I don't have the time," he jawed jokingly, looking up peevishly and more than a bit miffed by his detective's persistence.

"Funny man. Then if you won't send me, send Justin."

Powell wore the look of exasperation. "I just let you talk me into sending Barnes on some flight of fancy to half a dozen cities and states as far away as Florida. Before that, I let him go to Massachusetts, and look what happened. He comes back clueless."

"You know that's not true. He found the cartridge and the bullet."

"And a mutt, no less."

"Purebred."

"That he calls his partner."

"Because you don't give him one."

"Because he can't hold on to one. Like that Rubino woman he almost got killed a couple of years back but who's smart enough to have nothing to do with him."

"Come on, Lieutenant. He saved her life. She's a civilian he recruited with last minute notice."

"What the hell do you think *he* is?"

"Quite frankly, Team Three considers him one of us."

"Oh, really? And quite frankly I consider him nothing but trouble who will one day give Team Three and this entire squad a black eye. He's a renegade."

"Why, because he once walked the other side of the tracks?"

"That's an interesting way of putting it. No. Because he *lived* on the wrong side of the *law*. That's why."

"You don't think that man has proved himself ten times over?"

"The man's an opportunist as far as I'm concerned. Whatever way the wind blows. He got a lucky break and grabbed it. If it wasn't for my predecessor and your partner Brian, Barnes would be back in prison where he belongs. He's nothing more than a common killer, like the kind he delights in hunting down. An unbridled, unbranded range animal is what he is."

"You know, it amazes me that you can even think that way."

"What way? And like I really even care to hear your opinion. Like it's really gonna change the way I feel about a common felon, with the emphasis on common."

"I hate to sound trite, Lieutenant, but—"

"So then why don't you keep your mouth closed and let both of us get back to work?"

Detective Gary York framed the heavy black face before him. "Try looking in the mirror and ask yourself what breaks *you* were given and grabbed along the way, Lieutenant. Breaks that your brethren hadn't a hope in hell or heaven of *ever* realizing. Sure, Justin caught a break. A big one, I'll admit. And he worked it to his full advantage with some help from Brian, Kim, and endorsed by Detective Lieutenant Theodore Groche, your predecessor, may I remind you. Justin turned his life around for the better. You want to engage in name-calling? You want to peg him as a common criminal? A killer? How about calling him what he is? Our house assassin. Might just as well call a spade a spade. But he's really no different than you or I."

"Don't you dare compare—"

"Stop sounding like the inspector whose butt you kiss morning, noon and night to keep you seated in that chair. Just remember you're only as good as *we* make you look, inclusive of that range animal who you'd like to keep in check like the rest of us but can't because he'd tell you to kiss his black ass like he did once or twice before.

"And along those lines," Gary continued, working himself into a lather, "remember too, that it was Kim and me who put this thing in motion. And it was Mike Grasso who called it on the money for the team," he went on, directing his anger and argument back to the business at hand. "A 45-70 Government cartridge—found at a Big Stone Gap crime scene in Virginia," he fumed, pointing down at the far southwestern corner of the state. "Tri-Cities Regional Airport in Blountville, Tennessee services the area. About sixty miles from the murder. An hour's drive across the state line, and I'd be there in no time, Lieutenant."

"No time is exactly what I'm giving you, Detective. And that Grasso is a wacko who's just looking for some attention. You know he retires in a few months."

"What does that have to do with anything?"

"You mean the fact that he's a wacko, wants attention, or already put in his papers?" Powell jeered.

"How about the fact that he hit the nail on the head, or more accurately pointed out to us that the same firing pin struck all five cartridges found at four crime scenes? And now we got another. Six connected murders."

"But the lab told us that."

"The lab confirmed what Grasso suspected early on."

"Yeah, and he tells you he knows the make and model of the gun. Thompson/Center something."

"Encore."

"Give me a fucking break," the lieutenant swore. "That's nuts. *He's* nuts, I'm telling you. Why not a Smith and Wesson? Why not a rifle instead of a handgun?"

"Because of the left-hand rifling found on the recovered slug at Big Stone Gap. Smith and Wesson-type rifling spirals to the right, in answer to your first question. Because the lab now feels that the lands and grooves as well as their widths are consistent with Colt-type rifling fired from a *pistol* barrel of considerate length; that is, rifling spiraling to the left, in answer to your second question. That's why."

"So then why not a Colt .45 revolver or a semi-automatic pistol? Why Grasso's insistence on a single-shot Thompson/Center Encore?"

Having paid a subsequent visit to the firearms training supervisor's office earlier, Gary had the answer ready, quoting Grasso's reply to the same question. "For openers, Lieutenant, it's a 'break open' style piece. No extractor. No ejector. That's why there were no such marks found on the rim of any of the cartridges. Kind of narrows the selection, doesn't it?"

Detective Lieutenant Ethan Powell took a moment to mull things over in his troubled mind.

Gary helped him along.

"Her body and that of the fetus stopped the lead cleanly. It's the best evidence by far. There'd be no contest in matching the bullet to the barrel once we find it—and the frame."

"Same indentation mark as on the other five cartridges?"

Gary nodded solemnly. "I put the report on your desk myself this morning. Read it."

"This guy could be anywhere, Gary."

"So could my first wife. We'll find him. We'll find the barrels. We'll find the frame and close the case."

"You pushing on this because of the heat Brian's been getting from the Matucos?" Powell questioned with a grin.

Gary did not want to compound or confound matters by telling him that Michael Matuco was Mike Grasso's nephew by marriage. "I'm doing this because I'm a homicide detective and it's my job."

"Wouldn't be because this Virginia woman was both legally blind and pregnant, could it? I mean, I can't have you losing your objectivity, Detective."

Gary considered the question carefully before he answered. "Carla Banks. Her name is Carla Banks, Lieutenant. It took a very long time for her to die, but not so long before the wildlife got to her."

More than a moment had passed between them before the commanding officer nodded without expression. "Three days and I want you back here. Understand?"

"Can I take Justin with me then?"

"You may not."

Gary turned around and headed for the door.

"Justin Barnes has a mutt to take care of, unless you forgot," Powell barked. "And don't bother saying thanks or anything."

Gary had one foot out the door.

"Better bring me back a present from the airport. Hear?"

What the lieutenant heard was the sound of the door closing abruptly followed by footsteps swiftly moving down the hallway.

"Ingrate," Detective Lieutenant Ethan Powell mumbled under his breath. "Goddamn ingrate."

Chapter Twenty-Five

Detectives Brian and Kim Archer sat at home in their study. Brian doodled behind a mahogany desk. Kim sat alongside him at one end, polishing her nails with Dazzle Frost. It was three in the morning. It had been a long and tiring day. The two were lost in the moment, their thoughts and conversation wending back to the serial killer case.

"Making any headway?"

"Two more to go," she teased, holding a slender hand out at arm's length, admiring the silvery-green glitter.

Brian smiled. "I meant the handgun."

"Big Sister and I are busy profiling the guy."

"Maybe it's a female killer," he bantered, sketching the wings of a model plane upon a yellow-lined pad.

"A woman would never shoot a pregnant woman in the stomach like that."

"Oh, no? What if the shooter was the victim of a relationship gone sour? What if the shooter not only found out that she was being two-timed but that her beau had impregnated the 'other' woman? Might not she shoot the expectant mother as well as the unborn child?" he threw out for the sake of argument.

"Nope."

"No?"

"Nope. She'd put a bullet in her brain or back but never in her belly while the woman was carrying."

"Never?"

"Never ever," Kim stated unequivocally. "Terminate half the problem, not the pregnancy, then find the beau and terminate the other half," she nodded assuredly, finishing off the next to the last nail.

"What if the baby died as a result of shooting the mother?"

"Not the same thing, now is it? A female shooter would never *deliberately* take aim with intent to terminate both mother and fetus. That's the difference."

"They're some pretty sick women out there, o' wife of mine."

"Tell me about it. But none as sick as you guys."

"Hey. You turning this into an 'all men are beasts' dispute?"

"Just stating the facts. As sick as some women are, you guys are the sicker of the lot."

"That's not fair," Brian said with a scowl.

"Fair or not, it's a fact."

"Sorry I asked in the first place. You finished?"

"You brought it up."

"I meant your nails. Can I borrow that?"

"This?"

"Yes, that."

She handed over the bottle of Sally Hanson Hard As Nails polish.

"The brush, too."

She gave him the applicator with which he took and dipped the tip into the liquid, withdrew it, then started filling in the sketch of the wings of a fighter plane penned upon the pad.

"I rest my case," she said, laughing lightly, leaning over and running a set of fingers across her husband's scalp.

"I hope that's the dry hand, darling."

"If not, it'll hold together whatever hair you're losing, dear."

"Gee, thanks."

"Heard from Gary yet?"

"Well, he's down there. That's about it. Said he'd call if he had anything," Brian added behind a yawn. "Nothing further on the frame or barrels, huh?"

"You know you'd be the first to know."

"Yeah, like I was the first to know about your giving Mike a copy of the file."

"Not the whole file. Just what he needed to know."

"What about *my* need to know? Beforehand."

"You might have said no."

"Damn right I would have said no."

"Well, there you go."

"Pull a stunt like that again and *you* may be the one to go."

"And then where would you be? Hum? Tell me. Cooking your own meals and no further along in the case before Gary and I took the bull by the horns. That's where."

"You mean you'd leave me if I fired you?"

"You can't fire me."

"Oh, no?"

"No. Only the lieutenant can fire me."

"Is that a fact?"

"Fact."

"How about my *seeing to it* that you got fired?" Brian backed off a notch.

"He'd never fire me."

"How about transferred? You think I couldn't arrange that?"

"Nope. I'm indispensable."

"Wrong. Big Sister is indispensable. You're valuable, but you're not indispensable."

"The mainframe is only as good as the person who operates it. And quite frankly, I'm the best," she offered and smiled so prettily.

"Why are we quarreling like this?" Brian balked.

"*We're* not quarreling. *You're* quarreling because you're tired. You always get like this when you haven't slept."

"I'm not tired."

"No?" Kim removed the pad and applicator from his hands. "Look. You can't even stay within the lines. Lorna's three-year-old niece colors better than this."

"Lorna's niece has a jumbo box of sharpened crayons. All I get is a beat up brush."

"This is not a beat up brush. The bristles happen to be as sharp as your tongue. And give me back the bottle before you spill it."

"I'm not finished."

"You're finished, and we're going to bed. Tomorrow I'll buy you a big box of Crayola Crayons."

"And a sharpener?"

"It comes with a sharpener. Part of the package. With sixty-four colors to amuse even a big kid like you."

"Maybe Emily and I can have a coloring contest," he kidded.

"Who?"

"Emily. Lorna's niece. No?"

Kim was rolling her lovely dark eyes while shaking her head in answer. "That's Lorna's dog's name."

"Oh. What's the little girl's name?"

"Elizabeth."

"I was close."

"To bed. Now." Kim took the bottle and inserted the applicator, tightly closing the cap.

"Sixty-four colors, you're sure?"

"Sixty-four," she assured him with a patient smile.

"Listen. On a more serious note."

"What?"

"You're working up a profile on our guy, you say?"

"You bet I am."

"So tell me."

Kim shook her head. "I'll tell you in the morning."

"It is morning."

"Back at the office when you're bright-eyed and bushy-tailed. Now stop stalling like a child and get to bed."

"You first."

Kim got up and sashayed toward the bedroom, edging the straps of a peach lace baby doll off a pair of slender ebony shoulders.

"What just happened to a good night's sleep and all that baloney?" he stalked after her.

"Night's over, o' husband of mine," she purred.

Chapter Twenty-Six

Having spent the next few days relaxing, Sep Cramer had decided it was now time to turn serious and start the first draft of his address. He had spent the better part of a morning revising and proofing his speech. The hours flew by. It was getting late and the first opportunity he allowed himself to think about getting something to eat in town. He hadn't even unloaded his bags after returning from the trip days earlier. He'd secure his toys and tools and accessories, too.

Sep bounded down the cedar steps of his seven thousand square foot retreat in the foothills and marched up to the blue Mercedes van, unlocking the doors and sliding open the passenger side panel, removing and carrying his expensive leather luggage back to the house. Moments later he returned and threw open the two wide doors at the rear of the vehicle, unloading a pair of shiny aluminum cases: one that housed his handgun along with a selection of interchangeable barrels; a second case that contained several pistol scopes of various magnifications, along with the necessary tools to affix or detach the optics quickly. He'd come back for the steel box, which compartmentalized ammunition according to caliber and gauge, all packed neatly away in different size sleeves: .22-250 Remington, .270 Winchester, .308 Winchester, .45-70 Government and a box of .45 Colt/410 shotgun shells and cartridges.

After securing his toys, tools and accessories, hungry or not, Sep jotted down some additional thoughts for a second draft of his speech. His mind was racing a mile a minute. He was preparing for the summer gala at the Bohemian Club, an elite all-male organization comprised of the country's most prestigious politicos and corporate powerhouses. The festivities spanned three weekends annually around the twenty-seven hundred acre retreat in Monte Rio, California, seventy-five miles north of San Francisco. Sep was to be this year's keynote speaker, delivering 'The Spirit of Bohemia' speech before such prominent members as the past and present Presidents of the United States George and George W Bush, Vice President Dick Cheney, Secretary of Defense Donald Rumsfeld, Secretary of State Colin Powell, former House Speaker Newt Gingrich, Statesman Henry Kissinger—to name but a few.

Among the membership were other notables such as Gerald Ford, William F. Buckley, Jr., Casper W. Weinberger, Stephen Bechtel, Jr.—not to mention Danny Glover, not at all surprising when considering that Ronald Reagan had also been a member, though no longer active, ostensibly for reasons of ill health and perhaps the man's greatest performance of all. Sep smiled to himself with a degree of satisfaction, noting that all presidents, from George Washington to George W. *had* to be consummate actors as a matter of mere survival. Sep noted sadly, too, however, that Reagan was truly dying; the great communicator. Great men one and all. From the early days of Herbert Hoover, every Republican president belonged to the Bohemian Club, which the late president had emboldened as, "The greatest men's party on Earth."

Twenty-seven hundred plus members. Twenty-seven hundred acres in Bohemian Grove near the Russian River in Sonoma country.

Sep finished editing his second draft and was famished. He got up and walked out onto the spacious wraparound deck, backdropped by the highest point in all Kentucky, the Black Mountain—four thousand one hundred thirty-nine feet from surface to summit. Sep closed his eyes and imbued the surrounding areas bleak beauty located just across the bullet-ridden state line's WELCOME TO KENTUCKY-THE BLUEGRASS STATE sign that one would pass after leaving the southwestern corner of Virginia . . . amidst the desolation of downtown Appalachia along its border . . . among the storefront churches . . . around the mountain's rural roads with its notorious rolling coal trucks barreling by at breakneck speeds . . . beyond the dizzying drop-offs that either caught the infamous 'Cars in the Trees' or dropped the soaring auto bodies far below, unburied and left for decades in decaying rusty heaps.

Home.

Home away from all his homes and wives and children.

Then off and through Lynch he traveled; a four-mile drive to the nearest town. Continuing on for almost another thirty miles as the crow flies, he brought the Sprinter panel van up to eighty miles an hour and flew most of the way to Hazard for some of the best tasting fare around. He was starving but holding out for his favorite meal. Real Kentucky fried chicken. They prepared it quite well, too, at Big Stone Gap, Sep knew, but he wasn't heading back to Virginia anytime soon.

"Should I or shouldn't I?" he said with a sudden sigh. "Wait for the newspapers' accounts of the bloody murder of a mother and her unborn, along with all the local gossip, or turn on the local news and listen now?" the serial killer considered aloud. "Either way, some know-it-all is sure to ruin my meal. Then again, it's good to know *all* the facts beforehand," he chattered and laughed like a lunatic. "Danny Glover!" the madman yammered. "I think I'll ask him to introduce me to Mel Gibson. Then the three of us can sit around and discuss *Lethal Weapon* one through four," Sep declared and positively pealed, popping an M&M into his mouth to keep him going until he reached the restaurant.

Chapter Twenty-Seven

Detective Gary York sat on a stool eating a greasy cheeseburger and French fries at a diner in Big Stone Gap, Virginia, as Sep Cramer relaxed with an after-dinner drink in a comfortable booth following a delicious Southern-fried chicken dinner in Hazard, Kentucky, some forty miles away.

A diner employee cleared a table and counter and carried off a heavy load of plates, glasses and silverware in a deep bin that rattled as he walked briskly toward the kitchen. Another man ran a broom along and around a line of pedestals near people's feet.

Gary picked up bits of idle chatter that buzzed about the busy eatery. He listened intently to the conversation between two men sitting off to his right, discussing the brutal murder.

The younger man in dusty blue coveralls had a theory. The other, wearing a field jacket and jeans, disagreed.

"He's been acting very weird lately, I'm tellin' ya."

"He's been weird since the day he moved here. That's why they call him Weird Willy," the man put forth then sipped his coffee.

"Yeah, well he's certainly capable of something like that. Believe me."

"Maybe of shooting off his mouth. Not Carla."

"Do you know he tried to pick her up here one Sunday evening?"

"So has every male I know," the older man drawled, looking up from his coffee and over at his friend.

"Don't look at me like that. I never went near her."

"Not while she was pregnant, you didn't."

"You wanna wear that cup of coffee or drink it?"

"Hit a sore spot, did I Ted?"

"I don't know what in hell she ever saw in Garson in the first place," the friend stated emphatically, ignoring the comment.

"She couldn't *see* at all. That's the only reason why you thought you had half a chance when you hit on her yourself," he needled.

"I'm telling you, I never hit on her."

"I'm not going to tell Denise," Ted's pal promised rather loudly, crossing his heart with a tobacco-stained finger.

"Nothing to tell, damn it."

Denise came from the other end of the counter and poured both men a second cup of coffee. "Tell Denise what?" she insisted.

"We were just discussing who got Carla pregnant," the older man baited them both.

"Garson got her pregnant plain as the nose on your face," Ted declared matter-of-factly.

Denise leaned in against the counter before her husband. "Garson cut out on her little over a year ago. Carla was well into her trimester. Do the math, Einstein," the attractive waitress smirked.

"Ted's going to need the unknown factor in order to do the arithmetic, Denise," his good friend stated with a straight face.

The husband and wife glanced at one another then back at Benny.

"All right, I'll bite," Denise said. "What unknown?"

"Well, Ted first needs to know how long it takes to make a baby," the troublemaker chaffed and giggled.

Benny received the heel of Denise's hand solidly against his left shoulder. Ted delivered a more menacing blow to the opposite arm.

"Hey, watch the goddamn coffee, Ted, or you'll buy me a cup."

"Is that right?"

"Goddamn right that's right. This place isn't like it used to be, you know. Time was you'd get a second *free* refill. Now you get charged for another mug."

"Times change, Benny," Denise offered as an excuse, topping off his cup with a splash equal to the amount that landed on the counter, taking the time and trouble to wipe the surface clean as well as Benny's sleeve and sticky gravy fingers in the bargain.

"So, then who was it then that got Carla pregnant?" Ted

questioned rather seriously.

"I thought we settled that," Benny decided, not knowing when enough was enough.

"I'd like to know who *shot* her; never mind who got her pregnant," Denise remarked. "Gives me the willies."

Both men laughed.

"What's so funny?" she asked with annoyance.

"Weird Willy. Ted thinks Willy shot her."

"Oh, he does, does he? Well, there's one way to find out for sure."

"How's that?" Ben asked.

"By asking him yourself," the woman answered and smiled with a mischievous gleam in her eyes. "He just pulled up," she added, nodding toward the window behind the pair.

"Oh, shit," Benny frowned, watching as the burly figure stepped from his beat-up pickup truck. "I'm sure glad I finished my dinner."

"What about your coffee, Benny?" Denise teased and tested with a grin as wide as a cavern. "I still got to charge you for the first cup. Hang around awhile and finish up."

"Nooo thank you, Denise. Not on your life."

"That makes two of us, woman," Ted agreed. "Me and Benny's got some last minute molding we gotta put up. Ain't that right, Benny?"

"Molding at this hour?" she questioned with mock surprise.

Both men threw down a ten dollar bill upon the counter to cover the cost of their meals and coffee.

"Bye, honey," Ted waved. "See you back at the house."

"Keep the change," Benny decided, frowned then scurried toward the exit door.

Every customer and employee gradually grew quiet as Willy Hawkins walked through the front door then turned to watch the pair climb into Ted Holloway's work vehicle and leave the parking lot. A good minute had passed before the husky man moseyed on up to the counter, spinning the seat of a stool clockwise while plopping himself upon another—two seats away from Gary York. Another sixty seconds had elapsed when the eccentric six-foot-six sodbuster suddenly made an announcement, directing his full attention to the stranger sitting off to his left.

"I know who shot Carla Banks!" Willy declared in a voice that thundered throughout the length and breadth of the room.

"Then you tell us in a quiet tone or you're out of here, Willy," Denise warned. "And I'm not going to tell you again. Hear me?"

Willy got up and took a seat next to the Yankee stranger. "Outsider," he said in a tone just loud enough for everyone to hear. "An outsider murdered that woman 'long with the child she carried in her womb."

Detective Gary York kept his eyes fixed straight ahead.

Willy deliberately scanned the entire space, spinning himself around on the stool a full three hundred and sixty degrees before coming to an abrupt stop.

Every head except Denise and Gary's was lowered to the counter, table or floor, although their eyes darted about the room like dragonflies.

Willy leaned to his left, got up and took the stool next to Gary's, riveting a stare no more than a foot away from the stranger's face. "I said an outsider murdered Carla and the child she was carrying. You hear me, mister?"

From beneath a set of unused utensils before him, Gary withdrew, unfolded, and then wiped his greasy hands and mouth upon the clean white paper napkin. Reaching over to his right, he took and handed Willy his own folded napkin from underneath the setup.

"What's this for?" the big man growled, grabbing the napkin roughly from the suited fellow's fist.

"For the bloody nose you're about to receive if you don't get your face out of mine," the detective said in all seriousness, his dark eyes blazing with wild abandon.

Willy backed off, mumbling something incomprehensible.

"Can't hear you, Willy," Denise exhorted, pleased as punch that someone other than she had the nerve to stand up to the psychopath.

Willy got off the stool and sent the seat spinning violently counterclockwise, leaving in a huff before the noisy clatter ceased completely.

"Another cup of coffee, honey?" Denise offered and smiled alluringly.

"He got a bigger brother?" the detective asked somberly.

Denise laughed wholeheartedly, shaking her head in the negative. Customers and employees alike relaxed and went about their business, eating, laughing and talking quietly.

"No, not to worry," Denise promised. "Neither he nor his mom, who is waiting in the truck, will be back for a month of Sundays, you can bet."

"His mom bigger than him?"

Denise laughed without restraint, again shaking her naturally blonde head. "You really put his shit out in the street," she said when she finally calmed down. "You really did."

"Guess I'll have that second cup of coffee."

"Great." She filled his cup and slid over the milk and sugar. "Got half-and-half if you prefer."

"This is fine, thanks."

"You got a name, good-lookin'?"

"Gary."

"Just passin' through, Gary?"

"Well, I was planning on staying awhile, but this place is a little too wild for me."

"Where you from?"

"New York."

Denise giggled girlishly. "New York, huh?"

Gary nodded.

"And this place is a little too tough, you say."

"Well, put yourself in my shoes."

"Love to, Gary." Denise leaned into the counter.

Gary smiled handsomely. "I've been in this town twenty-four hours, and all I hear talk about is this Carla Banks murder. I'm not in here twenty minutes when that nut walks in."

"Weird Willy."

"Weird isn't the word. He kind of puts a damper on that expression you folks got down here."

"Southern hospitality?"

"Exactly."

"Well, I'll tell you what, Gary."

"What?"

"Drink that cup of coffee real slow, have a piece of fresh

homemade cherry pie, on the house, and I could be out of here in less than fifteen minutes."

"And then what?"

"Well, if you like, you could follow me in that rental you pulled up in, and the two of us could find ourselves a quiet little spot," she said in a sweet whisper that took Gary's breath away. "Sound inviting?"

"What about, Ted?" Gary questioned, lowering his voice to a sound barely above a whisper.

"Ted went back to work with Benny, or so he said. In any event, the two of them will be drunk within the next couple of hours. They headed east out of here. We'll go west. You'll leave first, after you finish your coffee and pie. Make a right out of here, and wait for me at the top of the hill. You'll follow me."

"And you'll be driving—"

"—me crazy," she swore and beamed most beautifully.

Chapter Twenty-Eight

Gary and Denise sat in the backseat of his rental. She with her blouse unbuttoned and bra pulled down; he with his fly open and penis erect.

"So, what is it that you need to know about Carla Banks," Denise asked seductively.

"Right at the moment, nothing," the detective decided.

"That's what I figured." She stroked him gently then lowered her face toward his lap.

Gary gave a shudder. "Christ!"

"Good?" she asked on the ascent.

"Shut up."

Denise did just that as Gary leaned forward and fondled her ample breasts.

Moments later, he ejaculated somewhere deep within her throat. A quarter of an hour had past when the pair suddenly exploded together, the two of them completely out of breath, sighing and moaning and murmuring. Neither of them spoke a word for several minutes. Denise was the first to elicit conversation, a chat she was sure would be but a mutually illicit exercise in mental masturbation.

"So, are you married, Gary York?"

"Was."

"Divorced?"

"Just about final."

"Got a girlfriend back in New York?"

"Too busy."

"Just hit the bars and diners up north for a quickie, I suppose?"

"Now and then," he admitted freely.

"Happy?"

"Who's ever really happy?"

"Your turn."

"My turn what?"

"Talk. Ask me what you wanted to ask me about Ms. Carla Banks, I suppose."

"She have any boyfriends besides this Garson fellow?"

"She had one, obviously."

"Unless it was a quickie," he responded along with a wink.

Denise laughed quietly and rather sadly.

"What?"

"Nothing."

"Tell me all about nothing," he insisted.

Denise needed to unload, and who better, she surmised, than a complete stranger on whom she had just performed fellatio followed by the act of screwing her brains out in every possible position the two could manage in the backseat of a coup. "Ted. My good old unfaithful husband, Ted," the young woman began.

"Ted and Carla?" Gary asked with some surprise.

Denise nodded, buttoning her blouse after pulling on her panties.

"How do you know?"

"How do I know? he asks. Carla's perfume on his hair and clothing. Carla's shade of pink lipstick on his overalls. I was the one who was blind at first."

"Anyone else know about this?"

"Benny suspects, I guess. That's the funny part," she stated with a scowl. "Ted would go to great lengths to hide his affair from his friends. He'd park his car across that meadow most afternoons and walk a half a mile to her house. But he didn't even have the decency to try and cover up the obvious from me. When I confronted him with the scent of her perfume and color of lipstick on his clothes, he outright lied and said that Carla dropped by this or that bar-and-grill or tavern for a drink with the boys. In truth, she'd never go near a gin mill or saloon. She never took a drink in her life. One day I followed the bastard at a distance and waited for him to return to the car. An hour and a half later, the two of them came back together across the meadow. Hand in hand. I never confronted him with that. It's one thing to *know* your spouse is fooling around. It's another to *see* them together. It broke my heart."

"Is this your revenge?" he asked bluntly.

"I never cheated on him even once until now," she answered, subtly brushing away a tear.

"That's not what I'm asking. Is this your way of getting even—now?"

Denise shook her head.

"Why do you stay with him?

"Why do I stay with him? he asks. Well, I think the answer to that has to do with demographics and geography."

Gary seemed impressed. "Demographics and geography? Explain."

"Where do you live in New York, Gary? The big city?"

Gary shoved in his shirt and zipped up his pants. "Suburbs. Long Island."

"The population here in Big Stone Gap is five thousand. Everyone knows someone who knows someone. Where would I go? What would I do?"

Gary had to laugh. "It's not like you'd starve if you left him. You could waitress here or anywhere. You told me you have no children or family holding you down. I don't get it."

"Maybe that's the real reason, Gary."

"What is?"

Denise paused. "I can't have any children."

"So you're blaming yourself? Is that it? You're punishing yourself and excusing him for his actions. You can't have children, but he can knock up some blind woman, and that seems to even the score in your mind?"

Denise said nothing.

"Maybe if she lived and had the baby, you and Ted could go over there and help feed and diaper the kid. Maybe that would satisfy your maternal instincts. Is that why you'd hang around here? Carla Banks is dead, Denise. Your marriage is dead. Wake up. Pick up and leave or stay and start a new life. You're a very pretty, intelligent, nice lady. A guy would be lucky to find a woman like you."

"Pick up and start all over, you say. Just like that."

"Yes. Just like that."

Denise looked at Gary for what seemed an eternity.

"What?" he asked uneasily.

"You wouldn't want to take a chance on a broken down thirty-one-year-old, would you? Maybe take me back to New York when you leave here?" she asked plainly and without emotion.

Gary thought for a moment then finally answered. "You wouldn't like what I do."

"I thought you said you were an insurance investigator. Investigating fraud in her family or something."

"I lied."

"You lied."

"Yes."

"Did you lie about not being married, too?"

"No."

"So what did you lie about? What is it that you do exactly that you're afraid to tell me, Mr. Gary York, fraud that you are?"

Gary took an uncomfortable breath. "I'm a Suffolk County homicide detective. Long Island. I'm down here investigating Carla Banks' murder."

Denise didn't seem at all surprised. "A bit out of your jurisdiction, no? I mean a big New York cop in a small town like this."

"Murder doesn't concern itself with geography or demographics," he put forth playfully.

"Nor statute of limitations, I'm told. See, I do know something about the law," she stated and smiled anxiously.

Detective Gary York was back on the job after slipping into his expensive leather Loafers and straightening his tie.

"I'm going to ask you four questions, Denise Holloway."

Denise sat upright at the sound of his tone. "All right, ask."

"Did you shoot Carla Banks?"

"I thought about it. Believe me. But no, I did not."

"Could Ted have?"

"Not in a million years."

"Is there anyone you know of who may have wanted to cause her harm?"

Denise shook her head. "No one. She was well-liked. No one," she repeated. "Not even Weird Willy or his mom."

Gary appeared satisfied, yet lost in thought, remaining silent.

"You were going to ask me four questions. Was Willy the other?"

Gary shook his head. "Willy Hawkins couldn't get out of his own way let alone shoot someone."

"He is a psychopath, but he'd never hurt Carla. I think he liked her like everyone did." Denise began to cry.

Gary handed her his handkerchief. "I'm going to need to talk to your husband, Denise."

"What about?" she questioned with a start.

"About Carla and that meadow down there. She might have been heading back home after seeing your husband off. Afternoons you said. That's where they found her. In that meadow, murdered in the afternoon, although they didn't discover the body till the following day."

"Yes, but—"

"But he's not a suspect if that's what you're worried about. Nor are you or Willy or his mom," he assured her. "We believe the killer picks his victims at random, moving from state to state."

"Oh, my God! How many people has he killed?" she exclaimed.

"Six that we know for sure. Ted may have seen or heard something."

Denise was shaking her head. "The police would have questioned him, no?"

"Would Chief Wilcox know about his affair?" Gary shook his head in answer to his own question. "I spoke to his people who interviewed more than a dozen folks. Ted wasn't one of them. But guess what?"

"What?"

"Benny was. And according to one of the officers, Benny saw no evil, spoke no evil, and heard no evil. But Benny is Ted's best friend; drinking buddies they are, indeed. And I'd bet you dollars to doughnuts, or some more of that cherry pie, that Ben, at the very least, just like you said, suspected Ted was having an affair with her."

"So what does that mean?"

"Probably nothing. Just that Ben's his good friend. In any event, I have to have a talk with Ted. And it might be a good idea if I have a word with Benny Rodgers in the bargain."

"I see you know all the players by their first and last names, including mine," she said quite frankly.

"Except the name I really need to know," he stated sourly.

"What about question number four?" she reminded him.

"Oh, that. Do you want to come to New York to live with me for the rest of your life? Of course, we'll have to change one of the player's names from Holloway to York. But not till after the divorce. Yours. Not mine. I've got the jump on you by a year."

"The sex was really that good, was it cowboy?"

Gary shrugged. "Not to worry. They say it gets better as time goes by."

The detective received a shot in the arm harder than she or her husband had given Ben back at the diner.

"Hey, I'd like an answer to my question. Not your abuse."

"Are you serious?" she asked sincerely, the intentness of his tone coupled to the proposal gradually sinking into her brain.

"I never kid a kid. Even a thirty-*three*-year-old," he scolded, removing a small pad from his pocket and showing her his notes. "It never ever pays to lie to the police," he made perfectly clear.

"Mother of God," the woman declared. "Chief Wilcox tell you that?"

"That and the fact that you knew Carla Banks better than anyone."

"I thought I did at first, Detective Gary York. We were once good friends."

"In answer to my question."

"He wants to know if I want to go to New York and spend the rest of my life with him," Denise said quietly to herself.

"Well?"

"When?"

"In a few days."

"Do I tell him?"

"Nope. You just up and leave when he's out drinking with Ben. We'll handle the rest from New York."

Denise nodded, pulling Gary tightly into her arms.

Chapter Twenty-Nine

The following day, Detective Gary York held a prearranged interview with Ted Holloway at a booth in the back of a bar-and-grill along the outskirts of town. Ted's friend, Benjamin Rodgers, sat pensively at the bar with a beer, waiting to be questioned by the detective, too.

"I don't know anything," Ted complained. "I hardly knew her at all. I don't understand why you would want to question me about Ms. Banks' death."

"Her murder," Gary clarified assertively. "And you'll understand better as we move ahead here."

"How come Chief Wilcox doesn't talk to me himself?"

"The chief is busy with the homicide investigation."

"But you said . . . I thought that's what you wanted to talk to me about," Ted uttered in confusion.

"I do. But there are some things I don't think you'd want the chief of police to know about."

"Like what?"

"Like for openers, withholding certain information concerning Carla Banks."

Ted looked uncomfortably from the detective over to Benny sitting at the bar with his back toward them. "Why can't my friend join us? Why do you have to talk to us separately?"

"Same reason," Gary offered nonchalantly.

"Well, maybe I don't want to talk to you at all. How does that grab you?"

"Fine. But then you and I will have to sit down with Chief Wilcox, and you'll have to tell him all about your affair with Ms.

Banks, and the fact that you impregnated her."

"You're crazy! I never touched that broad."

"Broad?"

"What are you, her father? You don't know what you're talking about, mister."

"Detective."

"Yeah, like I really give a good crap."

Gary maintained his composure and decided to take a shot in the dark. "I have a witness who saw Carla Banks leave the area where you parked the car across the meadow from her home on the afternoon she was murdered," he lied. "That same piece of shit Plymouth you got parked out there."

"Oh, you do, do you?" Ted said and smiled slyly. "So why don't you have the chief impound that piece of shit and see what they can see? Not a fingerprint other than mine they'll find. Know why? Because she never stepped foot inside that car. That's why."

"I didn't say she got in or out of it, asshole. I said I have a witness who saw her leave the area and head back to her house. The house you often visited. You can bet your ass the chief is gonna find a ton of prints in there. Yours, Ted. It'll put a whole new slant on how the chief proceeds with his investigation. Not to mention the fact that the story will be in all the local papers."

Ted looked away and back at the bar toward Ben. "That you're fucking witness sitting over there?" he snapped. "Well, is it?"

Gary said nothing, giving the man enough rope to hang himself.

"Hey, friend," Ted shouted over to Ben.

Ben turned around.

"You got a big fucking mouth, Rodgers."

Ben looked oddly at Ted and the detective. "What?" he asked in confusion, looking for some sort of explanation. "What?" he asked again.

"You know damn well, what." Ted rubbed his day-old growth of pepper-gray stubble and faced the detective. "Look."

"I'm looking," Detective Gary York said complacently.

"I didn't shoot her, all right?"

"But you were there that afternoon at the meadow, yes?"

"Yes, but I didn't shoot her, I said. She walked back to the car with me, and I left."

"Did you see or hear anything? Maybe a—"

"Nothing," Ted Holloway barked, bringing a tight fist down hard upon the rough-hewed polyurethane topped table. "She started walking back home. That was the last time I saw her. I swear it."

"What about while heading out? Did you see anybody on foot? Maybe fishing or taking a hike along that trail down there? Perhaps you heard what you thought was a car backfiring. A vehicle passing by in either direction."

Ted shook his head. "Absolutely nothing."

"How about on your way back to work? See anybody that you recognized? How about a stranger? An out-of-state plate? Anybody or anything at all?"

Ted was shaking his head emphatically. "When I rounded the top of the mountain, I saw Carla halfway across the meadow. That was the last I saw of her." Suddenly, Ted turned his head abruptly and began to hyperventilate.

"All right, just calm down now and take slow, deep breaths. Take a moment, and then tell me exactly what happened. But I want the truth, Ted. Tell me the truth and you'll be fine. Lie to me and I'll see to it that you're fucked. Can I be any clearer than that?"

Ted Holloway took a minute to catch his breath before he continued. "I waved good-bye, but of course she didn't see me. Two days later was when I heard the news," the man began to tear. "That's it. That's the truth."

"Let me ask you a personal question, Ted."

Ted wiped his eyes on a shirt sleeve and fixed his eyes on the detective.

"What were you going to do when she had the baby, Ted? What was in your head?"

Ted shrugged a heavy set of shoulders. "I don't know. I didn't want her to have it, but she insisted. It was the only thing we ever fought about. I don't know what I was going to do."

"Does your wife know about the affair and the fact that Carla Banks was carrying your child?" Gary tested with a degree of morbid curiosity.

"Denise?"

"Yeah, Denise," the cop snapped snidely.

"No-she-does-not," Ted Holloway tapped out with a stubby forefinger upon the thick thermoplastic finish. "And I want to keep it that way."

Well, you're even stupider than you look, the detective wanted to say, but didn't. Instead, he just nodded. "Want to call your buddy over here?"

"He's not my buddy anymore."

"I think he's the only friend you've got left in the world, Ted," Gary said and smiled sardonically. "I really and truly do."

The homicide detective called and waved Benjamin Rodgers over to the table.

Ben had changed earlier from a field jacket and jeans into a cheap but neatly pressed polyester suit in order to make a good impression on the detective. The carpenter's helper anxiously approached the booth as Ted took his leave and left the tavern. Neither of the men made eye contact.

"Sit down," Detective York said without ceremony.

Ben sat.

"You know that withholding information in a murder investigation is going to put you in a heap of deep shit. You know that, correct?"

"I—"

"Just listen carefully to me before you say anything perjurious. Okay?"

"Okay."

"I know you know about your friend's affair with Carla Banks. Yes?"

Ben lowered his head and nodded.

"And you knew that the child Carla was carrying was his. True?"

"Kind of figured that," he admitted, keeping his eyes glued to the top of the table.

"But you were just trying to protect your friend in not saying anything. Right?"

Again, Ben nodded.

"Yet, you were trying to get a rise out of him and Denise back there at the diner yesterday. Why?"

"Just kidding around, I guess."

But Detective Gary York was shaking his head. "No, I don't think so, Ben. You don't kid around like that. I told myself there has to be a good reason why a good friend of Ted's and Denise's would do something like that. And do you know what I came up with?"

Ben sat as still as a Buddha, though not nearly as bright or wise.

"What I came up with, Ben, is the possibility that you'd like to incriminate your buddy. Cause a bit of dissension in the Holloway household."

"And why would I want to do that, Detective?"

"Because you wanted the finger of suspicion pointed at Ted. Not only for fingering him as the father of Carla Banks' child, but for suspicion of murder as well."

"If I wanted to accomplish all that, all I'd have to do is go to Chief Wilcox and tell him what I thought. Which I didn't."

"Exactly. And there has to be a good reason."

"Such as?"

Gary reached inside the breast pocket of his suit and withdrew his notepad, flipping through several pages. "Note the time here," he said, pointing to the top of the page.

"What's that supposed to mean?" he asked fearfully, staring at the hour in question.

"It's the time you left the diner with two containers of coffee on the afternoon of the murder. One for you, and one for your pal, Ted."

"So?"

"So where did you go with the coffees when you left?"

"Back to the job to wait for Ted."

"Who just happened to be leaving Carla Banks' house, crossing the meadow where her body was found."

"If you say so, I suppose."

"And where was this job that you were doing, Ben?"

"The old Bickford Estate."

"And where is that estate located?"

"Top of the Gap."

"Top of Big Stone Gap?"

"Yes."

"And in order to get to the Bickford Estate from the diner, you had to take the mountain pass."

"Yes," Ben answered, having no idea where the detective was headed with his questioning.

"In other words, the road leading from the town of Big Stone Gap. Not the one out of Appalachia."

"Of course."

"So you had to pass anyone coming or going along that route. Correct?"

"I passed no one. I saw no one. I spoke to no one."

Gary smiled and consulted his notes. "That's exactly what you told one of the officers."

"Because it's true."

"What about when you reached the estate?"

"What about it?"

"Says here that you went to work immediately."

"Yes, Ted and I were putting up molding."

"Southeast window."

"Yes."

"Affording you a bird's-eye view of the valley."

"I suppose."

"And the meadow where Carla Banks was found."

"Yes."

"Yet you saw nothing."

"I didn't see Carla being murdered if that's what you're getting at. From up there, people look like ants."

"And vehicles look like shoeboxes I would imagine."

"If you say so."

"What if I were to tell you that I could tie you to the time of her death? What if I were to tell you that I could and *will* provide Chief Wilcox with a motive for your taking Carla Banks' life?"

"That's a lie!" Ben shifted his body anxiously in the booth. "I never touched her."

"That's funny because that's precisely what Ted was telling *you* back at the diner. Only he was full of shit."

"I never touched her *that* way either," Ben bellowed.

"What way is that, Ben?"

"Sexually or otherwise," he practically whispered as several people at the bar were looking over their shoulders.

"How about putting a bullet in her belly from a distance, Ben? You do that?"

Ben looked about ready to bawl, or blow, or both.

"Let me tell you about motive and opportunity, Benny boy. All right?" Gary continued.

"I did nothing."

"Precisely." Gary leaned in to the table. "You did nothing, and yet you did everything."

Ben stared in confusion.

"You were in that diner to stir up some shit between Denise and your good friend, Ted. You drew attention to the three of you in order to raise the question of Ted's affair in front of Denise's customers and some of the employees. Get them to gossiping. Why? Because in your sick little mind, you saw an opportunity to make a play for Denise. Don't give me that shaking of the head routine. I saw the way you watch her. There's your motive for murder: create a bit of suspicion referencing Ted's intimate relationship with Carla Banks. And if the police didn't go there after that, you'd help speed things right along. 'Fetus and forensics, guys? Your number one suspect is right under your noses, Chief Wilcox. My good buddy, Ted, I'm very sorry to say, is as guilty *as* sin or, at the very least, *of* sin. But I'm a good citizen and must do my duty to come forward.' And to Ted, what were you going to say? 'Sorry, good buddy. Them's the breaks. But not to worry. I'll take good care of Denise in your absence. After all. What are good friends for?'

"And now we come to opportunity, Benny my boy. Yours. Not Ted's," Gary labored. "You saw Ted's green Plymouth parked along the woodlot. You saw Ted and Carla heading toward the car. They said their good-byes. He drove off, and she started walking back across the meadow toward her house. That's when you came down—"

But Ben was shaking his head violently. "I was up at the estate," he swore. "I saw a vehicle pull out onto the road near the cutoff leading to the meadow. Heading east." Ben was shaking. "Then it just disappeared."

"You mean Ted's Plymouth."

"No, not Ted's. A van, I think. I didn't pay it much mind. Like you said, it was the size of a shoebox."

"Color?"

"Blue, I think."

"Solid? Two-tone?"

"Solid."

"Shade?"

"A darker blue . . . like a greenish-gray almost."

"Turquoise blue?"

"Yes! Turquoise. I'm pretty positive."

"Take a stab at the make."

Ben shook his head.

"Late model? Older looking? Wide body? What?"

"Shiny. That's all I could tell."

"Sound of the engine getting the hell out of there. Fast? Slow? Noisy? Muffled? Anything unusual? Anything at all?"

"Just normal as far as I could tell."

"A description of the driver? Number of passengers?"

"It was too far away."

"You're sure?"

"I'm telling you the truth."

The detective studied the man for a moment. Colleagues who knew Detective Gary York, knew him to be a human lie detector. His ability was uncanny. Yet, he wanted to be certain.

"Well, Ben. We went from, 'I heard no evil, saw no evil, spoke no evil,' to a shiny turquoise blue van traveling east at a normal rate of speed. That's quite a leap."

"I told you, I'm telling you the truth."

"So you say."

"I did nothing."

"Precisely what I said you did: nothing and everything. You didn't come forward or tell the police when they questioned you because you were hoping Ted would take the fall. Isn't that so, my monkey-suited friend?" Detective York smirked, covering his ears, then his eyes, and finally his mouth with two cupped hands. "Yes, Ben. You have the right to remain silent," he concluded the interview, lowering his palms patently to his lap.

"Am I under arrest?" Ben was sobbing.

"Nah, just under an arrested sense of judgment," the cop said appreciatively. "Now scram before I change my mind. And change or exchange that fucking suit while you're at it. You're really a field coat

and jeans jerk-off kind of guy."
    "Yes, sir."

Chapter Thirty

Kim Archer worked both Big Sister and herself into a tumult, tracking down late-model turquoise blue vans in the tri-state region of Virginia, Kentucky and Tennessee. The territory was vast. The list of vehicles was endless. Kim focused on the far southwest corner of the state where Carla Banks was murdered, hoping to trace such a van through the departments of motor vehicles, dealerships throughout the area, and both new and used car and truck lots. Learning the unique color description of the van that Benjamin Rodgers had given Gary certainly helped level the playing field. For this, Kim was somewhat thankful.

But the eyewitness's observation of "shiny" kept running through her mind. *Did that translate into a clean and highly polished older model, or something brand-spanking-new off the lot or out of the showroom?* she wondered, searching also for light to heavy-bodied trucks with and without four-wheel drive, in short and long beds, featuring factory installed as well as aftermarket cap conversions in case the man's powers of perception were off the mark. Kim was even considering tackling small trailers if vans and trucks did not pan out.

If only Gary's witness could have determined its make and model, definitive size or shape, or whether the vehicle actually was a van or panel van or truck, along with the number of doors and/or windows. How about a partial plate number just for giggles? the detective snickered with weariness, wishing to lead a charmed investigation for just once in her exhaustive exploration into additional minutiae that could make or break this murder case. *And what if the witness had been wrong altogether?* she entertained. *What if the vehicle was an SUV? What if Benjamin Rodgers had made up the story to get Gary off his back?* But Kim knew better because she knew her husband's partner had a nose and knack for sizing up situations and people whose lies were as large as their egos or as little as their self-esteem, from outright falsehoods to the tinniest of fibs. And he'd do it without the benefit of any electronic barometer, save the change in pitch of a person's protest, or perhaps a subtle facial expression or mannerism, but above all else, unquestionably through the telltale pair of panes leading to the interviewee's very soul; the eyes, those two extraordinary windows which paradoxically revealed as well as veiled an individual's secret, introspective world. He was rarely ever wrong. Detective Gary York could read a person as well as any psychologist or psychiatrist could interpret the underlying message, meaning or manner of a single look or statement. He was simply that good.

And if Kim were so lucky to pinpoint the vehicle in question for her colleague before he left the area, then what? Would the van be the vehicle through which they'd nab their culprit, or simply another lead on a very short list of leads that might move them further along the line of bodies the serial killer was chalking up through several states?

Stop supposing this and wondering that," Kim told herself through an amplified yawn. *Stop surmising and just do your job, girl,* she added, stretching a pair of slender arms high above her head. *But what if Ben is color-blind?* the computer maven momentarily marveled. "Did Detective Gary York, the embodiment of Mister Polygraph personified ever stop to think about that?" she asked aloud and smiled at the prodigious mainframe before her. "Hey, Big Sister? Can you answer me that one? Yeah, I know. Knowing Gary, he probably dragged the guy off to the nearest paint store to have him read a color chart," Kim went on, leaning forward, arching an aching shoulder, resuming her search while dancing eight silvery-green nails across the keyboard.

"Let's home in on a turquoise blue van, or a shade thereof, between the years 2000 and 2004. Ah, but what if the person had it repainted?" Kim questioned, continuing to torment herself. "Needle in a haystack? We'll just whittle down that pile, Big Sister. Damn if we won't, girl. Damn if we won't."

Chapter Thirty-One

Liza Downs returned home from town with newspapers, bagels and coffee. Robert Redler was upstairs brushing his teeth.

"Guess what?" Liza called out excitedly, setting aside the items then stepping through the kitchen and into the hallway.

There was no reply.

"You upstairs, Rob?"

Robert blasted the toothbrush with running water then closed the faucet.

Liza went over to the staircase and called again. "You hear me?"

Robert came down the stairs. "What took you so long? Thought you got lost," he griped.

"Grumpy when you first get up."

"I've been up."

"You weren't up when I went out."

"I was up half the night writing."

"What else is new? Now, do you want to hear some news or not?"

"I'd rather read it firsthand. Did you get *Newsday*?"

"Not there yet. I got you *The News-Review*, coffee and bagels. But boy, do I have news for you."

"Al-Qaida's backing John Kerry?" the writer toyed.

"The police found that missing woman, Vinessa Hoera."

Robert turned serious. "Found her where?"

"In the woods near Gabreski Airport."

"Didn't I tell you?"

"Her throat was cut."

"Jesus."

"Bet you won't read *that* in *Newsday* or *The News-Review*. Not this early in the game."

"Then where?"

"*The Independent. My* paper. And it's free, I'd like to remind you."

"So that's what took you so long. You were busy looking through the newspapers and gossiping at the store."

"The guy the police are holding in Riverhead jail as good as confessed."

"You'd confess, too, if they were holding you."

Liza was shaking her head. "Listen to me. He told the father where to find her body, and they did."

"The same guy they found in a burning car after he torched hers, I'll bet."

Liza nodded anxiously.

"Just a reminder that I called that one, too."

"And that's not all. That '99 Shantay Moore murder case?"

"What about it?"

"Keisha Topping's conviction was overturned. She'll get a new trial."

"Wow."

"There's more. The Marvin Tolliver case that Sidney Schatz had eons ago?"

"Who insists the kid is innocent."

"Apparently he is."

"Yeah, I was in Schatz's office when he told me that of all the cases he's ever had, he absolutely believes Marvin is innocent."

"There's a witness, a man who supposedly drove the real killer or killers to the Tolliver home that night."

"I knew that one was in the works."

"But I'll bet you didn't know that Shelly's Deli was hit again last night," she zinged him.

"What!?" Robert looked at Liza incredulously.

"Last night when Steve was locking up."

"He all right?"

"He's fine. Everybody's fine. And guess what? They caught the bastards."

"Who? How?"

"The police. That's who. How? A patrol car was cruising by the deli."

Robert laughed. "Police headquarters is set behind Town Hall, which is one building over from the deli, Liza. A patrol car is *always* cruising by."

"I sure as hell wish you would have remembered that the last time you took a gun and matters into your own hands."

"Let's just drop it. Okay? That business is behind us now."

"I certainly hope you're right."

"You see Steve there?"

"No, but Shelly and Albert were on. And you want to know another piece of news?"

"How many more reports are you holding in that pretty head of yours?" Robert teased through an affectionate smile.

"This one's a secret."

"Well?"

"Promise not to tell a soul?"

"I promise, I promise," he swore impatiently.

"It seems that Albert tipped off the police."

"Really? Who told you that?"

"Shelly, while Albert was back in the kitchen. It's all hush-hush."

"Who were the guys?"

"Two black kids. Eighteen and twenty-two."

"Customers?"

"Shelly didn't seem to think so. She said the police showed her and Albert pictures of the perps."

"So, Albert's a hero, I guess. I wonder how or what he knew to tip off the police."

"Well, he's not acting like a hero according to Shelly. He seems very upset, she said."

Robert recalled the words of one of the holdup men he shot dead while coming out of the kitchen with the large coffee can of money under his arm . . . mumbling something about Prince Albert in a can. "I think Albert was somehow involved in that first attempted robbery," the writer said suspiciously.

"Oh, is that so? Well, I think you think the worst of everyone," she whined.

"Not everyone. But you know full-well that I'm almost always right about people."

"Not in this case you're not. Albert's one of the nicest young people I know."

"*Young* might be the key word there."

"What do you mean?"

"Young people are prone to making mistakes."

"Oh, I see," she responded good-humoredly, taking Robert by the arm and leading him over to the counter. "Let's have our coffee while it's still hot. I bought nice onion bagels, and we have some cream cheese and chives left over."

"Any lox?"

"You finished the lox last night."

"Let me see those papers."

"After breakfast."

"Why not now?"

"Because you'll bury your face in them, and I won't get to see you again until lunchtime. That's why. And that's when you're not writing. Besides, I've already given you all the news."

"All the local news for sure it seems. But what about al-Qaida backing John Kerry?" Robert teased.

"Don't kid yourself, dear. Bernard Kerick's comment out of California probably has cleric fundamentalists around the globe doing exactly that."

Chapter Thirty-Two

Barret Dexter and Terrance Lincoln were being held in Riverhead jail after their arraignment in First District Court in Central Islip on charges of attempted robbery. In a small room off a holding cell at the facility, Detective Brian Archer sat across from the teenager.

"So, I understand you have some information that might be useful to us," Brian began.

"In exchange for dropping these made-up, Mickey Mouse charges," Barret bargained.

"Made-up? Mickey Mouse?" The detective smirked. "I don't think so, fella."

"You don't think so?" the young hoodlum snapped belligerently.

"First off, they're not made-up. Secondly, they carry a pretty stiff sentence, Mr. Barret Dexter."

"That a fucking fact?"

"That's a fact," he said, unruffled by the hooligan's arrogant behavior.

But Barret was shaking his head. "Let me tell you what the facts are in this bullshit case. One: I never touched or threatened that guy who's making all the noise. My word against his. Two: It'll never get to court. You're gonna see to that. Three: If you don't deal, and push comes to shove, my mouthpiece will see to it that my cousin Terrance takes it on the chin and up the ass, seeing that I'm younger, prettier, and this is my so-called first offense." The youth smiled winsomely. "Ya dig?"

Brian smiled back. "The correction officers told me you were a brash young man."

"Correction. Eighteen-year-old kid. Young and very impressionable. Terrance Lincoln misled me down the primrose path while I always tried to follow the straight and narrow."

"That's why you were arrested with a weapon, I suppose."

"His weapons. His gun. His knife. Me? My weapon is my personality and charm."

"Both of you were armed with .38s, Mister Charisma."

"Both his, in addition to a knife. He handed me his second revolver as the cops were coming around the corner."

"You mean around the corner from the rear of the deli the two of you were planning to rob."

"Only thing I ever planned in my life was a sports career. Now, listen to me and maybe you'll learn something. There's a big difference between attempted robbery and the actual deed. An even bigger difference between actually being in the building we was *al·leged·ly* planning to rob and my being apprehended in the fucking street."

"Rear of the building," Brian reiterated.

"Terrance Lincoln may have been at the back of the building, Detective. Me? Like I told you. I always try and follow the straight and narrow. I was in the street," the teenager recited.

"I got a call that you had valuable information. So let's hear it now or I leave."

"You leave, and you leave here empty-handed. You broker my release through my attorney with an ironclad agreement, and I hand you a piece of gold."

"Tell me what you got."

"You know exactly what I got or you wouldn't be sitting here, chump."

"I want to hear it from your lips."

"I give you the make, model, color and year, along with a partial plate; the direction the vehicle headed after it left the deli on the morning my stepfather and uncle was murdered, not to mention my cousin's brother-in-law."

"Along with a description of the driver of this mysterious vehicle?"

"Whattaya want? Blood from a stone? It was dark and he had a hood on or something—moving fast. You make the car, you got the killer. Deal?"

"Leniency. Best I can do. And that's after I speak to the D.A.,"
Detective Brian Archer hedged.

"Leniency's cool," the prisoner nodded. "Time served," he
added coldly. "That's all I'll agree to. Not a minute more."

Brian laughed. "You've been here three days."

"Another day and the deals off the table, whitey. Got it? Then
I'll roll the dice. And guess what? The odds are in my favor I'll walk
away with probation. And you'll walk away with zip like I said. I'm
the house, Detective Archer. I'm holding the ace in the hole in this
shithole."

Brian pulled his chair closer to the table and leaned forward,
taking the overbearing adolescent into his confidence. "I'll let you in
on a little secret, you piece of garbage. First off, I couldn't care less
about you or any member of your family. More specifically, I couldn't
give a good fuck about your uncle or your stepfather. As far as I'm
concerned, they both deserved what they got. The same goes for your
cousin's brother-in-law. Quite frankly, the person who shot them
deserves a medal. I don't see the perp as a criminal. You want to know
what I see the guy as?"

Barret Dexter shrugged indifferently.

"A good Samaritan," the detective stated evenly through
clenched teeth. "That's what."

Handcuffed, Barret leaned back in his chair. "To tell you the
truth, Detective, I couldn't give a crap about them either. Stepfather.
Uncle. Cousin-in-law by marriage. None of them was any good. That's
why I won't take your head off your shoulders for bad-mouthin' them
like that. You wanna say somethin' 'bout my mother, though? You
wanna open your mouth like that again? Put you through that fuckin'
wall behind you 'fore you could bat an eye. Wanna try me?"

Brian didn't blink.

"Didn't think so, tough guy. By the time those flunkies out
there got to me, you'd be ground-up dog meat. One hundred percent
lean. You got that?" Barret Dexter smiled and winked, leaning in
toward the table before bringing his handcuffed wrists down upon the
surface in a clatter. "Now, back to the main discussion, Detective. Your
personal feelings or mine 'bout family really don't mean dick-shit.
Understand? You wanna let a murderer go free? That's your business,

Mister Lawman. But the day I walk the fuck outta here, I'm heading for the news desk at the *The New York Times* with my lawyer and tell them all about our little tête-à-tête. That's French for a one-on-one, Detective Brian Archer. *Parlez-vous Françias?*"

Brian stood. "Tell you what, hotshot. You give me the info you got, and I'll go to the D.A. today. Right now as a matter of fact."

Barret laughed quietly. "Tell *you* what. When you get real, you come back and see me. Remember. Twenty-four hours. Meanwhile, you say hello for me to that pretty mama of yours. Oh, I don't mean your mother, Detective. I'm talkin' 'bout that black bitch you call your wife."

Brian lunged for the prisoner as Barret laughed.

In an instant, the detective found himself facedown upon the table with his neck in a makeshift noose of steel bracelets and three-inch chain.

"Say uncle," Barret Dexter tormented as the door to the room flew open and two correction officers rushed in. "Another step and he's dead; I swear it!" the prisoner challenged the duo as Archer struggled violently with flailing fists and legs and powerless prying fingers tearing at his own throat.

One of the men had a hand on the butt of his billy club.

"Go ahead. Raise it, and I snap his neck," the prisoner warned.

The uniformed pair stood frozen in time.

Brian was rapidly tapping Barret's muscular shoulder.

The prisoner put his ear close to Brian's mouth.

"What?" the young man whispered maniacally.

"Uncle," Brian barely whispered back.

Barret smiled and released his death grip from around the man's neck and throat. "Be smart," the powerful and lightning fast teenager told the detective as he helped Brian into an upright position. "Be smart and go make that deal. I can—"

Barret never finished his sentence as the two officers rushed him. One wielding his truncheon. The other flailing his fists. A dozen correction officers stood funneled just outside the doorway. Across the threshold, two more officers invaded the claustrophobic space.

"Stop!" Detective Brian Archer commanded the personnel.

But Barret received several severe blows from four officers.

"Stop it!" Brian shouted at the top of his lungs, which

amounted to no more than a hoarse shriek. "I SAID STOP IT!"

Suddenly, the men listened up and ceased.

"I will handle this," Detective Brian Archer assured them all. "Believe me. I will handle this," he repeated, helping a bleeding, subdued Barret Dexter to his feet.

Chapter Thirty-Three

B arret Dexter was sitting in solitary confinement. Terrance Lincoln had been brought over from the general prisoner population and was now sitting in the same room from which his cousin had been torn thirty minutes earlier. He sat before Detective Brian Archer. Terrance Lincoln couldn't take his eyes or mind off all the blood. Even as he spoke, his dark curly head darted back and forth among the freshly imbrued red blotches stippled along a white cinder block wall, a corner of the table, as well as the floor beneath his feet.

"I don't know nothin' 'bout no car leavin' any scene."

"Not *any* scene, Mr. Lincoln. The scene in which your unarmed brother-in-law was murdered by some stranger coming out of Shelly's Deli after he shot and killed Barret Dexter's stepfather and uncle."

"I wasn't there," Terrance said flatly.

"Look at me. Forget about the blood and look at me."

Lincoln looked.

"Do you know anything, anything at all about those shootings that occurred at the deli?"

"No, sir."

Brian thought for a moment, figuring that a picture was indeed worth a thousand words. "All right. You can look."

"What?"

"I said you can look. Look at your cousin's blood. Barret lied to me. That's what happens when you lie to me," Detective Brian Archer fibbed. "You don't believe me, do you? You think this is all part of a script, don't you? DON'T YOU?" Brian shouted and hammered a corner of the table with an angry closed fist as though the piece of furniture were an anvil.

Terrance bucked in his seat from the sound.

Two court officers immediately entered the space.

Brian spun around to face them. "Get Dexter back in here now," he demanded.

"I believe he's waiting to go to the infirmary, Detective," one of them stated truthfully.

"I couldn't give a flying fuck if he was in the middle of an operation. I want him in here, now!"

The two officers stepped outside the room and closed the door.

"A good buddy you think you got there, right? He wants you and you alone to take the fall for his actions, claiming you brought him along to the deli the other day without his knowledge of what was about to go down. He wants to cut a deal. A description of the vehicle along with a partial plate number in exchange for *his* freedom. Not yours. Is he blowing smoke up my ass? Well, is he?"

"I'm telling you the truth. I don' know anything about that. I wasn't there that day."

"Could Barret have been?"

"I don't know. He wasn't with me. I think he would have told me."

"He's either got a bargaining chip or he's full of shit. What do you think?"

The prisoner shook his head.

"You prepared to do some hard time upstate? You know you're going away for a while. Don't you?"

Terrance nodded, staring down and around at the bloody walls and floor.

"Want to make things a bit easier on yourself?"

The twenty-two-year-old looked up.

"I want you to level with me, Terrance. First I want to know what you know about the attempted robbery. Not yours and Barret's lame attempt. I don't give a crap about that at the moment. I'll let the Robbery boys and girls worry about that. Right now I'm concerned with homicide. Yours if I feel your dickin' me around."

Terrance Lincoln stuck to his story, changing the subject and putting the onus on Barret Dexter as the leader and himself as a helpless follower. "Kid's positively crazy. Just ask anyone."

Minutes later, the door opened and Barret Dexter was escorted to the threshold, limping in leg irons with handcuffs coupled behind his back. The prisoner's face was badly swollen. A bloodstained sweatshirt dominated the boy's powerful frame.

"Thanks, fellas," Brian said satisfactorily. "Now get him the hell out of here. And do not enter this room again unless I call you. I don't care if you see a river of blood running under the door this time."

One of the officers rolled his eyes, shook his head and sighed in exasperation, turning the prisoner back around. Barret took tentative steps as he shuffled and swept the chain noisily down the corridor. Another officer closed the door with a note of finality, leaving Archer and Lincoln to themselves.

"So. What's it going to be? Truth or consequences?" Brian bellowed, immediately standing up and sending the legs of his chair scraping backward across the tile. "Let's see how tough you are without your knife. I hear you're a real cutup, kid."

Terrance instantly began to bawl. "I swear on my-my mother, I know nothin' 'bout what you're askin', man. Noth-nothin' at all. All I know is Curtis drove the car and Taiquon and Moses went in," he swore. "I hear some guy comes out of the deli after shootin' Barret's stepfather and uncle then wastes Curtis. I never ever knew the deal was goin' down."

"Did Barret?"

"I tol' ya. I don't know. He don't tell me shit."

"Who set up the job this time around?"

"Tol' ya. Barret. It's always Barret. We paid Fat Albert a little visit at the deli to find out where the owner stashed the cash."

"And?"

"And Fat Albert tol' us after we leaned on him a bit. 'Money's in one of the broken ovens in the kitchen,' he said. But we never got that far because he went and tol' the police we was comin'. They was waitin' for us. I pity Fat Albert when Barret gets out. I don't wanna be and won't be a part o' that. Barret will kill 'em. He tol' me so."

"How many jobs you and your cousin work together?"

Terrance Lincoln clammed up and simply shook his head.

Brian went over and turned the young man briskly about, taking him by the handcuffs locked at the small of his back, another hand gripping the collar of his shirt, putting the prisoner's head an inch away from the wall.

"What are you doing?" Terrance protested, dropping to his knees while getting a very good idea of what was coming.

"It's my counting game," the detective explained. "I smash your head into this concrete wall until you come up with a number. If I feel the number is too low, I—"

"Four!" Terrance shrieked. "Four jobs we pulled. That's it. I swear it."

"Break-ins?"

"Walk-ons."

"Walk-ons?"

"Barret likes to call them walk-ons."

"Stick-ups."

"Yeah, stick-ups."

"How many guys?"

"Jus' me and him."

"Who sets them up?"

"I told you. Barret does."

"And where are you and Barret when you pull off a job. You both go in or what?"

"I go in alone and put a knife or gun in some fucker's face. Barret waits outside."

"A lookout."

"Yeah, a lookout." Terrance Lincoln sobbed. "Nobody ever got hurt."

"You think he might have been a lookout on the day of those shootings, Mr. Lincoln?"

"Could have been. But I don't know. I tell you, he doesn't tell me jack-shit."

Brian lifted Terrance gently and sat him back in the chair. The lead detective seemed somewhat satisfied.

Chapter Thirty-Four

From her desk at police headquarters in Yaphank, Detective Kim Archer spoke to Detective Gary York at a bed-and-breakfast in Big Stone Gap, Virginia.

"You awake, Gary?"

"Barely," Gary groaned.

"Big night, buster?"

"Big night and day."

"Alert enough to listen?"

"As long as I don't have to move."

"Maybe move the point of a pen or pencil and write this down."

"I'll remember if it's not too long."

"Turquoise blue panel van, vanity plate CAPITOL 1; that's o-l, like the building in Washington; vehicle registered to a Sep, S-e-p Cramer—"

"Wait a sec."

"That's what I thought."

Gary reached for a pad and pen. "Cramer with a C?

"C-r-a-m-e-r."

"Go ahead."

"101 Black Mountain Road, Lynch."

"Lynch, where?"

"Where horseshoes are lucky," Kim both stated and smiled. "Right across the border from your B 'n B. He's worth a visit. As a matter of fact, he's worth plenty."

"I'm listening."

"Big bank account. Big home in the foothills. Big reputation in

D.C. and California. Big Mercedes-Benz Sprinter panel van."

"Sprinter?"

"As in running."

"Never heard of it."

"Probably because they're not entirely manufactured in this country. The parts are shipped from Germany, assembled by Freightliner in Gaffney, South Carolina, and purchased through select Dodge dealerships."

"Huh. How'd you come up with a Sprinter, Kim?"

"Well, after exhausting the truck market from Avalons to Yukons, I homed in on the type and color turquoise like your witness said. Actually, Big Sister walked me through it. But not without a glitch or bitch or two because they don't offer that color here in the states. Believe me, there are not too many factory-painted turquoise blue panel vans found rolling through the Blue Ridge Mountains of Virginia and the Appalachian area, you can bet your boots. Or in your case, your Versace Loafers. Anyhow, if I were to run a check on all the boxy blue bodies we got listed, Big Sister and I'd be here till the cows came home. You with me so far, or drifting off someplace?"

"Good work, Kim."

"That's it? 'Good work, Kim.' I find you a true-blue turquoise panel van in the middle of a million mountains—which is the equivalent of your needle in a haystack, mister—and all you can say is 'Good work, Kim'? You owe me a steak or lobster dinner when you get back."

"What do you make of this Cramer fellow?" Gary yawned in her ear.

"I don't know, sleepyhead. Upstanding on the screen before me. Outstanding according to his peers and the press. It appears he has the ear of the president and others on the Hill. That's Capitol Hill. Hence, the vanity plate."

"Number one, huh?"

"Probably thinks like Hertz instead of Avis."

"You're probably right."

"Just be careful, okay? Not like Brian, yesterday."

"What about Brian and yesterday?"

"He tangled with a prisoner over at Riverhead jail."

"He all right?"

"Sore neck, throat and shoulder, but otherwise he's fine."

"What the hell happened?"

"That deli in Riverhead. Shelly's."

"What about it?"

"It was almost hit again. Two black youths were arrested by the locals who received a tip. One of the punks wants a deal in exchange for info on the shooter who fled the scene. Says he can identify the vehicle and hand over a partial plate."

"You think he knows anything?"

"Brian thinks he knows too damn much. Like having a 'black bitch for a wife,' quote-unquote."

"It's those goddamn court and correction officers, not to mention several clerks who have big mouths over there, Kim. Trickles down from the troops to the trash."

"Seems they're everywhere as well. Over in Nassau, they refer to Brian and me as the black-and-tan, I heard through the grapevine."

"We're not talking about the brightest or the best, I know you know."

"I know, but it still hurts."

"Fuck 'em, if you'll pardon my French."

Kim laughed hard and loud.

"It wasn't that funny," Gary said through another yawn.

"No, no. Not you. Your partner and the perp who almost broke his neck. He was speaking French to Brian."

"They found an interpreter in Riverhead who speaks French?"

Kim was hysterical with laughter. "A word here, a phrase there," she told her colleague after catching her breath. "Forget it. I'll explain it all when you get back."

"Then you'll have to explain it to the two of us," Gary said enigmatically.

"What are you talking about?"

"Forget it. I'll explain it all when *we* get back," he parroted.

"Who's we?" Kim insisted.

"You'll see," he said happily. "It's a surprise."

"Oh, my God! You're coming home with a dog like Justin did."

It was now Gary's turn to become hysterical. "She'd be very upset to hear you call her that," he managed through his tears.

"It is a dog, isn't it? Tell me."

Gary shook his head and terminated the conversation, placing the cell phone back in its case and wondering what he'd be dealing with in Lynch, Kentucky. Another dead end? A possible witness who just may have seen something? Or perhaps the vehicle belonging to the serial killer himself? "Yeah, right," he spoke aloud and smirked in the mirror above the bureau after getting up and out of bed. "If only they were all that easy," he said to his sleepy reflection.

Team Three now had two mystery men and two vehicles to locate. One: a serial killer of unsuspecting innocents. The other: a shooter of the sinful. The first: a man moving around from state to state. A man of means, he was sure. The second: a man from the Riverhead area he was pretty damn positive. A villain and a good Samaritan as his partner, Brian, had put it several times. A villain and a vigilante were probably more to the point, the homicide detective decided while pulling on his pants.

Chapter Thirty-Five

Detective Gary York rang the bell, waited, then knocked loudly on the front door of 101 Black Mountain Road in Lynch, Kentucky. Gary stood in awe of the magnificent grounds and splendid log cabin home of Sep Cramer. The cabin alone had to sit on at least five cleared acres, the detective figured. The prodigious post-and-beam construction certainly covered a good seven thousand square feet, he calculated while peeking through one of the many expensive Marvin windows.

After several more rings and knocks upon the door, Gary took the liberty of taking a walk around the property. At the rear of the house, he spotted movement just beyond the woodlot. Heading toward him in the distance, coming down a mountain trail, an apparently tall man sat high in the seat of an open green and yellow vehicle. Gary immediately recognized the unmistakable color scheme as that of a John Deere.

As the man and machine drew closer, the fellow gave a friendly wave. Gary waved back. A moment later, the two were shaking hands. York identified himself and chatted briefly while admiring the Trail Gator HPX 4x4, its tires and chassis covered with mud and dirt and dust, obscuring a decal of a leaping deer, the trademark symbol for which the company was well-known.

"Nice piece of machinery, Mr. Cramer," the detective said appreciatively, observing the cargo the cart was carting.

Sep smiled happily. "Just doing a bit of planting up there. Clover and sorghum. I like to keep the deer around," he explained.

"You hunt them?'

"Oh, good heavens, no. I don't care for guns or hunting. No, I just sit back and watch them come down from the mountain in the early mornings and later on in the evenings. Soothes the savage soul," he said through a grin. "They're such beautiful creatures."

"I see you have some alfalfa and sudan grass to go," Gary noted among the series of rakes, pickax, shovels and spade. "But I don't think you're going to bother with that bag of Triticale till the fall," he pointed out.

"I'm impressed, Detective."

"And I'm impressed with this machine."

"Well, thank you kindly. So, how do you come to know about such plants and things?"

"I worked at a nursery as a kid."

"Where?"

"Long Island."

"Where on the Island, if I might ask?" Sep inquired politely.

"Calverton and Jamesport. Jockeyed back and forth between those towns."

"Long Island's quite beautiful. Especially out east."

"Been back there recently?" the cop asked casually.

"Oh, not for some time now. I grab the ferry once in a blue moon when I don't feel like fighting city traffic. Guess I don't really take the time to stop and enjoy the East End like I should. Say, would you like to come inside for some lemonade and a special dessert I made? Poronui Lemon Pudding. Not an original creation, but delicious. When I was vacationing at the Poronui Ranch in New Zealand, they served it there. I actually bribed them for the recipe, and I do mean bribe," Sep said and winked, rubbing the tips of two fingers against a thumb. "And guess what?"

Gary shrugged, smiled and shook his head.

"The same recipe appears in an Orvis catalog I just received, sitting on a pile of mail."

"You were away, I take it?"

"Boston, on business."

"And you just got back?"

"Few days ago."

"Fly?"

"No. Drove. Why?"

"I assume you didn't hear about a young woman's murder over

in Big Stone Gap. Carla Banks."

"Goodness no. To tell you the truth, I've been so preoccupied with a speech I'm preparing for a conference, I haven't had time to listen to the news or even look at a newspaper. First real break I took was to go up there and put in some plants."

"Guess you still got a few plants to go."

"Yes, indeed. I saw someone in back of the house and came back down. You," Cramer said straightaway, smiling most amicably.

"Sorry I pulled you away from your work."

"No problem. So, when did this murder occur, Detective?"

"Three days ago. Wednesday."

"That's when I came home," Sep said with sudden realization. "Is this why you're here?"

"Can you tell me as accurately as possible what time you passed through Big Stone Gap?"

The man gave the appearance of mighty thought, as if ruminating in deep consideration. Sep's brow furrowed while the corners of his mouth folded in kind. "Let's see, now. It had to be around four or four-fifteen in the afternoon because I arrived here about four-thirty. I was so exhausted, I went straight to bed."

"Did you see anyone or hear anything suspicious along the mountain road leading into or out of town that afternoon? Especially overlooking the meadow from the summit, Mr. Cramer? A gunshot? Maybe a speeding vehicle? Perhaps a jogger? Hiker? Fisherman? Anything at all?"

Sep Cramer searched his mind considerably but slowly shook his head. "To tell you the truth, I was so damn tired all I wanted to do was head home and get into bed. But I certainly would have remembered a gunshot, a speeding car or something unusual like that. No one passed me on the road, nor did I notice anyone walking about, Detective York."

"You're sure?"

"Pretty damn sure."

"Well, I want to thank you for your time, Mr. Cramer."

"Sep," Sep said, extending his hand. "Please call me Sep. Everyone does."

Gary withdrew his card and jotted a name and phone number on the back. "If anything pops into your head, please give Chief

Wilcox over at the Gap a call."

"Sure will. You're sure you won't come in for at least a lemonade before you leave?" he asked, turning over the card.

"Thanks, but I really have a few things to attend to before heading back to New York."

"Ask you something?"

"Sure."

"I'm curious. Why do they send a detective from New York all the way down here to investigate a homicide?"

"There are several cases up north that we believe could be connected to the woman's murder here," Gary answered directly.

"I see. I think I did hear a couple reports on the radio up in Boston. So we're talking maybe a serial killer?"

"May be," Gary said benignly.

"Permit me one more quick question before you run?"

"You bet."

"How did you happen to wind up here? I mean here at my home, Detective York? I guess you must have known I drove through the area about the time this woman was found murdered."

"Murdered but not found until the following day," Gary clarified. "A witness spotted your Mercedes Sprinter," he magnified. "Turquoise blue. Kind of hard to miss."

"How was she murdered?"

"Shot in the stomach while carrying practically to term. Blind woman."

Sep Cramer stood in absolute shock. "Oh, my God! How positively dreadful. How old a woman?"

"Listen, gotta run. You can catch all the grim details on the telly, which you left on in the den, Sep." Gary headed back toward the front of the home as Cramer followed him with dark penetrating eyes. "Wilcox, if you think of anything," Gary reminded the owner, waving good-bye without turning around.

"Right," Sep replied, staring down at the card. "Wilcox," he said, popping several M&Ms into his mouth.

Chapter Thirty-Six

Justin Barnes stooped and peered over Kim Archer' shoulder, fixing his eyes on the computer screen. Leaving nothing to chance, Kim tapped the keyboard and again brought up a list of late model vehicles inclusive of mini, mid-sized and heavy-duty trucks, sport utility vans, panel vans and otherwise: crew cabs, extended cabs, long and short-bodied pickups with factory and aftermarket caps. There was even a station wagon, a conventional trailer, two motor homes and a fifth-wheel thrown in the mix for good measure. Just for giggles, in order to keep her sanity, Kim threw in a taxi and a bus, which she quickly deleted.

Armadas, Astros, Blazers, Broncos, Canyons, Cherokees, Colorados, Concept SUTs, CR-Vs, Durangos, Envoy XUV, Escalades, Express', Explorers, 4 Runners, Frontiers, a Freightliner and Frontline, G-Class', Highlanders, Land Cruisers, Muranos, Navigators, Odysseys, Pathfinders, Pilots, Quests, Rams, Rendezvous CXL's, Sequoias, Siennas, Sierras, Silverados, Sprinters, Tacomas, Tahoes, Titans, Tundras, Trailblazers, Villagers, VUEs, a Winnebago, XTERRAs and a plethora of Yukons were alphabetized and pictured from A to Y.

A list of licensed owners now included eastern central United States. The compilation was long and seemed endless. The color selection the factories offered were equally staggering. The color blue classification alone gave Kim and Big Sister the blues while matching shades to models to manufacturers to customers through the departments of motor vehicles as well as several other sources.

Considering the atmospheric conditions on that murderous afternoon in Big Stone Gap, Kim ran the entire spectrum, reflecting on the weather and its effect on a body of metal when viewed from mountain to meadow. What color vehicle did Benny Rodgers truly see that afternoon: admiral blue, aqua, aquamarine, azure, blueberry, cornflower, French blue, gray blue, clear blue, coal black blue, cobalt, indigo, marlin blue, midnight blue, navy, royal, sapphire, sea blue, sky blue, sage, teal, *truly blue*—she chuckled beneath her breath—turquoise, turquoise blue, voyage blue. Kim worked from a weather map, satellite and aerial images of the area, and vehicle manufacturers' color charts. She labored indefatigably until she thought her brain would cloud over. Still, she persevered.

Buick, Cadillac, Chevrolet, GMC, Oldsmobile, Pontiac, and Saturns topped the list of General Motors trucks. Ford and Chrysler were first and second runner-ups respectively, along with a multitude of foreign challengers that underscored the Big Three; namely, another paradoxically intrinsic trio: Toyota, Honda and Nissan. Among a smattering of imports stood Mercedes-Benz.

Kim cross-referenced the lists, creating her own database, cautiously eliminating what wouldn't fly, carefully retaining what would—even remotely—in accordance with Gary's questionable eye-witness, Mr. Benny B. Rodgers, from Big Stone Gap, Virginia. On the other hand, Benny was and had been a carpenter's helper for many years; a house painter, too. Who better qualified to recognize a work vehicle or its color when considering the distance of mountaintop to meadow, the computer maven mused.

Kim had been at it for many hours over the course of two days.

"How the hell do you do what you do, Kim?" Justin marveled.

"I'm the mother of patience."

"What the hell are G-Classes?"

"Shh."

"Hear from Gary lately?"

"No, and I said, shush."

"Sprinter I never heard of either until yesterday."

Kim looked up annoyingly from the monitor.

"What happened to the mother of patience?" Justin questioned, exhibiting his pearly whites.

"Spinach."

Justin scratched his head. "Spinach is a shade of blue?"

"Between your teeth. Spinach. Now, what is it? You can see

that I have work to do."

"What are G-Classes?" Justin persisted, passing a tongue then running a pinky nail between his teeth.

Kim hit a single key. "There."

Justin focused stilly on the silent screen.

"G 500 SUV and the G 55 AMG SUV; Mercedes-Benz," Kim explained.

"Can I get one in spinach?"

"You can get out of here and let me work."

"Yesterday you were all hepped up on that Mercedes Sprinter. What happened?"

"Today's another day."

"Be serious."

"I'm always serious. Except when I'm delirious. Like now."

"I think you need to take a break."

"All right. I can see there's going to be no peace. You want to listen and learn? Pull over a chair and stop breathing down my neck."

"Yes, ma'am."

"You see that G 55 AMG SUV Mercedes?"

"Clear as the pretty nose on your face."

"I'm going to report you to Brian," she promised.

"Brian's in conference."

"Get smart with me and I'll tell the lieutenant."

"That's who he's in conference with at the moment."

"You're bad, J," she scolded.

"Few know how bad I can really be."

"And live to tell about it," she remarked in kind.

"Hey! You're crossing the line now, girl. Hittin' below the belt."

"Just sit there and shut up. All right?"

"All right."

"A vehicle like that one was registered to a Mr. Samuel Carper of East Marion. Bought new in Amityville in 2000, then sold to a William Tafferty in California a year later."

"Turquoise blue?"

"Coal black."

"I don't get where you're headed."

"There was a black Mercedes SUV, similar to the one pictured there, seen leaving an area where a body was found in Van Buren, Maine." Kim flashed an image from the crime scene: the man's upper body wrapped in a colorful cloth, lying in a culvert. "Shot through the back of the head. Right along the Canadian border. May of 2000. The case remained unsolved until two years ago when a young Canadian man was arrested, tried, convicted, sentenced, and then released when a judge reversed himself after being hit over the head with new and overwhelming evidence. The guy was released, and the case went cold again."

"I thought we're looking at a person of interest named Sep Cramer who drives a turquoise blue Mercedes Sprinter panel van."

"We are."

"So how did we get to a coal black boxy rig like that? You're telling me there's a connection?"

"How about a month later, a thirty yard shot in broad daylight taking down a woman who was walking her daughter home from preschool? The mother caught the bullet smack in the middle of her forehead. Again, a black SUV—no make or model identified this time —was seen in the vicinity. Sound familiar?"

"Cartridge?"

"30/06 Springfield re the mother; a .22 Hornet re the guy in the ditch."

"I don't know, Kim. Seems like you're all over the map. Literally."

"So's this nut."

Justin nodded and rose from his seat, digesting the information. "So you're thinking this Samuel Carper and Sep Cramer might somehow be connected?"

"Maybe working in concert, or maybe—"

"—the same person?"

"It's a possibility."

"DMV would answer that one for you in a heartbeat."

"Tell me something I don't know."

"I'll let you get back to work."

"Gee. Thanks, sport."

Justin put the chair back then headed for the hallway, stopping in mid-stride, pivoting back around on the soles of his sneakers. "Kim."

Kim ignored him.

"Where is this guy Sam Carper from again?"

Kim sighed. "East Marion."

Justin stepped in close and placed both hands squarely on Kim's shoulders.

"What now?"

"Type."

"Type what?"

"Their first and last names. One above the other."

Kim ran a flashy set of painted nails across the keyboard.

Samuel Carper
Sep Cramer

"Just the shortened nickname, Sam."

Kim backspaced and deleted u-e-l.

Sam Carper
Sep Cramer

"Ain't you the mother of unscramblers. You do that Jumble puzzle in the paper every day. Right? I'll go take a ride out to East Marion while you play around with those two names. And do yourself a favor and check with DMV. See what you can turn up."

"That's what I was about to do next. I think my brain is fried. Too many friggin' vehicles. I feel like I've just been run over by an eighteen-wheeler. Tell me this is all just a coincidence."

"Can you get me Gary? Got a question or two for him before I leave."

Kim punched in her colleague's cell phone number. "He was on his way over to Sep Cramer's last I spoke to him, then heading back here. I wanted to give him the update, but I couldn't reach him." Using a landline while holding the other instrument to her other ear, she placed a call to Gary's room at the B&B. After a moment, she got the front desk. "Gary York, please. Room 323. .... You're sure?" Kim abruptly thanked the clerk then hung up the receiver. "He's already checked out." Detective Kim Archer kept the cell phone pressed to her ear. "He's not picking up."

"Probably a poor signal or something."

"Did he ever say anything to you about wanting a dog?"

"A dog?"

"Yes, a dog. He told me he had a surprise when he got back. He was all excited. I figured you put a bug in his ear. You came back with a dog, so I figure he was talking about a pet or something. He said he'd explain it all 'when *we* get back.' Quote, unquote."

Justin had to laugh. "The only thing Gary gets excited about is a broad."

Kim frowned and closed her cell phone. "Broad?"

"Sorry. A woman in waiting is what I meant to say."

"Incorrigible."

"But cute. Yes? Very cute." Justin displayed his pearly whites.

"Seriously, J. I'm a bit concerned. I need him to hear and see this latest business; speculation at this point or not. I need to bring him up to snuff. I'm wondering if I should call Chief Wilcox."

"I wouldn't. I'd wait."

"Why?"

"Just a feeling. This guy Cramer is very powerful, I'm learning by the minute. You don't know how far his tentacles may reach."

Kim nodded, staring intently at the two names.

Sam Carper.
Sep Cramer.

"Hold on a minute, J." Tired but anxious the computer whiz let her fingers do the walking, striking a BUILD WORD LIST letter-key on a Game Menu, entering Sep Cramer's name consisting of nine characters, the maximum that the program would accept: s-e-p-c-r-a-m-e-r. Kim hit ENTER twice. A series of consecutive numbers flashed in place upon the screen then disappeared at 130, indicating the number of words that could be formed from the entry. The word **sera** appeared as the first selection. Kim smacked her right hand hard against her forehead. "Names," she chastised herself impatiently. "I need names, not words. I'll just bet he's using more than one alias, J. Wanna bet me?" she said excitedly, about to start running through the list.

Justin reached around Kim's shoulder and hit the '**?**' key for the first definition. The screen flashed WORKING . . . then the word **sera** appeared again, followed by its definition.

sera:

1. serum (noun)
serums or sera:
watery part of blood
serous (adjective)

"Can you show me the next word on the list, Kim?"

Kim's brightly colored nails flashed across the pad before striking the ↓ key. The word **serape** appeared.

Justin immediately hit the '**?**' key for its definition.

serape:

1. colorful woolen shawl worn by Mexican men

The two looked at one another queerly before Justin spoke. "Like this fellow you mentioned murdered in Maine in 2000, found wrapped in a colorful cloth, lying in a culvert. Yes?"

Kim nodded anxiously.

"Changed my mind. Call Chief Wilcox," Justin said quietly. "Tell him what you got so far, and that we're concerned about Gary. The sheriff's office down there also. Tell the Chief you already notified the troopers. I'll call the Feds and fill them in. Tell Wilcox all that, too—just to keep all of 'em on their toes in case there's any game playing—meaning one faction purposely keeping another out of the loop."

"Maybe we should first tell Brian."

"Just do it. This Sep Cramer's a player, Kim."

"This could all be just one big coincidence, J," she reconsidered, backpedaling a stroke.

"Too much of one if you ask me. Please. I'm a bit worried now myself."

Kim nodded.

"Jot down that address in East Marion for me, and work those names, words or whatever, every which way but loose while you're downloading and awaiting photos from DMV. I think you're onto something, Kim."

"As we speak." She handed him the street and number then continued working the rather extensive list.

"I wouldn't take the bet you wanted to bet me, Kim, because I'll bet you're gonna get other hits that somehow unquestionably connect. Call me the second you've got something solid. If you don't hear from Gary by the time I call you, line up a flight and a rental car for me."

"To where?"

"Closest airfield to Black Mountain, Kentucky. But first I'm gonna pay a visit to this Carper residence."

"Fine, but you know I can't authorize a flight."

"A private plane if you have to. Put it on my credit card."

"The lieutenant will kill you. What do I tell him if you go without his blessings, let alone Brian's permission?"

"Tell them sick leave, vacation, anything you want. And if the lieutenant wants to kill me, tell him that I neither forgive nor forget," he said, smiled and saluted adieu. "Oh, and I'll need a file of whatever you got on this Carper dude, including those pix, which should prove interesting unless we're dealing with some master of disguise."

"Oh, boy. Here we go again." Kim booted up another mainframe and immediately went to work on Justin's requests. "Better be damn careful out there, damn it," she ordered. "Hey. You hear what I'm saying?" she called out as Justin disappeared around the corner and down a staircase.

Chapter Thirty-Seven

It was a warm and pleasant afternoon with temperatures in the mid-seventies when Detective Gary York collected Denise Holloway at her home, both knowing that her husband would be working up at the Bickford Estate. Denise had but a single, small piece of luggage, which she immediately dropped into the trunk as Gary released the latch from inside the rental sedan. Denise closed the lid and quickly came around to the passenger side, opened the door, slid in, and in seconds the two were heading out of town.

"Jesus. When I said to pack light, I didn't mean a pair of panties and a toothbrush," he joked.

"You'd be surprised what I crammed into that bag."

"Did you remember my cell phone?"

"Sure did, and I thank you for letting me borrow it. Ted's so damn cheap that he wouldn't let me pay the bill for several months, so they finally disconnected us. Then he complains that he doesn't get enough business. How do you run a business without a phone?"

"I thought you said you were having trouble with your phone."

"Money trouble. I didn't want to get into it. Anyhow, thanks again. I called who I needed to call."

"No problem. Did I get any calls or messages?"

"No."

"You sure?"

"You showed me how to use it and told me not to answer it. No calls. No messages."

"May I have it, please?"

"It's in my bag in the trunk."

"Panties, a toothbrush, and my cell phone."

"Sorry. Need it right now?"

"I'll need it when we stop."

"Please don't stop until we're miles away from here."

"Worried?" he asked with some concern, watching her absently picking away at a cuticle with a forefinger.

"Scared to death."

"Everything's going to be all right," he promised.

"I know."

"If you knew, you wouldn't be worried," he pestered playfully, trying to have her relax.

"I feel like I'm running away from home."

"You are."

"I mean like a little kid."

"Well, you're not a kid any longer," he reminded her. "So. How old are you?" he questioned in terms of a test.

"Stop it."

"No, tell me."

"You know how old I am."

"I want to hear it from you lips."

"Thirty-three. Happy now?"

"You're sure?"

"Yes, I'm sure. And you? You never told me."

"You never asked."

"I'm asking."

"Nineteen."

"Not on your life!" she made clear through a laugh.

"Well, I feel as though I'm nineteen. That's got to count for something."

"Count for what?" she asked, her eyes attentive to the cars passing them in both directions.

"Count for the fact that I can shave at least a decade off my age since I met you. You're my Fountain of Youth, Denise."

Denise turned quiet.

"Hello in there."

"Sorry."

"Don't be sorry. Don't be nervous. Don't be sad. All right?"

Denise smiled. "I'll try."

The two remained silent for several minutes.

"Do me a favor?" she suddenly asked.

"Anything, princess."

"Princess? I don't think anyone has called me a princess since the day I left Windsor Castle," she teased, taking Gary's free hand into hers.

"Oh, Prince Charming threw you out?"

"No, I left of my own accord, just as I'm doing today." The pretty woman smiled affectionately.

"Huh. Anyway, princess, what can I do for you? Clean the moat when we get to where we're going? Actually, it's not really a moat. It's a kidney-shaped swimming pool that's filled with a million decaying leaves because I lost the cover this winter, along with any ambition to repair or have it replaced."

"I need to stop at Wal-Mart in Bristol."

"What is it that you need, princess?"

"Things."

"What kind of things?"

"Your princess needs some feminine hygiene articles, toiletries —girlie things like that. It'll take ten minutes."

Gary looked at his watch. "We've got plenty of time before we have to be at the airport, so no problem. I think I remember seeing a Kmart in Bristol when I was heading up from Blountville the other day."

Denise firmly shook her head. "It's got to be Wal-Mart. Ten minutes. Promise."

"Fine by me. Did you remember to change the flight from two to four o'clock and book yourself a seat?"

"I took care of everything. We're sitting together in first-class. Eating at five o'clock. You'll even get to see a murder mystery to make you feel right at home. It's a new release, so I know you haven't seen it before. And you better not figure it out. But if you do, don't tell me because that will be our first real fight."

"Can I tell you what does and doesn't work as it moves along?"

"Only afterwards. I'll kill you if you ruin it for me."

"I have a partner who will track you down."

"Well, I have one who will take your partner out. So there."

"Oh, yeah? What's his name?"

"Prince Charming."

"I thought he dumped you."

"I just told you, I dumped him."

"And this prince would do your bidding after that?"

"I have men wrapped around my finger."

"Oh, you do, do you?"

"Absolutely."

Gary suddenly reached across her knees and opened the glove compartment, withdrawing a small wrapped box with a teeny bow. "Then try this on for size. Go ahead. Open it."

Denise sat transfixed.

"I said open it."

Denise Holloway unwrapped the tiny present and popped open the blue velvet box. "Oh-my-God! How did you . . . where did you . . . ?"

"Of course, you'll have to unwrap all those other men from around your finger first, or it'll never fit."

"Whoosh, they're gone forever," Denise swore in a single breath, waving a hand through the air as if holding a magic wand.

"Put it on. I'm not going to bother to wait until after your divorce."

"You're supposed to put it on for me," she insisted.

"While I'm driving? You want me to have an accident?" he scolded playfully, taking the silver and gold banded two-caret diamond-studded stone from her slender fingers, slipping it onto the ring finger of her left hand. "I now pronounce us permanently hitched."

"Not exactly a whiz with words or timing, Detective Gary York, but I accept," she proclaimed, leaning over and giving him a quick but serious kiss upon the corner of his lips.

"Good, because I ain't turning this crate around to return it."

Denise suddenly began to tear, removing a tissue from a blouse pocket, dabbing the corners of her blue-green eyes.

"You want me to turn around and return it?" Gary pretended to cringe.

She shook her head.

"Then why the tears?"

"Happy."

"Oh, I get it. You laugh when you're sad and cry when you're happy."

Denise laughed lightly.

"So now you're just a little sad."

"Shut up and drive."

"To Wal-Mart."

"To Wal-Mart."

"Do princesses really go to Wal-Mart? Maybe Bath and Body, I'd believe."

"Princesses go anywhere they please."

"Makes sense to me," he said with a shrug.

An hour later, the couple pulled past a large parking area filled with trailers and motor homes.

"Courtesy of Wal-Mart," Denise expounded. "Vacationers can stop here when touring around the country, free of charge, staying over for a night or two. Smart business if you ask me. Practically everything folks need they shop for inside. My sister and brother-in-law take full advantage whenever they travel. They have a good-size camper." She directed Gary to a secluded spot toward the back of the building. "I'll fetch your phone."

"Why do you have us stopping here?" Gary questioned as he parked and hit the trunk release. "I always drop my princesses off at the front door."

"You never know who's watching," Denise said decidedly, stepping to the rear of the vehicle and reaching for her bag, snapping it open and removing Gary's cell phone before closing both the single piece of luggage and the trunk. She went around to the driver's window and handed him the instrument. Denise feigned a frown. "Make your calls. But not to any other princesses. I'll be ten minutes."

"Take twenty, but just remember we have a plane to catch."

"Roger that," she sounded and saluted.

Gary looked down oddly. "Where are you taking that bag?"

"With me into the store."

"Why?"

"Because I'm leaving you."

"Already? After I give you an expensive diamond ring? I thought we were engaged at least. Oh, I get it. You're really a shoplifter and expect me to bail you out if you get caught. Well, let me tell you something, sister. You've got another thing coming," he warned.

"Not another *thing*, Detective Gary York. Another someone," she taunted with a haunted look in her eyes. "Look. Over there," she pointed.

Gary looked over his left shoulder as Denise walked leisurely away, examining the brilliance with which the light of day lit the precious stone.

Sitting squarely at a small bench-table in the back of a turquoise blue Mercedes Sprinter panel van, its wide back doors open fully, Sep Cramer aligned the cross hairs of his weapon and touched off a single round from the Thompson/Center handgun, the slug from the .45 Colt cartridge catching Gary York in the middle of his forehead in the time it took for the homicide detective to blink.

A Thompson/Center select for the center of Detective York's furrowed brow, the serial killer thrilled in triumph, popping several M&Ms into his mouth. Within seconds, he pulled the van doors closed. "Right between and an inch above his bushy black brows with a bullet that would blow out the back of a barn," he vaunted happily. "A weighty piece of lead that couldn't get out of its own way past sixty yards yet could take down a wall at thirty," he exaggerated with glee. "But that kill-shot had to be every bit of a hundred and fifty feet, I'd bet a yard," he punned merrily. "Had to be. Just had to be."

Chapter Thirty-Eight

Justin sat down with Karen Carper in the comfort of her cozy East Marion home on the North Fork of Long Island. The attractive woman's two daughters were sound asleep. The woman was wide-awake and apparently quite uncomfortable, fidgeting with a tie from her apron, which she promptly draped over the back of an antique wooden chair standing in a corner of the living room.

"I'm not supposed to have anyone in here while Sammy's away," she began. "Especially a stranger. I'm sure you can understand."

"Especially a black stranger who comes knocking at your door after ten o'clock in the evening," Justin made clear and nodded knowingly.

"Anyone," Mrs. Carper stated flatly. "Anyone at any hour. Night or day. Black or white or purple. You see, we're very private people, Mr. Barnes. We keep to ourselves and mind our own business."

"And this is certainly a very private area, I can see. Remote would size it up quite nicely, I guess."

"We have a neighborhood watch committee," Karen threw out haughtily. "I'm surprised no one stopped you driving through to get here."

"Not a soul around except for two pretty good size deer," he assured her. "So much for your watch committee," he added rather sorrily.

"Oh, we have plenty of them around here for sure. The deer, I mean. And I'm sure other eyes were watching you as well," she countered with canniness. "So, Mr. Barnes. I'm sorry to have you standing out there while I phoned and checked with headquarters.

Detective Archer told me that this visit of yours is very important and that it couldn't wait until morning."

"That's quite true."

"And that it concerns my husband."

"Yes, ma'am."

"And that's the only reason why I'm seeing you, I want you to understand. That and the fact that she threatened to send a patrol car out here and bring me into Yaphank to speak to your lieutenant."

"I'm sorry."

"Detective Archer also informed me that Sammy is all right. Is that true, Mr. Barnes?"

"So far as we know. And I can assume from your question that you haven't spoken to him. Is that correct?"

"He's extremely difficult to reach."

"Is that correct, Mrs. Carper?" Justin pressed politely.

"Yes, that's correct. I haven't spoken with him."

"Have you tried to reach him since after you spoke with Detective Archer, perhaps leaving a message? It's important that you answer me honestly, ma'am."

"He's my husband, Mr. Barnes. He has a perfect right to know that the police want to question me as to his business and whereabouts or whatever it is you're after."

"I know that Detective Archer told you very clearly that it wouldn't be the prudent thing to do."

"I have a duty as a wife, Mr. Barnes."

Justin nodded. "I understand, ma'am." He thought for a moment before opening his mouth again. "You seem to me to be a very candid woman, Karen Carper. I'd like for you to tell me truthfully if you left word with anyone who might contact him that we're interested in speaking to you. A simple yes or no. Please."

"I tried to reach him directly, yes. I was unable to; therefore, I left no such message. Now. I have a question for you. And I expect you to be equally honest."

"Yes, ma'am."

"Karen, if you like."

"Fine, Karen."

"Exactly how are you connected with the police? I don't quite understand."

"I'm a liaison."

"Detective Archer told me the same thing. But she wouldn't tell me anything beyond that. I feel I have a right to know what's going on. Who are you exactly? Why do want to question me about my husband? What is so urgent that this couldn't wait until morning? Is Sammy in any sort of danger? Well, is he?"

"I'll try and answer some of those questions as we move forward, Karen. That's the best I can do for now. But you're going to have to answer mine. Does your husband drive a blue turquoise Mercedes van, Karen?"

Karen stared at Justin for several seconds before she responded. "Yes."

"And last you heard from him?"

"Three weeks ago."

"From where?"

"He called from up north and spoke to the girls briefly. Sammy told me he had an unexpected assignment."

"Did he say what kind of an assignment it was?"

"Just that it had to do with the infrastructure of our economy," Karen offered rather pompously.

"The economy?"

"Mr. Barnes. Some people build homes, tunnels, bridges, skyscrapers. Some people come in and save corporations from collapse. My husband helps repair the foundation of floundering, falling or fallen governments on the local, state and federal level. That's what he does. As a result, he has many enemies. People who would try to push him out of power. Even people in his own party. People, Justin Barnes. Politics." She shook her head sadly. "It's an ugly mix. Because of his dedication and devotion, his family hardly ever gets to see him."

"Seems to me to be his choice, Karen. No?"

Karen shook her head. "You seem like a nice enough fellow, Mr. Barnes. But like so many, and I do mean the masses," she added pretentiously, "you're naive."

"Naive?"

Karen nodded. "Yes, naive."

"Maybe you could explain," Justin invited.

The comely woman accepted. "I'll give you a quick insight

into government—all democratic governments, in fact. It doesn't really matter which: local, state, national. Just before an election, it's one party in the throes of battle with the other. Republican and Democrat alike. Tearing at each other's throats. Winner take all. After the election, it's no longer one party vying against the other. Know what it is?"

Justin shook his head.

"It's those two parties against the people. A two-party dictatorship if you will. Keep that little lesson in mind, and you'll put politics in its proper perspective. My husband works 24/7, Mr. Barnes."

Justin nodded politely. "Did your husband ever mention a Sep Cramer, Karen?"

"Sep Cramer?" she searched her memory for a moment. "No. Not that I can recall. Who is he?"

"Someone who we believe knows your husband quite well," he toyed.

"Wouldn't surprise me. My husband is a very important man, Mr. Barnes. Behind the scenes but indispensable. Few people are, you know."

Justin had noted several photographs of Karen and her two daughters when he first entered the home. In separate poses as well as all together, the stolid female family stood. Absent from the array was the man of the house.

"Would you happen to have a picture handy of your husband, Karen?"

"Be right back." Karen got up and went into another room, returning a moment later with a heavy silver framed portrait of a rather young man, which she handed over with aplomb.

Justin had to smile. "Don't you have a more recent photograph?"

"Just that one. Sammy doesn't want his picture taken or displayed openly."

Justin couldn't help but wonder if Karen's young daughters were permitted to carry around pictures of their father in their pretty little heads. It was, perhaps, the proper time for Suffolk County Homicide's liaison to awake the alluring yet unsuspecting head of household—in her husband's absence—to certain facts. Justin opened a folder and removed a single image.

"Here's a more recent picture of Sep Cramer, Karen. Recognize him?"

Karen Carper took and held a likeness of her husband up to the light. "So?" she said, seemingly unimpressed. "My husband sometimes uses several names in the sort of business that he's in, Mr. Barnes."

"And how *exactly* would you categorize that business, Karen?"

"I'd have to say that he's a *liaison* between government and the real people in power," she offered smugly. "There's a big difference."

Justin looked down at his handwritten list of additional names that Kim had provided him via phone on the drive out East. "It might interest you to know some of those aliases, Karen. Actually, Sep Cramer is your husband's legal name. Sam Carper is fictitious. So are Mac Pace, Marc Espe, and Case Reece. They're all one in the same person. I'm sure we'll discover others as we continue our investigation."

Karen smiled with mild amusement. "And I'm sure you'll come to learn that your information is just a bit mixed up. It may be that Sep Cramer is one of my husband's aliases. Samuel Laird Carper, however, is my husband's full and legal name. Again, the others may be fictitious. But so what? Those names wouldn't interest me at all. Not in the least. Why should they?"

"Because the same man with five different names has taken four different wives in four different states. That's why, Karen. There's a Karen Carper of East Marion—that's you," Justin said so sadly, "a Rebecca Pace of Maryland, a Sharon Espe of Maine, a Brenda Reece of Virginia—who by the way has been missing for close to a decade— and a Lynda Cramer of Kentucky who supposedly committed suicide some fourteen years ago."

Justin took back the DMV photo of Sep Cramer, put away the list of names along with a page of notes and then closed the folder.

Karen digested the information and swallowed uncomfortably.

"There's no confusion or mistaken information in that folder, Karen. I'm very sorry."

Justin's cell phone sounded followed by a low whine from just outside the home.

"Did you here that?" Karen asked with some concern,

disregarding the call while pointing toward the front door, listening for the noise anew.

Justin smiled. "That's just my partner out there getting a bit impatient. Excuse me a minute." Justin answered his cell.

Karen got up and went over to a window, staring out at the car parked in the driveway with a shadowy figure moving back and forth along the front seat.

Justin listened to Kim's trembling voice as she broke the horrifying news. He blotted out the details after hearing that Gary York was dead. Numbness took hold of him as he awkwardly rose from his seat. He heard Wilcox's name mentioned then something about reporting immediately back to Yaphank.

"No. You get me a flight number and have a car in place when I arrive," was all that Justin could manage.

Several seconds passed without a response before Brian came on the line. "You get back here, J. That's an order. Hear me?"

"I'm going."

"Going where?"

"For some mountain air."

"No, you're not."

"I'm going," the maverick stated calmly, controlling his breathing before terminating the conversation with the case detective. "Put Kim back on."

"You get your ass—"

"Put her on or I'll drop this cell in the nearest toilet. I mean it, Bri."

"I'm here, J," Kim responded.

"You get me that plane and car or I do this on my own."

"Chief Wilcox and—"

"Fuck Chief Wilcox and everyone else!" he shouted, speaking into the mouthpiece at arm's length.

Karen studied the angry man standing before her.

"I'm going down there with or without your help," Justin swore quietly, realizing Karen's children were sleeping. "Just tell me how it's going to play, Kim."

There was a moment of silence then muffled arguing on the other end of the line.

Justin disconnected the call and started to make his apology to the woman.

"What happened?" Karen interrupted. "Please tell me."

Justin shook his head. "There's been an accident. Not your problem."

Karen's home phone rang and she picked it up immediately. "Hello?" She listened carefully to the instruction and handed over the phone.

"Yeah," Justin said evenly.

"She okay?" Kim asked with grave concern.

"Fine."

"She know?"

"The polygamy part."

"Just the polygamy part?"

"Right."

"Keep it that way."

"Right."

"Brian and I and the lieutenant say go with God. Start heading for LaGuardia. I'll call you en route."

"Thank you."

"Are you taking Pug?"

"Wouldn't leave home without him."

"I figured that. It'll be late, but I'll try and arrange something on the other end. How's that?"

"Great."

"Sep Cramer's very powerful and unbelievably connected. You've got to be extraordinarily careful, J."

"I know."

"No, you don't know! You won't get near him. He's insulated with lawyers from the foothills to Capitol Hill. He's got a solid alibi if that's where your mind is working. Forget arrest. Forget bigamy, polygamy or whatever else you think you can prove. You won't. His people will see to that. He's dangerous, J."

"I'll be careful. All right?"

"Gary promised me he'd be careful, too, and look what happened."

"I think Gary had his head in another direction. He wasn't careful."

"A broad, you said," Kim reminded herself through her tears.

"Correct. Like I told you before, only thing that would ever distract him."

"He was involved with a woman, not a pet?"

"Something like that."

"You keep that firmly in mind and your wits about you at all times. Do you understand that?"

"I do."

"We'll watch the house from the moment you head out."

"Good."

"I love you, J. You know that."

"I'm going to report you to Brian the second I get back," he promised with a broken smile, damning up a tear or two with the edge of a finger.

"He's standing right here, and he wants you to know that he feels the same way, too. We all do."

"Gotta go." Justin put the receiver down and headed toward the door.

"Hold on a second, please," Karen practically pleaded. "I have something for you to take." The pretty lady disappeared for a full minute then returned with two small packages wrapped in foil. "One's for you; the other one's for your friend waiting in the car." The woman forced a smile.

Justin thanked her. "Look at me, Karen."

Karen tried to look but couldn't. She turned away.

"Then listen," Justin insisted. "You and your daughters are going to be okay."

Karen quickly nodded.

"Double-lock this door behind me. A car will be watching the house from the second I drive away. And I'm not talking about your neighborhood watch committee either," Justin affirmed.

Karen forced a crooked smile and saw the man out. She was staring at the dog peering over the steering wheel at the two of them.

Chapter Thirty-Nine

Sep Cramer, assuming the name of Ace Reaper, rendezvoused with Denise Holloway in a hotel room in War, West Virginia, just across the state line from Cedar Bluff, a little more than an hour's drive from her home in Big Stone Gap. Denise had told her husband that she was spending a few days with her sister and brother-in-law. Traveling. Sep told his lawyers that he had business in Charleston, some eighty miles to the north.

Sep and Denise had a quiet dinner at a nearby restaurant before returning to their room for the evening. The two took a shower together then got into bed.

"Do you know what kind of room this is, Denise?" Sep asked, switching off the night light. "Aside from a hotel room, it's a war room," he said and smiled complacently there in the dark. "A room in which we'll plan our strategy for the next battle. How does that grab you?" he asked and answered his own questions, clutching her panties, pulling them off her slim trim hips, down along a pair of lanky legs, quickly removing her silk cami. "I asked you a question."

"Like a military operation, General. Am I your second in command?"

"First things first," he whispered, flipping her over on her stomach and applying a generous amount of a syrupy substance along his erect penis before mounting her forcefully from behind.

"Ohhh," she said shivering, arching her back to meet a continuous series of pounding thrusts. "What-ev-er-hap-pened-to-fore-play?" Sep's accomplice protested in ambivalent surrender.

"Went-out-with-chiv-al-ry," the serial killer concatenated each and every syllable in kind.

"Harder . . . faster. I want that how-it-zer-up-my-ass till *I* shoot," she practically shouted.

Sep suddenly stopped.

"What?"

"A howitzer's a short cannon, Denise. Got that?" Sep made clear, followed by a snicker, pausing just long enough to catch his breath. "You making fun?"

"Keep that long gun coming," she insisted. *Putz*, she thought but resisted. "Stop again, and I'll cut your balls off, fucker. You got that?"

"Who did or does it better? Tell me," he commanded. "Detective York? Or-yours-truly?" Sep hammered her buttocks hard and heavily for a full minute and a half.

Denise said nothing, burying her face into a pillow, moaning with pleasure as he exploded seconds before her.

"Well?"

"Well, what?"

"I asked you a fucking question. Who *is* the superior cocksman?" the debaucher demanded to know.

Denise rolled over onto her back, smiling up at the man's insistence. "Well, let me put it to you this way, darling. Gary York surely had his moment, but in the end, he was certainly outgunned."

The pair stared at one another for what seemed like an eternity before they both erupted with laughter so loud that the guests in the adjacent room started knocking on the wall.

"Shh," Denise managed pulling the pillow over her face to control herself.

"Shhhh," Sep mocked, pressing a foam pillow down forcefully upon her face until her arms and legs flew out in all directions before allowing her to catch her precious breath.

Chapter Forty

Justin Barnes and Pug arrived at Tri-Cities Regional Airport in Blountville, Tennessee during the wee hours of morning. The new dog owner had little choice but to place Pug in a kennel in Bristol on the way to Big Stone Gap. It broke his already broken heart. Kim had made the necessary arrangements. Both man and man's best friend had spent a restless night at a bed-and-breakfast and Paws N Claws, respectively. Justin's accommodations were in the same area where Gary had stayed. In the morning, the maverick was briefed by police, rather briefly he imagined, about the facts surrounding the detective's murder.

"I'd like to speak to Chief Wilcox," Justin finally said to their one and only police sergeant.

"Not available now," the burly man answered.

"Then when?"

The cop shrugged.

Justin turned to the lieutenant. "Give me the chief's cell phone number."

"Don't happen to have it handy."

Justin walked directly up to the man. "Listen, Lieutenant. I really don't expect you to keep too much in that head of yours, but your desk is right across the room. I'm sure you have it written down there somewhere."

"Chief'll call in when he calls, and I'll give him your message. You can leave a number where you can be reached."

"I see." Justin scratched his head in annoyance. "You know, I had this funny idea that you fellas were holdin' back, not tellin' me everything I need to know. And you just confirmed it. So, I'm gonna tell you what I'm prepared to do, Lieutenant Garvey. I'm prepared to sit behind that desk of yours and wait for your phantom chief to call or show. You got one detective who gave me the bum's rush but asked that your sergeant here cooperate and give me what you got; two other detectives unaccounted for who don't return my calls; some bimbo secretary who can't even get a coffee order straight; ten full-time sworn officers, I hear, four that I dealt with who know little or next to nothing about the case, one who didn't even realize a murder was committed while the other dunce showed up at the wrong Wal-Mart in Bristol, Virginia when my colleague's body is in Bristol, Tennessee—eight fucking miles away from one another; and a records clerk who's about as useless as teats on a bull and still hasn't returned from a coffee break, and that was over forty minutes ago." Justin went over and plopped himself into the lieutenant's chair, folding his arms firmly across his chest.

"You can't do that."

"Do what, Lieutenant?"

"Sit there like that."

"How 'bout like this?" Justin dropped his arms and clasped his hands politely in front of him. "Betterer?"

"Listen, hotshot."

"I'm listening."

"We've got every available swingin' dick out there investigating this, including the sheriff's office, CID and Intel. Understand? My men are on this thing 24/7 like glue on flypaper, and we're gonna stick it good to that fuck."

"What fuck? You can't even manage a search warrant for Cramer's home. Have you even spoken with the boys over in Lynch? That's just across the western border in Kentucky, a stone's throw from Big Stone Gap. I mention it in case you don't know exactly where you're standing at the moment and have a bit of a problem with geography. Have you personally contacted the police in Bristol? The one in Tennessee? That's on your southern border, Louie. I'll tell you what your swingin' dicks are doin'; doin' anybody they can pin this on without doin' what they should be doin', and that's focusing on your prime suspect."

"No, Barnes. *Your* prime suspect. Not ours. You're way off base with Cramer."

"Oh, am I?"

"Yes, you are. He may be what you claim he is in part: a bigamist, but—"

"Try polygamist for openers."

"Whatever. But that's a far cry from a murderer. Sep Cramer happens to run in the finest of circles."

"So did Ted Bundy, Louie," Justin countered with a sneer.

"I am not Louie. I am Lieutenant Bryce Garvey, and you'll respect my rank and address me as Lieutenant. You understand me, Mr. Barnes? Mr. Hotshot nig . . . nobody from the north."

"What was that, Louie?"

The lieutenant fixed his eyes on Justin. "Just get the fuck out of my seat."

"No, what were you about to say? Hotshot what?"

"I called you a hotshot nobody from the north. Don't like it? I'll let you in on a little secret, Barnes. You're down here because your lieutenant and my chief decided to placate you."

"No. I'm down here because I choose to be down here. With or without anyone's blessing. Now, back to name-calling. You were about to denigrate me as some nigger from the north. Why don't you be man enough to admit it?"

"I asked you to get out of my seat. I'm not going to say it again, Barnes," the lieutenant stated angrily, glancing at his sergeant.

Sergeant Baker took a tentative step toward Justin.

Justin thought for a second, nodded politely, and then stood, walking over to the secretary's vacant desk. He roughly pulled open the bottom right-hand draw and withdrew a black Rolodex with a series of typed white cards.

"Just what the hell do you think you're doing?" Lieutenant Garvey blew.

"I guess you thought I didn't see your secretary's little disappearing act, discreetly dropping this in here before she disappeared for coffee," Justin accused, searching unsuccessfully through the W's, continuing counterclockwise and stopping at the C's, pulling out Chief Wilcox's card with a list of phone numbers and a home address. As the maverick put the card in his coat pocket, Sergeant Baker suddenly charged forward. Justin withdrew his weapon and leveled it before the man's massive chest. Baker froze.

"You're making a big mistake, Barnes," the lieutenant swore. "Big mistake."

"Licensed to carry and kill at will if I feel my life is being threatened in any way, shape or form, flunkies," he announced, glaring at the two of them. "Actually, I don't need this piece to whop your sorry ass, Sergeant. But I'm short on sleep and patience, long on bad memories of having to explain myself in court and private hearings. *Always* more difficult when there's a second version for a judge and jury to hear," he blared. "So I'd just as soon waste you right here, Baker. And as for you, Louie, I'd put a bullet in your brain just for the hell of it. Now go sit down in that seat of yours and keep your trap shut before I have second thoughts about how to handle this matter at hand. Baker, better step back the hell away from me or a bullet with your name on it will do it for me. This northern nigger ain't fuckin' 'round with you, asshole."

Sergeant Baker stepped back, and Lieutenant Bryce Garvey took a seat in his chair.

"You drew your weapon and threatened two law enforcement officers," Garvey stated with ire.

"That's your version, Louie. Mine is that you provoked me by calling me a nig and then sicked your two-ton sergeant on me. I was acting in self-defense. I'd even take a poly. Would you?" Justin questioned. "How 'bout you, Baker? You see, guys, I'm in the enforcement business, too. Whether it's lawful or not is in that gray area. Gray," Justin repeated for emphasis. "Dat's dat neutral color between black and white," he jawed. "Neutral," he reiterated. "So what say we cool our jets? Or this can all turn into one big fucking ugly mess. And then where are we? Think about that. Think about this, too. Detective Gary York was the case detective's partner on these handgun homicides. Brian Archer. Brian Archer recruited me. Feel free to call him, Lieutenant. You're probably right about my lieutenant and your chief placating me, but speak to Archer on this serial killer case we're working. I'm sure you'll come away with a different slant. I don't think your chief is sharing everything with even you because he's under pressure from the mayor's office. But what else is new, right?" Justin holstered his weapon and locked his eyes on Sergeant Baker. "Baker, my man. A dozen less doughnuts daily, and I think you'd be on the road to recovery in no time, buddy."

Chapter Forty-One

S ep Cramer and Denise Holloway ordered breakfast at a diner in Welch, West Virginia, ten miles north of War.

"There's a pesky nigger down from New York, nosing around your neck of the woods," Sep said, abruptly putting away his cell phone.

"Pesky?"

"Troublesome."

"Don't you mean pesty?"

"No, I mean pesky," Sep said nastily.

"But pesty's the right word, too. Right? Pesty. Like a pest. No?" she persisted.

"As an alternate, all right? Pest is a noun. Pesky is a modifier."

"Modifier?"

"Adjective."

"And pester?"

"That's what you're doing to me now."

"No, seriously. Pester's a verb, right?"

"A transitive verb."

"You know I don't understand all that business. A verb's a verb. No?"

"There are transitive verbs and intransitive verbs. Got it?"

"What's the difference?"

"Forget it."

"No, I want to learn."

"Transitive verbs take a direct object from which a passive can be formed."

"Huh?"

"Like I said. Forget it."

But Denise shook her pretty head. "I said, I want to learn."

"I'll make you a deal."

"Tell me."

"You help me with this pest, and I'll teach you basic grammar. How's that?"

"You'll be patient with me?"

"I'll be patient with you."

"Promise?"

"Promise."

"How do I help you with this pesky nigger from New York? Set him up at Kmart for you next?" she tested with a titter.

Sep laughed, too, and shook his head. "No, but you're warm."

"J.C. Penny," she teased.

"Target."

"Target?"

"Target," Sep affirmed. "The one down in Johnson City."

"A target at a Target. Neat. But why Tennessee again? Why not another state? And why fuck around with another cop? I think you're playing with fire. No?"

"He's not a cop, Denise, but an adjunct."

"Adjunct?"

"He's their in-house assassin. All rather hush-hush," the serial killer explained clearly and coldly.

"Assassin?"

"He does their dirty work."

"I don't understand."

"It's very simple, my simpleton. He kills killers for the police that for one reason or another they don't want to arrest and/or have prosecuted."

"Why?"

"Why? she asks."

"Tell me."

"Because of the possibility that people like me will one day walk free, or at least still breathe behind bars whereas their victims will never take another breath again. Is that so hard to understand?"

"How do people like that nigger get away with it?"

"Power behind the throne."

"Aren't you just a bit concerned that this guy—what's his name —might find and kill you?"

"Not if *we* kill him first. And his name is Justin Barnes."

"Fine, but let me tell you right off the bat. I don't fuck niggers."

"You won't have to."

"What do I have to do?"

"Just serve him coffee—black—and some homemade cherry pie."

"You're asking me to poison him back at the diner?" she queried with a cheerful smile.

"No, but I'm glad to see that you're thinking and getting into the spirit of things."

"How do you know that he'll come to the diner?"

"Maybe not the diner, but he'll come all right. Especially when you call and tell him you're the prize that Detective Gary York was bringing home."

"Are you serious?"

"As serious as a funeral director."

"I don't know if I want the role. And why would he believe me? Because I don't think anyone knew about York's proposal and plans."

"Maybe, maybe not. But they're going to know soon enough if they don't already."

"How? I covered my fingerprints with clear nail polish like you told me to."

"I'm talking about the ring."

"I took it, along with the box it came in. I told you all that."

"What about the receipt?"

"What receipt?"

"The receipt for the ring that the police surely found in his wallet or a pocket. You don't know what York said to the salesperson, or anyone else for that matter. It's best to be on the up-and-up."

Denise thought about the implications. "And Ted? What if he finds out?"

"He probably won't. Especially if you go to the police or Barnes first. They'll be discreet if you bat your eyelashes."

Denise nodded her understanding. "And just how do I lure

Barnes to Johnson City for you?"

"You don't. I lure you."

"I don't follow."

"You will."

The pretty woman made room on the table as their waitress lowered two large oval plates and then left. "Why are we doing this exactly?"

"The game. Tell me you don't enjoy it."

"I love it, Sep."

"Ace. Ace Reaper."

"I love it, Ace," she said sincerely, directing a knife and fork toward her perfectly prepared eggs over easy and very rare steak. "I absolutely love it."

Chapter Forty-Two

K im Archer contacted Justin on his cell phone and began relating the most recent updates with regard to Sep Cramer's past and present wives. Detectives from Team Three's homicide squad had traveled north and south to interview two women.

"Brian personally spoke with Rebecca Pace down in Denton, Maryland; Vic with Sharon Espe up in Millinocket, Maine," Kim expanded. "They talked to scores of neighbors and merchants, too."

"And?"

"And Sharon Espe just gave birth to a premature girl, which Sep Cramer—as Marc Espe—had insisted on naming Karen. Karen, as you know, happens to be the name of Carper's/Cramer's wife you interviewed in East Marion. Anyway, Sharon Espe and Sep Cramer had a big fight before he left Maine because the bastard promised her he'd stay home until after she had the baby, Vic said. Carla Banks, I don't need remind you, was eight months pregnant when she was murdered."

"Whoa there, Kim. You're sayin' that the Banks woman's murder wasn't random?"

"I don't know, J. Just keep it in mind. How are you making out with Chief Wilcox's boys?"

"Not so good. They're blowing smoke up my butt."

"Not surprising."

"I told Lieutenant Garvey to speak to Brian. Seems their chief and our helmsman want me out of the picture, although they're putting on a different face."

"What do you expect? You went off half-cocked."

"Listen to me, Kim. You and Bri should be glad I'm down here.

These Big Stone Gap guys are a cut above the Keystone Kops. Got the picture? They're looking in a completely different direction. Sep Cramer seems to be their fair-haired boy."

"You've got to understand something, J."

"Like what?"

"Like a spokesman for the state department telling Chief Wilcox he better show cause to even *imagine* bad thoughts about Mr. Sep Cramer. *You* got the picture?"

"What about beating them over the head with marriage records and affidavits showing that he's a polygamist? We can start there."

"And it'll end there. You really think they're going to bring Cramer in and interrogate him on what *we* suspect? Gotta get real, J. He cooperated when Gary interviewed him in Lynch. It's in Gary's notes. Next time it will be with Cramer's lawyers you can bet."

"He owns and operates a blue turquoise panel van seen in the vicinity where the Banks woman was murdered that afternoon."

"And Gary walked away after interviewing him, seemingly satisfied."

"Then winds up dead."

"Push the envelope and there are going to be repercussions. Big repercussions, I hate to tell you. Powell told Brian to tell me to tell you to back off. You're down there as an observer only. That's all. If Wilcox wants to share something with you, that's fine. If he doesn't, that's it. When they release Gary's body, the show's over. You get him and your ass back here pronto."

"Kim."

"What?"

"Never mind."

"I mind every nuance. Tell me."

"It's got to be Cramer. The turquoise van. The timing. Everything."

"I wish we could prove it."

"If only someone could secure a search warrant. I'd bet big bucks they'd find the goods. The frame. The barrels. The ammo. The whole nine yards."

"It's not going to happen."

"I could make it happen, Kim. I could."

"Now, you listen to me, and you listen up good."

"I'll bet you dollars to Sergeant Baker's doughnuts Cramer's got a cache in his home or somewhere on that property."

"You stay far the hell away from there. You even think about a visit or a break-in, and I'll break your neck. You find out what you can through Wilcox. It's home for you as soon as they're done with Gary. I'm not going to lose you, too. And those are orders from the top on down. Hear me?"

"Yes, ma'am."

"I mean it, J."

"I heard you.

"And who's this Sergeant Baker?"

"A nitwit with a waistline you could wrap around a city block. He's Wilcox's and Lieutenant Garvey's impenetrable wall."

"I see."

"Anything else you can tell me?"

Kim hesitated.

"Give. I know that sound of silence," he coaxed.

Kim pressed one corner of a saddened smile against the mouthpiece. "According to Gary's notes, Cramer's a speechwriter and speaker. And a damn good one from what information I could gather. He'll be delivering the keynote speech at the renowned Bohemian Club in San Francisco during mid-July, rubbing elbows with the aristocracy. I'm talking George W. Bush, Cheney, Rumsfeld, Powell, Kissinger and heavyweights like that."

"Jesus, Kim."

"Christ would probably be there too, if available. Only I don't know whether the members would listen up or carry Him back to a cross."

"History does repeat itself, I'm told."

"You were told correctly. Got one more. You writing all this down?"

"Every syllable. Are Brian and the lieutenant beginning to see the light regarding those murders dating back to 2000?"

"They feel you can read what you want into anything when you start playing around with words like sera and serape. But they couldn't argue over Cramer's aliases that I unscrambled, of course: Sam Carper, Marc Espe, Mac Pace and Case Reece. All letter formations of Sep Cramer. I had them eating crow over those, especially when our investigators returned from Maine, Maryland and Virginia. But those words, J. I sometimes tend to doubt myself. Anyhow, I borrowed a program from the feds that's the equivalent of FORTRAM, only it analyzes and solves linguistic problems. It's very sophisticated."

"Borrowed?"

"Well, more like broke into," the computer wizard admitted.

"So look who's calling the kettle black," Justin jabbed.

"Never you mind. It's one thing to break into a system; another to enter a home illegally."

"I see," Justin said unheedingly, standing in a tree and raising a pair of binoculars, focusing upon the man riding up a mountainside on his green and yellow John Deere Trail Gator.

"Where are you now, J?"

"About to sit down to lunch."

"Remember. As soon as they release Gary's body, you and Pug are out of there."

"Yes, ma'am."

"I mean it. You be very careful."

"I will, indeed."

"Take heed, and take care. Oh, and don't worry yourself none about puppy. I called the kennel, and he's doing fine."

"To tell you the truth, Kim, I think I had more of a chance of getting fleas than Pug. That was some room you booked me."

Kim allowed herself a little laugh. "Sorry, champ. Best I could do on short notice as there is a convention going on, you know."

"Right."

Justin put away his cell phone, reached over and pulled a green apple from a branch near the top of the tree before lowering his body to a sitting position upon a thick bough, taking a bite of the bitter fruit.

Chapter Forty-Three

Big Stone Gap's police chief had reached Justin by phone in his motel room late in the evening, promising the interloper a piece of interesting news that Wilcox felt sure would satisfy Barnes and send him packing, especially since authorities and forensics were finished with Detective Gary York's body. Chief Wilcox personally invited Justin to come by bright and early the following morning, 7 a.m. sharp, to meet and interview the last person who they believed saw Gary alive; the killer notwithstanding.

Justin arrived a few minutes before seven with containers of fresh coffee and a box of doughnuts, the latter of which he slid across a conference table toward Sergeant Baker as the big man ushered him past the chief and into a room near the end of the hall.

"Peace offering," Justin offered, flashing and flaunting a bright, white set of healthy teeth. "Assorted, so I'm sure you'll find your poison. Five black coffees with a container of moo to help balance the mother lode. And here's some sugar and Sweet 'n Low," he chattered away, digging into the bottom of the cardboard cutouts after removing the Styrofoam cups from the tray. "So where's this mystery guest?"

"She'll be here in a minute. Why don't you have a seat," Chief Wilcox bade politely, stepping into the room.

"A she," Justin echoed with little surprise. "Very pretty, I'll bet. On the slim side. Five foot eight to ten. Dark hair. Brown eyes. Fairly intelligent. Good sense of humor, but no nonsense. How am I doing, guys?"

Sergeant Baker and Chief Wilcox looked at one another momentarily before setting their eyes back on the thorn in their sides.

"Oh, I can see from your expressions that I can't be very far off the mark. Yeah, that's how Gary liked them, all right. Tall and dark haired. Me? Blonde and buxom," he needled. "Actually, Gary liked them all. But if he bought a ring like that for her, well, she had to fit a certain criteria. That's my new word for the day. Criteria," he said and smiled disarmingly. "Every day, whether I'm home or away, I learn a new word."

Lieutenant Garvey escorted Denise Holloway into the room and quickly made the introduction.

Justin appeared impressed.

"Before we get started, Barnes," Chief Wilcox said, "I want to make it perfectly clear that it was Mrs. Holloway who came forward voluntarily with information. We did not seek her out."

"Missis?" Justin remarked with some surprise.

"Why don't we all sit down?" the lieutenant suggested.

Justin immediately pulled out a chair for Mrs. Denise Holloway and waited for her to take a seat before taking a chair for himself. "There's coffee and doughnuts, ma'am," he invited.

"No, thank you," Holloway responded politely, her voice hardly above a whisper.

"Chief? Lieutenant?" Justin redirected their attention. "Real police fodder, fellas," the maverick funned. "Plenty to go around, fellas."

The two superiors declined.

"Well, that just leaves you and me, Sergeant Baker," Justin yawed and yawned again. "You'll have to excuse me, folks. I had three sour apples since yesterday afternoon and a bad night's sleep. Cup of java and a jelly doughnut ought to pick me right up in a minute, though. Might have to arm wrestle you for the cruller, however, Sergeant; that is, if no one changes their mind."

Baker and Barnes helped themselves to coffee and a doughnut as the police chief began the informal interview.

"Denise, I know this is very hard for you, especially having to go through this ordeal a second time. But it's important. Mr. Barnes, here—"

"Jesus Christ!" Justin suddenly interrupted.

"What is it?" Lieutenant Garvey snapped.

"No napkins. I told the woman to make sure there were napkins. Damn. Jelly and cream-filled doughnuts and no napkins," the maverick complained, licking his fingers as the lieutenant got up, walked out of the room, then returned in less than thirty seconds with a new roll of paper towels, which he placed abruptly in the center of the table. "Thank you," Justin ranted, reaching for the Bounty and tearing off the plastic wrap. "You've got to watch them like a hawk. I'm surprised the bimbo even got the order right," he raved, surveying the entire order. "Good thing I ordered all black and everybody puts in their own cream and sugar. You sure you won't have a doughnut and coffee, Mrs. Holloway?"

"I'm sure, thank you," the woman declined, fidgeting with the strap of her purse.

"Sorry," Justin apologized, noting Wilcox's annoyance.

"Why don't you begin at the beginning, Denise. Nothing you say here leaves this room. You didn't witness the murder nor hear anything, so you won't be called to testify. This meeting is off the record, and Ted will never know unless you decide to tell him yourself."

"Thank you, Chief Wilcox." Denise put forth her best choked-up expression of grief and sorrow.

The woman began her story from the moment Detective Gary York entered the diner and her life, until the final hour that she had stepped from the detective's rental car at Wal-Mart in Bristol, Tennessee.

"And that's when I went into the store. When I came back out, not ten minutes later, Gary was nowhere to be found," Denise declared with a sob. "I thought he changed his mind and drove off. I had no idea what happened until later in the evening when I listened to the news."

"You said to one of the officers that you took a taxi home," Justin questioned politely, consulting his notes.

Denise nodded and blew her nose into a tissue.

"It's all checked out, Barnes," Lieutenant Garvey interjected. "Believe me."

But Justin waved away the reassurances. "How long did you wait before you called a cab, Mrs. Holloway?"

"Maybe another ten minutes. I'm not sure."

"And you looked around the parking lot for Gary when you left the store?"

"Yes."

"All around? The front? The side? Near the back of the building where the car was found with his bleeding body?"

"The front, where he dropped me off."

"Mrs. Holloway," Justin carped with a disingenuous smile. "Detective York just buys and hands you a diamond wedding ring appraised at well over four thousand dollars; you admit to a rather short but passionate affair; you're about to run off with him and leave your husband for good, and you look and wait for your lover out front of Wal-Mart for ten minutes?" he asked with mocking incredulity.

"Maybe it was longer. I told you, I'm not sure. I was in a state."

"Yeah, the state of Tennessee." Justin sallied and snickered for Wilcox's benefit.

"Excuse me?" Denise Holloway snapped. "We were to catch a plane in Blountville, bound for New York. We had to be there early. When I came out of the building and saw no car, no Gary anywhere, I panicked and believed that he had gotten cold feet and left for the airport without me."

"And you never called the airport to confirm whether he was on that flight."

"At that point I was angry. What would it have mattered anyhow?"

"Didn't it occur to you that if he had a change of heart, he wouldn't have picked you up at your home in the first place? You were the one who asked to stop at Wal-Mart, you said."

"Men can sometimes be just as fickle as they claim women are," was the waitress' reply. "I'm in the food service industry, Mr. Barnes. I see how unpredictable they can be."

"You know, that's so true, Mrs. Holloway. Why, less than fifteen minutes ago I was in a coffee shop, and I ordered these five coffees and a dozen doughnuts to go. 'Go where exactly?' was the young woman's question. Like if I had told her, she'd know exactly how everyone here took their coffee et cetera, being a small town and all, I guess. Black. Light. Regular. Milk or half-and-half or maybe those international coffee creamers in lieu of one or two sugars. Cream-filled doughnuts, jelly, plain or powder coated to choose from, too. She really caught me off guard; I couldn't think straight. You see, I was thinking all about this mystery person and our meeting here this morning. I saw a copy of the receipt for the ring Gary gave you. It's one of the few things the police in Bristol shared. Of course, they didn't know who you were either. No lead even after they spoke to the owner of the jewelry store. So it's really swell that you came forward early and cleared this up for everybody. Oh, back to the young woman in the coffee shop, spelled with two p's and an e at the end; that's: s-h-o-p-p-e. Adds a little class to the place," Justin jabbered. "Anyhow, she suggests five black coffees with all kinds of fancy creams or milk to choose from. But I said, 'No thank you; just milk will be fine. On second thought, make that half-and-half,' I decided. But then I thought about health and diet conscious people, and I was having trouble making up my mind again. I guess you can call that being fickle. Well, you know what she did after I finally decided on medium-sized cups?"

"Barnes!" Chief Wilcox said in exasperation.

But Justin bought another minute with a single digit pointed around the table at everyone.

"I'm coming to the good part," he insisted. "Just bear with me a moment. Please," he practically pleaded. "It's important."

Lieutenant Garvey raised his eyes impatiently to the ceiling.

Sergeant Baker was well into his fifth doughnut and third cup of coffee.

Denise Holloway stopped fidgeting with her purse and was listening carefully.

Chief Wilcox sighed. "Go on, Barnes."

"Well, the young woman poured the five black coffees, filled the sixth container with both milk and half-and-half and a splash of flavored cream, put twelve different doughnuts into that box and sprinkled half of them with a powdery white shower of fine sugar, getting it all over the counter and herself. That's when it hit me. Well, not exactly then, but when she handed me back change from a twenty." Justin paused for the full effect.

"What hit you?" Sergeant Baker asked, polishing off the doughnut while staring indecisively at the box.

"The young woman's prints from the fine white powdery sugar were all over the dollar bills. You see, the boys in Bristol found not a single fingerprint from around the front passenger area of my associate's rental car belonging to any person other than Detective Gary York, excluding a fellow from the prepping detail who had

ArmorAlled the dash, along with an assistant from Alamo who put paperwork into the glove compartment. Didn't you tell us that Gary had you open the glove compartment and remove the gift of a wedding ring? Why weren't your prints found there or on the inner or outer door handles? How about the trunk you closed after throwing in your bag? I'm sure you have a very good explanation for that, Mrs. Holloway."

Chief Wilcox, Lieutenant Garvey and Sergeant Baker were staring intently between Barnes and Holloway.

Denise Holloway lifted her eyes from her purse and set them confidently on her interrogator. She slowly and deliberately unclasped the black leather bag and reached inside, withdrawing a pair of short white satin gloves. "I was wearing these from the moment Gary picked me up at the house until the time I got home. They went with my outfit."

"Well, Barnes?" Wilcox said rather satisfactorily. "Do you have any further questions for Mrs. Holloway?"

Justin wouldn't take his eyes off the woman.

"I'm very sorry about your friend, Mr. Barnes," Denise said comfortingly. "I know that you and he were good friends because Gary spoke fondly of you. He told me there were four people in the world he would trust with his life. Brian, Kim, yourself . . . and me." Denise wept and wrung her hands together. "I'm so sorry. I loved him dearly al-although we-we only met. It seemed like we kn-knew one another for a lifetime." The woman's shoulders shook and shivered as the chief and the lieutenant rose from their seats and came to comfort her.

"This meeting is over, Barnes," the chief said coldly. "We've made arrangements for you to take yourself and Detective York's body back to New York this afternoon: depart Blountville 3:06 p.m.," he read off an index card; "arrive Pittsburgh 4:40 where you'll lay over for an hour. You'll reach LaGuardia shortly after seven this evening. If you have a mind to, try catching the evening news. We're about to make an arrest in this case. I'll be sure to send a press release your way."

Sergeant Baker reached for a sixth doughnut and a fourth container of coffee.

"You coming, Barnes?" the lieutenant asked sharply.

Justin remained in his seat, refusing to take his eyes off Denise

Holloway as she was promptly escorted from the room, her two sympathizers sandwiching the waitress between them with Baker languidly taking up the rear, doughnut and coffee in hand, returning a second later and greedily sweeping up the entire box into his arms.

"Peace offer accepted," Baker said and smirked broadly, breaking wind loudly as he turned back around, stinking up the room. "That's another new word for you for the day. Try and spell that one," he added with a chuckle, releasing another rush of air. "Hotshot. Just like the lieutenant said." Sergeant Baker simply shook his head disparagingly before waddling out of the room, into and down the corridor.

Chapter Forty-Four

Justin drove from Big Stone Gap, Virginia, to Bristol, Tennessee to fetch Pug from the Paws N Claws kennel. The pup looked no worse for wear, the anguished recalcitrant determined. Having no intention of continuing on to the airport in Blountville, the maverick headed west, back along the Virginia border on U.S. 421 toward the corner of the state, northwest on Alternate 58 through Pennington Gap, and on toward Harlan, Kentucky, making a wide semicircular sweep to the north on U.S. 119, away from Big Stone Gap, then on to Lynch, before dropping south into the foothills of Black Mountain. Home away from home to Sep Cramer.

"Well, we'll be there in a few minutes, Pug."

The terrier lay with his nose a foot away from Justin's leg.

"I know you're not too happy with me, fella. Leavin' you all alone like that. But it just couldn't be helped. And it's not that I really left you. True? I flew you down here with me. Did I not? I mean, it wasn't first class or anything, but if you saw what I had to put up with in tourist, you'd understand. Damn right those people should pay one-and-a-half or double for the price of a seat when they weigh in at close to three hundred pounds. But the nerve of the airline charging one hundred dollars each way for a ten-pound pup is absolutely outrageous."

Justin threw the car into low gear and ascended the mountain.

"And talk about lodging, you had it twice as good as I did, Pug. Trust me on that. You may have had a flea or two, but I had bugs and beetles in and beneath my bed. Gigantic ones!"

Pug lifted his head as though he were sizing up the big picture. When he settled back down, his nose nestled against Justin's knee.

"And chow? You had it ten times better than me. I mean, *I*. Do you know that in the last twenty-four hours I had three sour apples, one doughnut, and maybe a half a cup of black coffee? Of course you don't. But you can bet your bottom that I know what you had. Two squares a day. Would have been three, but Kim says you're getting too fat because I overfeed you. Not as fat as that fuck on the plane comin' down here, or Sergeant Baker. Oh, you'd like Baker. He farts when and where he feels like it, too. Just like you. Although you're much better with two meals in your belly instead of three, I can see. And you're not bothering me as much either about having to stop to piss and shit. No, you ain't half as bad as Baker. I'll tell you that. That's one shithead they got for a cop. I shit you not."

Pug inched over and up, resting his head on Justin's lap.

"So I guess we're buddies again. Yes? And while we're on the subject of cops, I've got an assignment for you. I'm gonna make you into a police dog yet. And don't you worry none because I'm gonna back you up one hundred percent. That's what partners are all about. I just want to see the look on Sep Cramer's face when he sees the look on yours. I know you didn't forget Ellis Everett or the scene at that overlook; those cliffs where he put your ol' pal down. I'm sure you saw him shoot your partner and will never, never-ever forget. The only problem there is that your testimony can't be used in a court of law. Not that we're even headed in that direction if that be the case."

Justin and Pug reached the top of the mountain and surveyed the panoramic blue-green vista dotted with stands of unblossomed goldenrod and American flowering dogwood before starting their descent.

"We just have to bide our time till we're absolutely sure. There's supposed to be an arrest today. And I have a pretty good idea of who the poor unfortunate soul is who's going to be blamed for the Carla Banks murder, if not Gary's, too. Anyhow, you and I are here to rattle Cramer's cage. Should prove pretty interesting. If he's not in, we'll wait rather than leave our calling card. If he is in, we'll do what we have to do and catch the next flight out. We missed the three-o-six. Gary will just have to travel home alone, but I can promise that I'll make it up to both of you or die trying."

Pug and Justin watched a Kentucky cardinal fly into a tulip poplar.

Chapter Forty-Five

Sergeant Baker sat with his arms folded across his massive chest. Chief Wilcox stood over him, reading the cop the riot act. Two of Big Stone Gap's seasoned detectives filled the corner nearest the door of the small office.

"Didn't you hear what I just said, Sergeant? He's not on that plane. I specifically instructed you to follow him."

"But I did," Baker said defensively. "I absolutely did, Chief. I swear it."

"To the airport, Sergeant? Did you follow Barnes all the way to the airport or not?"

"To Bristol."

"But what were your instructions? What did I tell you, man?"

"He stopped in Bristol to pick up a dog."

"A dog?"

"Yes, a dog."

"He bought a dog?"

"No, sir. He brought it with him and boarded it for three days. It's *his* dog."

"He brought a dog down from New York and kept it in Bristol for three days?"

"Paws N Claws."

"Why?"

"I don't know, Chief. I thought it was odd that he'd stop by a kennel on his way to the airport. So I waited till he went in and watched as he came back out with the dog. That's when I went inside and spoke with an assistant to the owner. She didn't know anything other than he'd brought a dog in at three a.m. three days ago."

"What the hell is a kennel doing open at three in the morning?"

The sergeant checked his notes. "Let's see, that was on—"

"I asked you what a kennel is doing open at that hour in the morning."

"She didn't know, except that arrangements had been made beforehand with the owner of the shelter."

The chief of police gestured to one of his detectives, and the man stepped into the room.

"And then what happened, Sergeant?" Wilcox demanded.

"Then?"

"Yes, then."

"I left the shelter, and when I got back outside, Barnes was gone."

The detective standing in the corner of the chief's office laughed quietly with a hand covering his mouth.

"Knock it off," Wilcox snapped. "Sergeant?"

"Yes, sir?"

"Did you follow him after you got out? Did you try to catch up with him to see if he went to the airport?"

Sergeant Baker remained mute.

"Well, did you?"

Baker shook his head.

"So you don't know where this maniac and his mutt disappeared to, do you?"

"I assumed it was to the airport."

"You assumed?"

"He had a flight to catch, Chief. He picked up his dog, and I thought he was headed to the airport. I know that he made a right out of there. That's in the direction of the airport."

"In the direction of the airport," the chief soured.

"Yes, sir."

"But he never got on that plane, Sergeant; with or without his dog."

"Sir, can I say something?" Baker balked.

"What can you say other than you screwed up?"

"Sir, Detective York's body was sent to the airport at one o'clock this afternoon, and it was Barnes' responsibility to see to it that the body was shipped back to New York. I just assumed—"

"Did Detective Gary York need a babysitter at that point, Sergeant? Is that what you're saying?"

"No, of course not, Chief."

"How long have you been a sergeant, Sergeant? Tell me."

"Eleven years."

"And how many more years do you have before you're up for retirement?"

"Nine, sir."

"Then guess what?"

"What, sir?"

"Get out of my office."

Baker did an about-face and headed for the door.

"Sergeant!"

The police officer stopped in his tracks.

"When you left the kennel, where did you go? I want the truth," Chief Wilcox insisted.

Sergeant Baker hesitated before he spoke, dropping his voice to a whisper. "Lunch," the big man said, lowering his eyes to the floor.

Wilcox slowly shook his head. "Nine long years or ninety pounds, Sergeant. Whatever comes first. Follow what I'm saying?"

"Yes, sir," Baker mumbled beneath his breath.

"What?"

"I said, Yes, sir!" the angry man bellowed.

"Now, get out of my sight."

Chapter Forty-Six

Justin and Pug arrived at Sep Cramer's residence and found the turquoise Mercedes panel van parked in the driveway. The home and property looked even more spacious than it had when Justin viewed it from the mountainside a day earlier.

"Well, here we be, buddy. You and me. Gonna be a scene. But like I said, not to worry. I got your ass covered, fella. But before you say or do anything foolish, let me be the first."

Justin pulled alongside the vehicle before swinging a hard left, lining up the rear of his vehicle with the van's driver's side door. "Come on up here, boy. Come on," he said, slapping a knee in invitation.

Pug quickly obeyed, practically jumping into Justin's lap.

"That's a good dog." Justin praised the puppy, wrapping an arm firmly around the animal's body for its protection as well as hugging privileges. "Now we'll just pull forward a bit like this." The renegade gently pressed the accelerator and drove ahead several yards. "There we go. Now we're loaded for bear. Brace yourself, Pug. Ready?" Justin shifted into reverse and hit the gas. The rear bumper of the rental crashed solidly and rather loudly, burying itself significantly within the lower panel of the Sprinter's sliding door. "Whoops."

Pug looked up at Justin with some confusion, recovering quickly with a lick to his partner's face.

"It's what we'll term rebel rage. Actually, it's just a fender bender. Insurance covers it. I never go for the added coverage, but I was thinking well ahead. With this monkey you've got to. Now, let's go see what kind of damage we did. I say *we* because you're what us humans call an accomplice. Like it or not."

Justin pulled straight ahead and then clipped a leash onto Pug's collar before stepping out of the sedan. "We don't want to escalate this from a fender bender to having *you* impounded. Now do we? Because the way my luck's been running lately, Sergeant Baker would be the one to show up on the scene. Oh, I'm telling you you'd love Baker. That is until you decided to share his treats. You'd have to fight him for whatever scraps or— Uh-oh. Here comes trouble on the double."

Justin stooped to examine the damage, keeping an eye on Cramer as well as the deep crease in the door.

"Who the hell are you, and what are you doing on my property?" Cramer cringed. "Look at what you did to my van!"

Justin stood and smiled, fixing his eyes keenly on Sep Cramer, as did the dog. "Oh, I'm sure—"

Pug actually lunged at the tall figure, barking away insanely while Justin held the dog at bay. The terrier went positively wild, flashing its teeth while fighting fiercely against the leash, whipping his wispy frame from side to side before the startled man.

Justin reined in the pup, sweeping him up with a single hand before bringing him over to the rental, setting the snarling animal down upon the front seat, swiftly closing the passenger door so that he could hear himself above the ruckus.

"As I started to say, Sep, I think you know who I am. And in case you don't know who that dog is by now, it belonged to a Mr. Ellis Everett of Massachusetts."

"I asked what you're doing on my property . . . and just look what you did to my van." Cramer did a slow burn.

"Oh, that? That ain't nothin' compared to what it would have been with you in it because I know what you did."

"I don't know what you're talking about, and I'm going to call the police."

"But that dog sure knows what *he's* barkin' about. Look at him. He hasn't behaved like that since the day I took him in."

Pug's paws tore away at the back window; his spittle and angry breath covered the glass.

"Never mind that mutt. Just look at what you did to my van. I'm calling the police," he repeated.

"That there *is* a po·lice dog without the proper papers, you asshole-motherfucker. And I'm a po·lice·man without a proper badge."

"I know exactly who you are."

"Now, didn't I just say that, dick-face? Didn't I? So you know who I am, and I now know who you are for certain. But before all this, I was just ridin' 'round and happened to make a wrong turn. Pulled into your driveway and had a little accident. Accidents do happen, you know. Anyone can have them. And I can assure you that you're going to have a big one in the very near future. I want you to think about that."

"And I want you off my property this minute."

Justin consulted his watch. "Oh, dat give us forty seconds to hash this down to the bone. And if I let dat dog out in the next ten, I'd guarantee you one of your legs would be mincemeat in less than thirty. You see, I'm very good with numbers, Seppy. Practicin' my vo·cab·u·lary, too. My latest word is agenda; a-g-e-n-d-a: dat be a list of things to do," Justin concluded, pointing a gun-finger at Cramer's forehead before returning to the car, opening the door quickly and jumping in behind the wheel with Pug barking away at the top of his voice.

As Justin turned the car around, the two men fixed their eyes icily on one another.

"I SAID I WANT YOU OFF MY PROPERTY. NOW!" Sep Cramer screamed.

The maverick suddenly dropped the gear into drive and peeled out across the manicured lawn, leaving two twenty-yard tracks on newly installed sod for which Cramer to remember the dog and his new master.

"Better than any calling card," Justin swore, smiled and waved good-bye in the rearview mirror. "I know, I know," he said with complete understanding, glancing over at Pug. "You want instant justice or immediate satisfaction, called revenge. Actually, they're one in the same thing, for your information. Punishment, pure and simple. Me? I want that, too. But in a real man's world, Pug, you learn to wait and pick your fights. After all, we're not animals, you know," he kidded, grinning from ear to ear. "Now, simmer down some."

Chapter Forty-Seven

Justin was surprised to learn that Gary's body did not leave as scheduled on the 3:06 p.m. flight out of Blountville, but was being held over until he arrived to sign papers of release. Lieutenant Garvey suddenly appeared at the reservations desk as Justin was putting Pug into his Traveler, handing it over to a young male attendant who disappeared around the counter.

"Louie!" Justin exclaimed and smiled handsomely. "Is this an official send off, or what?"

"You've got seven minutes to get on that plane and the hell out of here, Barnes. The paperwork is taken care of. All you have to do is sign. I took the liberty of booking this flight for you. If you're not on it, Kentucky, Tennessee and Virginia State Police have been notified to pick you up and arrest your sorry ass. I cut you some slack, slick. So don't mess things up for yourself."

"Arrest for what?" the maverick questioned, scanning the manifest, which an attractive, uniformed, red-headed female counter clerk set before Justin.

"Trespassing, harassment, leaving the scene of an accident, destruction of personal and government property for openers," Garvey rattled off. "Not to mention your Alamo rental, jerk-off."

"I didn't mention it at all, Louie. Wish you wouldn't. Those rental folks are about as observant as the Big Stone Gap Po·lice Department. Besides, I'm covered. And what's this crap about government property?"

"Cramer owns the home. The government owns the property. He has a hundred-year lease."

"Huh. You learn something new every day. Anyhow, there was

no No Trespassing sign posted out front, and harassment is generally defined as continual torment, but I only just met the gentleman for less time than I have to get on that plane. Cramer insisted I get off the property immediately, which is what Pug and I did, Louie. Listen up." Justin whipped out his recorder and hit the reverse button, backing up to the homeowner's last words: *I said I want you off my property now!* "Note that he said it was *his* property, Louie. Rather deceptive to downright dishonest of him if you ask me."

"Sir, would you please sign here," the pretty reservations clerk said and smiled in mild amusement. "I don't think you want to miss your flight."

"So, let's see, here, Doreen," Justin replied, reading well beyond the buxom woman's U.S. Airways nametag. "Body bag and container containing the 'Human Remains' of one Detective Gary York; a pet carrier containing Pug, which the handler assured me wouldn't wind up in Cincinnati along with my associate's personal effects or—" Justin suddenly stopped reading and jabbering and looked up. "Why my carry-on bag, along—?"

"—along with your automatic weapon, which I'll relieve you of now, Mr. Barnes, civilian," Lieutenant Garvey insisted. "Hand it over."

Justin stood firm. "No, sir. I'm licensed to carry my weapon via special permis—"

"Horse manure. It's going into your bag, which will be stored with Detective York's effects. Any lip, and you'll be detained and escorted by security and myself to a waiting room where you'll be arrested by the state police. You behave yourself and get on that plane in the next three minutes, and you can pick up your bag in Pittsburgh, where you have an hour layover. Visit us again, Barnes, make sure it's a one-way ticket. Round trip would be a total waste of time and money for you. Now, hand it over."

Justin covertly removed his weapon from a shoulder holster as passengers and personnel passed by unaware. He handed the pistol and carry-on to the lieutenant who took both items, unzipping the canvas travel bag, placing Justin's weapon within.

"Add those to the manifest, Doreen," Garvey instructed.

"What do I write down, Lieutenant?"

The law enforcement officer furtively cradled the piece. "S&W

4040PD. Serial number, KAP, with a K, 0010."

"Yes, sir."

"Why a three-and-half-inch barrel, Barnes?"

"I like to get up real close and personal, Lieutenant. Don't need nor wanna carry 'round no cannon like yours."

"It's not a cannon, Barnes."

"Oh, no?"

"No. Show him what a real cannon is, Doreen. Go ahead. Make his day."

The lieutenant placed Justin's bag atop the counter so that Doreen could clandestinely display her stainless steel S&W model 500 Magnum 15 revolver along the marble edge.

Garvey grinned. "That's an eight and three-quarter inch barrel, Barnes. It's the most powerful production revolver around."

"Around for what?" Justin asked with hesitation. "You expecting al-Qaida or Godzilla?"

"Northern vermin," Doreen assured him with a grin, lowering her weapon below the counter and out of sight.

"Just in case we had any serious trouble here this afternoon, Barnes, we have Sergeant Doreen Michaels to help handle things for us."

"Sergeant Michaels." Justin couldn't help but smile. "Well, I'll be damned. A notch up from Baker in any case, I'd have to say. Just love that southern drawl, girl," he flirted. "Undercover in a uniform. Ain't that a kick."

"Airport security, hotshot," the lieutenant clarified. "Doreen, why don't you personally escort Mr. Barnes to his seat. He has one minute. I'll take care of this bag. If he gives you any trouble, whip him," Garvey ordered with even a wider grin than Doreen was wearing.

"Not with that cannon, I hope," Justin whined and winced in exaggeration.

"Up close and very personal, Mr. Barnes," Doreen assured him. "I'm trained in jujitsu as well as judo and karate."

"What degrees?"

"The highest." Doreen bowed politely, stepping around the corner and taking Justin firmly by the arm.

Justin turned and frowned at the policeman. "And I thought

this was the beginning of a beautiful friendship, Louie. Gotta watch *Casablanca* if you haven't, Lieutenant. Bogart and Bergman. You'll love it. You even look a little like Claude Rains, but without the mustache."

"You think?"

"Let's go," Doreen insisted, marching the man briskly away.

"Forget what I said earlier today about blonde and buxom, Louie."

Lieutenant Garvey waved. "Bye, Justin,"

"Did you hear that, Doreen? Louie and I are finally on a first name basis. Say, can you loosen your grip on my arm, please? Say something nice. I may never see you again."

"I like your dog better than you," Doreen declared, hurrying her charge toward the loading gate.

Chapter Forty-Eight

When Justin was finally buckled in his seat and settled back, the aircraft rolled smoothly along the runway before lifting and taking to the sky. Not ten minutes later, a strained but familiar female voice immediately off his left shoulder sounded in his ear.

"May I sit down here?" she asked civilly, her face red from crying.

Justin looked up in amazement. "Mother of God! I don't know how many more surprises I can take in one day," he responded. "What are you doing on this plane?"

"May I sit down? Please."

Justin got up and stepped into the aisle.

"You don't want the window?" Denise Holloway asked courteously.

Justin didn't bother to tell the woman that it took all the courage he could muster to even get on a plane, let alone take a window seat.

"Sit down," he insisted uncomfortably if not irritably.

Denise climbed in and moved over to the window.

"You're the last person on earth I'd ever expect to see on this flight. What are you doing here?" he repeated.

"I promised myself I'd be with him for better or worse. I can't think of anything worse. Can you?"

Justin remained silent.

"There were so many things I wanted to tell you this morning. But I couldn't," she broached.

"Why, because you were coached?"

Denise Holloway nodded nervously.

"Like what?" he asked suspiciously.

"Like the fact that my life is being turned upside down," she responded evasively.

"How so?"

Denise took a tissue from her purse and dabbed her eyes. "It's a long story, Mr. Barnes."

"It's a five hour flight with a stopover. What is it that you want to tell me?"

"I don't want to tell you a damn thing, but something inside me tells me that maybe I should."

"Really?"

"I'm hearing different stories, and I'm all confused."

"No, shit?" Justin said in the snidest manner he could muster.

Denise started fidgeting with the strap of her purse. "You don't like me very much, do you?"

"That's an understatement, Mrs. Denise Holloway."

"Then why did you allow me to sit here?"

"Because I believe in getting to know my enemies very well. And I also figure you could give me a hand job in short order or maybe some head after we depart Pittsburgh, assuming you're going all the way. I mean, after all, you went all the way with Gary in less time than it takes to whip up bacon and eggs in that greasy spoon you work in, I'll bet."

Denise stood up to leave.

"Sit the fuck back down."

Denise sat.

Justin let out a forceful stream of breath.

"I'm not a whore, Mr. Barnes."

"No? What are you then?"

"A woman who needed a push to leave her husband. A woman who fell in love with your associate. Deeply in love."

"In twenty-four hours?" Justin sneered.

"In less time than that," Denise confided. "But we both knew it was immediate and very real."

"That a fact?"

"That's a fact."

"Let me ask you something. Would you have left your husband if Gary hadn't come along?"

"Probably not."

"And if it wasn't Gary? How about some other pair of pants?"

Denise Holloway held Justin in her eyes with sheer hatred and pure contempt.

"Oh, that's a stumper, I can see. What if Gary worked the grill at Burger King instead of pulling down six figures?" Justin waved away the question. "Bad analogy. You'd probably tell me next you two would pool your resources and open Denise's B 'n B. And if you couldn't make a go of it with breakfast, you'd make up for it by taking your customers to bed."

Justin grabbed her wrist as she was about to make contact with his face.

"Oh, I thought that was a better analogy. No? What if Gary was a ditch digger with a bad back?"

"I'd have him if he was penniless and a paraplegic."

"Funny, 'cause that's the same way I feel about you, sweetheart. In other words, suck my cock."

Denise Holloway turned as wild as Pug had several hours earlier . . . before a purser put a stun gun between the couple's face.

"It's okay—okay?" Justin quelled the situation, holding both her wrists in a vise-like grip, his leg across a pair of shinbones, holding her firmly in place. "She's just upset with me because I told her this interracial arrangement is over with and that I—"

"You're Mr. Barnes, is that correct, sir?" the man asked directly, putting away his battery-powered equalizer.

"Yes, sir."

"And this is your seat?"

"Yes, sir."

"And, ma'am, where do you belong?"

"Back there," she pointed.

"Then I suggest you get back there and stay back there."

Justin relaxed his hold, and Denise Holloway stood up to leave, brushing briskly by the two men.

"Barnes?"

"Yes, sir?"

"You're trouble. You were trouble before you got on this aircraft, and you're trouble now."

"She came on to me, mister. Most women do. I don't know

what compels—"

"Barnes, listen to me carefully. If there's another commotion before we reach Pittsburgh, I'm going to have you arrested when we land. You've been warned on the ground, and I'm warning you up here."

"She came over—"

"I don't care. I don't want any more trouble out of you."

"Just have her stay in her seat and there won't be any."

"Trouble may seem to find you. Fine. Don't perpetuate the problem. Call me if anything happens, or speak to a stewardess."

"I'll do that."

"Any questions?"

"Yes, will I get to see the crack in the Liberty Bell when we get to Pittsburgh?"

The purser looked at Justin Barnes queerly. "Sir, the Liberty Bell is halfway across the state in Philadelphia."

"But the woman at the counter told me the bell was in Pittsburgh, Frankie."

Frank, the purser, thought for a moment. "Maybe she was referring to the crack in your head, Barnes."

"Not nice, Frankie," Justin replied with a wink.

"Behave yourself. Hear?"

Chapter Forty-Nine

After an hour-and-a-half flight from Blountville to Pittsburgh, Justin had sixty minutes to kill, wanting to kill, instead, the figurehead in charge of airport security. Unable to retrieve his weapon as promised because of the incident on the plane, the rebel drowned and downed his woes with two Scotch and sodas at the terminal bar, accepting a third round on the house and leaving the attractive and affable bartender a ten dollar tip.

Back aboard the Boeing 737, after being assured that Pug was doing fine and that the pistol would be returned at LaGuardia after clearing customs, Justin saw Denise Holloway coming down the aisle from the rest room. Catching the woman off guard, he quickly stood and pivoted her past him, back into the seat against the window where they had fought earlier.

"They're going to throw both of us off this plane," Denise protested, struggling to retreat.

"I'll scream discrimination if they do."

"Let me out, damn you."

"If you run, so help me I'll scream rape."

"Let go."

"But if you rape me, I'll help you."

"You're drunk."

"I only had *free*," Justin hiccupped, holding up three fingers. "And the lady bar-bartender was nice enough to buy me one *three*," he said stupidly, twisting his words as well as screwing up his face.

"You can't even talk straight."

"So, I'll sit and listen."

"I can smell it on your breath."

"The peanuts or the pretzels?"

"The whiskey."

"Top whiskey. Scotch shelf."

Denise couldn't help but laugh.

"What's so damn funny?"

"You. You mean, Scotch whisky. Top shelf."

"That's what I said."

"You said—never mind."

"I said never mind what?"

"Forget it."

"You're right. I can't remember."

Denise giggled but then turned dead serious. "You said some pretty nasty things to me."

"I was drunk."

"No you weren't. You're drunk now."

"You mean you can tell the difference?"

"Yes, and I think I like you better this way."

"Fine, then I won't apologize."

"I think you should."

"For being drunk?"

"No, for some of the things you said before."

"Before we landed in LaGuardia?"

"We haven't even taken off yet."

"Good, then we can still get a drink aboard this crate."

"I think you have had quite enough."

"Just one for the road, or the airway, or wherever the fuck we are."

"Watch your language."

"Do you know that I make it my business to learn a new word every day?"

"Really?"

Justin nodded and practically nodded off.

"What's your word for today?"

"What?"

"I said, what's your new word for today?"

"Dewar's."

"Why am I not surprised?"

"Highlander."

"What was that?"

"Highlander. A colorful figure of a guy at the top of the label."

"What label?"

"White Label."

Denise shook her pretty head in mild amusement. "Dewar's White Label, I suppose."

"All right." Justin turned to the aisle. "Miss," he called. "Stewardess, over here, please."

The stewardess came immediately over to their seats. "Yes, sir?"

"Two Dewar's and—" He turned to Denise. "Soda, water, rocks?"

The flight attendant smiled. "Sir, we're still on the ground."

Justin looked down at his feet

"Please put your seatbelt on. As soon as we lift—"

"—and thrust?" The incorrigible passenger swayed toward her.

"As soon as we take off, I'll be back to take the order. As a matter of fact, why don't you give it to me now," *so I don't have to deal with you later*, she thought to herself and winked at the woman. "Ma'am?"

"Neat."

"Make it two," he burped, holding up a set of fingers.

"Yes, sir."

Shortly after the stewardess took her leave, and the plane lifted smoothly off the runway, Justin launched into a treatise on the Scottish Celts or Highlanders as alluded to earlier.

Denise seemed quite impressed.

When their drinks arrived, Justin opened the miniature bottles of Scotch and poured the contents into plastic glasses, handing one to his companion.

"Here's looking at you, kid," Justin toasted.

"I'm surprised you can even see at all."

Justin swilled his drink and delivered a sigh of appreciation as well as one of weariness. "Maybe I'll see things a lot clearer now."

"You look terrible."

"Haven't had much sleep over the past three days."

"Neither have I."

"What are you going to do in New York?"

"Pay my respects and then head back home, I guess."

"Back to your husband?"

Denise turned taciturn.

"Don't want to talk about that, do you?"

"I wanted to talk before, but you didn't want to listen."

"So I'm listening now."

"I don't think Ted's going to be there when I get back."

"How come?" Justin asked but believed he knew the answer.

"I think he's going to be arrested."

"For what?"

"For Carla Banks' murder and Gary's"

"Chief Wilcox tell you that?"

"One of his detectives."

Justin signaled the waitress for another round.

Denise declined. "I'm fine."

Justin raised a single finger. "One."

Denise sipped her drink and Justin grew serious, leaning toward her. "You know that your husband didn't kill either of them, don't you?"

Denise shrugged. "The detective said they believe he did. They asked me a million questions. Told me a few things, too."

"Such as?"

"Such as Ted's having an affair with Carla behind my back. He may already know about Gary and me. Gary questioned him about her murder shortly before he was shot."

"The person who murdered Carla and Gary is the same person responsible for the deaths of several other people in several states."

"A serial killer they say you insist. But the detectives say no."

"The detectives are mistaken."

Denise said nothing.

"It would be nice and convenient for you if your husband was out of the picture altogether and in lockup, wouldn't it?"

"You starting again? People do outgrow one another, you know. People move on. People fall out of love."

"And those people wind up getting a divorce or having an affair. No one I know runs off and leaves their husband for a man they just met, with the emphasis on the word *just*."

"Well, *just* for your information, Mr. Barnes, Gary surprised the hell out of me with his proposal, with the emphasis on the word *proposal* and an engagement ring in the glove box."

"Which I don't happen to see on either hand."

Denise opened her purse and pulled out the small blue velvet box which contained the ring. "See? Did you think I pawned it?"

"The thought did cross my mind."

Reaching back into her purse, she removed a sealed envelope, which she tore open, handing him a letter. "Read it. Go on. It's to his sister. I don't even know her name. But I plan on giving it to her at the funeral, along with the ring."

"That's your business."

"No, I insist. I really want you to read it. Then maybe you and the others Gary worked with will better understand. Here."

Justin took the letter and read it slowly and carefully, and then he read it once again. "I'm sorry," he finally said.

"Sorry, or sorry for me?" She started to tear.

"Maybe a bit of both. He was a good man."

"Yes, he was. You had a few years to judge that for yourself. I had but a few days, measured in hours, actually. Yet, they were the happiest hours in my entire life, Mr. Barnes."

"I'm terribly sorry," he said sincerely, for he was powerfully moved, handing her back the letter.

Denise took the diamond ring from the box. "Just in case," she punned playfully, brushing away several tears, "should we see if it cuts glass?" the pretender put forth, setting the sparkling stone against the window of the plane.

"Why, do you think Gary gave you paste?" he snapped.

"That's not what I meant. I was talking bait-and-switch—on my behalf."

"You wouldn't get away with it anyhow."

"Why not?"

"I'd tell Edna to have it appraised."

"Who's Edna?"

"Gary's sister."

"You know her?"

"Very well."

"You're kidding."

"Why on earth would I kid a kid?"

"Maybe because we're both off the planet," she remarked, blowing her nose and drying her eyes. "Though only temporarily."

"You may be quite right about that, Mrs. Holloway."

"Denise. Please."

"All right, Denise."

"How do you know Gary's sister?"

"Through the job. Family barbecues. Picnics. Times and places like that."

"Do you have family, Justin?"

Justin smiled. "I sure do. And you're going to meet them when we get back."

"Me?"

"Yes, you. In fact, you even know of them through Gary."

"Ah, I see. You mean Kim and Brian Archer and several others who Gary talked about."

"That's exactly who I mean. We're all one—not really big—very happy family."

"Do you think Edna and the others will like me, Justin? Or am I going to make everyone feel uncomfortable? How do you think Edna will react when I hand her this?"

Justin smiled sadly and took the ring and blue velvet box from Denise, placing the band on the ring finger of her left hand. "I think I know her well enough to tell you she'd tell you to keep it right there. Also, that she appreciated reading your letter once she sees it. And do you know how I know that?"

Denise shook her head in wonder.

"Because Edna is my fiancée, and I know that she's going to embrace you with open arms. How's that? Guaranteed."

Another stewardess came with Justin's drink. "Well, I'm glad to see that you two are getting along a little better," she remarked, looking down at the rock on the passenger's finger along with the blue velvet box in Justin's lap. "Frankie told me to keep an eye on you, Mr. Barnes. But from the looks of things, I'd say you two worked out your little differences." The stunning light-skinned Jamaican woman winked.

"Oh, then I take it you approve of interracial marriages. Yes?" Justin inquired.

"Oh, sure." The woman lowered her voice. "Just so long as

both my husband and I are dead and buried, my daughters and son can do what they damn well please."

Her candor took Justin and Denise completely by surprise.

Justin pushed the envelope. "Live and let live. Yes?"

"Over my dead body is what I'm trying to get across, Mr. Barnes. It's not that I'm prejudiced, being an island girl and later growing up on the streets of Brooklyn. It's just that I've seen it all." The outspoken woman leaned toward them and whispered. "Been there, done that. Doesn't work in this world of ours. Stay with your own kind and you'll be much happier. Sex on the side with any color is much healthier. Marriage in and of itself is enough of a challenge. Believe me. Mix it up with race and, like me, you'll need a good psychiatrist. Think about that."

"Is your shrink black or white?" Justin asked, slurring his syllables.

"I played it safe and picked a Chinaman out of the Yellow Pages," she quipped with a straight face.

Denise giggled.

"Did he help?" Justin pressed.

"We never completed the therapy."

"How come?"

"He committed suicide before we were halfway finished. I know it was about the halfway point because he said to me in one of our early sessions, 'Belle, you stay with me two year, I make you new woman. You see.' Anyhow, I have most of my marbles and figure I'm way ahead of the game."

"You're a very funny and fascinating woman, Belle," Justin remarked.

"And you're very drunk. That's why I'm telling you all this. You won't remember half of it in the morning. But your partner here will. And if she has any sense at all, she'll tell you that she's quite flattered but taking the advice of a woman who's been around a Brooklyn block or two. It's not going to work between you. I can just look and tell. I know trouble when I see it. But if you decide otherwise," she offered, addressing Denise with more than a hint of disappointment, "I wish you both the best of luck."

Belle opened and poured Justin's drink, collected the empty bottles then headed down the aisle.

"Do you believe that woman?" Denise whispered, even though the stewardess was far enough away so as not to hear.

"I certainly do, Denise. And I have to inform you that our engagement is off effective immediately. We can talk about an arrangement when I can talk at all. Besides, I don't think I could even make it down *this* aisle."

The two laughed heartily for a full minute before either of them could catch their breath.

"Tell me all about Edna," she said when they finally settled down. "Did Gary approve?"

"He didn't know. No one does. She wants it that way. We just plan to go off and get married next month."

"What do you think would have happened if Gary knew?"

"There'd be a homicide."

"That's not funny."

"It wasn't meant to be."

"But Gary told me he likes you, that he'd trust you with his life."

"With his life, yes," Justin swore. "But not his sister," he clarified, spilling several drops of liquid on his jacket.

Denise gently took the plastic tumbler from his hand and set it down upon the folding tray.

"So, you still haven't answered me, Denise. What are you plans after the funeral and you head on back to Big Stone Gap?"

"I'll take your lead and get drunk, I suppose," she answered so sorrowfully, taking a long pull on her Scotch, then picking up Justin's drink.

"I'm serious."

"So am I."

"You'll go back to the diner?"

"For a while, I suppose. I've got a job waiting for me out in California, if I want it."

"Doing what?"

"Hostess," she said, taking another sip. "A man made me an offer I couldn't refuse."

"Well, that didn't take you very long."

Justin received a solid punch in the arm. "The offer was made to me some time ago, only I never took the guy up on it. Two weeks in

Sonoma country. Four thousand dollars plus all expenses. Overtime at time and a half if I choose. He said I could easily come away with six grand. No strings attached. I was going to call him about the time that Gary showed up at the diner, turning my whole life around. And now it's totally upside down."

"When is this job for?"

"July."

"And where in California is this place?"

"Someplace north of San Francisco." Denise dipped into her purse for the caterer's business card. "Here. Monte Rio Caterers, Monte Rio, California. I had a girlfriend check them out. She said they're legit."

"Did the caterer give you this card?"

"No, the fellow who'll fly me there and back did."

"What's his name?"

Denise went back into her bag and drew out another card. "Ace Reaper." She handed it over and eyed Justin carefully. "The way you're staring at the card, it's like you know him."

Justin looked keenly from the card to Denise. "Denise, do you know a man by the name of Sep Cramer?"

"I don't think so. Why?"

"You sure?"

"Lots of men come into the diner. Most of them I know by name. Some I don't."

"Would you recognize this Ace Reaper fellow if you saw him again?"

"Absolutely. Nice looking fellow. Handsome in fact."

"Did he ever come into the diner?"

"That's where he made me the offer."

From inside a jacket pocket, Justin withdrew a photograph of a man standing in the shadows on the back deck of his commodious log cabin.

Denise nodded. "That's him. Without question. Who is he?"

"Sep Cramer," he answered, studying her reaction as soberly as a savvy homicide detective like Gary York could observe a suspect's body language and lying eyes.

"Oh, my God!"

Gary would know in a heartbeat if the woman was the genuine

article or a fraud, Justin mulled over in his muddled state of mind. But his brother-in-law to be was surely dead . . . his body lying in a bag within a compartment inside the belly of the plane, somewhere beneath them . . . resting peacefully in a temporary wooden box . . . listed on U.S. Airways' manifest as Human Remains. He was starting to feel sick.

"How many times did this man come into the diner, Denise?"

"Just that once that I know of."

"Did you ever see him before or after that?"

"Never."

"Speak to him on the phone?"

"Yes, as a matter of fact. About a week before Carla was killed. He asked me if I was still interested in his offer, which I told him I was. He said he'd like to meet with me and discuss it further."

"At the diner?"

"No, in Johnson City."

"Where in Johnson City?"

Denise shrugged. "He said he'd call back."

"When?"

"Soon."

Justin tried to think but his brain was on overload. Saturated, in fact. Figuratively. Literally. He fought the need to close his eyes and rest.

"When we get to New York, I want you to call him and tell him you'd like to meet when you get back. Would you do that for me if not for Gary's sake? Set it up? You won't be going, of course. This man's extremely dangerous, Denise."

"I'll do whatever you ask of me if you think it will help. But what are you going to do?"

"I'm not sure yet. But for now, I'm going to catch twenty winks."

"We have a good hour and a quarter before we land. You rest."

Justin leaned back in his seat, and within sixty seconds he was sound asleep.

Chapter Fifty

The parking lot at Atkinson & Son Funeral Home in Bellport was filled beyond capacity with vehicles of every shape, size and cylinder, spilling over into the streets, lining the perimeter of the building, continuing east along the serpentine path leading through the nearby churchyard and adjacent cemetery. From a distance of several blocks away, drivers and passengers, young and old alike, wives and lovers, husbands and hooligans, brothers and sisters, mothers and fathers, relatives and distant relations wended their way toward the stone walkway and up the porch steps of the two-hundred-year-old funeral parlor. From as far away as Europe, patriarchs of the church and adjoining properties mingled in a corner off the Doric columned entranceway. Just inside the doorway, to the right, police hierarchy gathered from all five boroughs. Commissioners and inspectors spoke quietly among themselves. To the immediate left, huddled in the opposite corner, stood several members of Team Three's homicide squad; among them were two women. Their commanding officer, Detective Lieutenant Ethan Powell, headed toward the group.

Moving somberly through the brass strode retired Lieutenant Theodore Groche, former commanding officer of Suffolk County's Homicide Squad. The man spoke with and listened most carefully to one of the inspectors before making his way through a crowd of past associates, erstwhile companions, friends and family forevermore. Groche went back outside and approached one of the venerable old men from his native home of Belfast, whispering in the octogenarian's able ear. The older gentleman turned to his comrades and spoke quietly, addressing the four men from Londenderry, Galway, Dublin and Cork. Three immediately nodded in agreement. The other shook his head then shrugged with cautious disappointment. Theo returned to the anteroom, winked and nodded at Powell. Two members of Team Three neither expressed their gratitude nor revealed their inner excitement. The others remained totally in the dark for the moment. Brian Archer took his wife's hand into his. Kim's heart returned to a normal beat as members of Teams One, Two and Four converged around the others.

Hand in hand, Edna York and Justin stood off to one side of Gary's closed casket. Edna smiled bravely through her tears and received the throngs of people who came to pay their last respects. Justin's jaw was locked in place like granite.

Kim walked over to the pair after a quarter of an hour and politely pulled Justin aside. "People are going to get the wrong idea," she said cagily.

"Just tell me what you have on Denise Holloway is what I need to know for now," he sounded off in a calm and purely businesslike manner.

"One traffic ticket and behind in a few bills. Otherwise, good as gold and pure as mountain snow is all that Big Sister and I come up with."

"Then I suggest you forget digging up old records and start panning for iron and copper in the valleys."

"And what is that supposed to mean?"

Justin glanced over Kim's shoulder at the woman sitting alone in the last row to his right. "Fool's gold, perhaps."

"Ah, we'll see. Any contact with Cramer yet?"

"She can't reach him but left a message for him to call her. How about Ace Reaper? Still no hit?"

"Not one that reaps us any benefit. But we're still searching. He probably hasn't set up good housekeeping with a new mate as yet," she stated glumly.

"And he probably won't at this point. Such an obviously phony name. Like the Grim Reaper, I guess. I'm trying hard to figure his game."

"You think maybe she's really his next target?"

"I don't know what to think, except I know Sep's our boy. Pug confirmed that as far as I'm concerned."

"It appears as though the upper crust within our circle agrees with you, up to a point."

"What do you mean? Who?"

"It's not important. What's important is that you have the lieutenant's blessing to move ahead with your *own* investigation of Sep Cramer and Denise Holloway, wherever that may lead you. Powell just gave the green light."

"Yeah, right. I thought I had it last time out, thank you very much. Remember? 'Go with God,' you told me both he and Brian said. Only I met with opposition instead of cooperation, supported by that two-faced fool. Powell, that is; not your own sanctimonious single-minded fool. Not only did Virginia police, in cahoots with airport authority, take away my weapon, the police on this end at LaGuardia refused to return my bullets when they reluctantly handed the piece over with an empty clip. I'm surprised they gave it back at all. And that's only after half a dozen phone calls."

"Well, I can assure you that won't happen this time out."

"Really?"

"Really."

"How come?"

"Be in the lieutenant's office tomorrow morning at seven sharp and you'll learn how come. Okay?"

Justin nodded skeptically.

"Another thing."

"Yeah?"

"When you hold Edna's hand, do it like you're commiserating, not like you want to drag her off to home and into bed."

"Am I really that transparent?"

"Maybe not to the others. But you forget who knows you best and loves you, baby," she reminded him and smiled warmly.

Justin nodded a hint of thanks. "How's Brian doing, really?"

"Really down and out."

"You tell him for me that I'll take care of business."

"Just be sure you see the lieutenant first before you leave this time."

"Leave for where?"

"Johnson City, I suppose. Just as soon as Denise Holloway hears from Cramer."

"How did you happen to hear about Johnson City so fast? I

didn't have time to update anyone. And that could change in a heartbeat."

"Powell interviewed her himself yesterday afternoon. I guess you heard about her husband's arrest."

Justin turned and stared through a crowd of teary-eyed mourners as well as the woman in the back row with her nose buried in a lace handkerchief, her shoulders trembling from apparent grief. He looked back at Kim. "What's your take on all of this? Tell me."

Kim looked over at Denise then back into Justin's dark and weary eyes. "I don't know. I can only tell you what I told you earlier. Be very careful."

Justin shook his head. "What does your *gut* tell you is what I'm asking. Never mind what's in your pretty little head."

"Again, I just don't know, fella. I really and truly don't."

"Neither do I, kid. Neither do I. And that's what worries me."

"We'll put it together. I know we will. Meanwhile, I'll work Big Sister to the bone."

Justin nodded appreciatively and went over to Edna, taking her by the hand to meet Denise.

Suddenly, Denise's borrowed cell phone beeped. She pulled it from her bag and answered . . . standing abruptly. "Yes, it's nice to hear your voice, too … Ah, huh …Yes, I am interested, but I need to know if the offer you made me still stands, Mr. Reaper." She pulled Justin into a neutral corner, sharing the instrument next to his ear.

Justin listened intently, his head pressed firmly against hers.

"Please, call me Ace," Sep Cramer said with delight. "After all, we're going to be traveling together to California in July."

"Then I can take that as a yes, Ace?" she said excitedly.

"Well, I don't know how much plainer I can put it. Yes, you have the job. Third week in July. But first I'd like to meet with you as I mentioned. Would that be all right?"

"That would be fine, sir."

"Ace."

"That would be great, Ace. I'll be here in New York for a few days, but I'll be home by the end of the week. When would you like to meet?"

"How about a week from Friday? Would that be too soon?"

Denise looked at Justin for confirmation. "No, that would be fine."

"Good. I could swing by Johnson City around noontime. Sorry we can't meet in Big Stone Gap, but I've got some other appointments."

"No, that's fine, really. I don't mind the drive. I'll do some shopping while I'm there."

"Terrific. There's a great Japanese restaurant on North Roan Street. Got a pen?"

"Got it."

"That's 1805 North Roan. Twelve o'clock. You like sushi?"

"To tell you the truth, I never had it. But I'll give it a go."

"Maybe we'll do Charlie's Steakery instead, or the NASCAR Cafe."

"No, no. Sushi will be fine. I'm a trier. Truly."

"Well, there are other things than raw fish on the menu. You'll love their tempura or steak teriyaki. Trust me."

"I'm sure I'll be fine."

"Do you know how to get there?"

"I'll find it. I live with a Hagstrom."

"Better yet, why don't you meet me in the Target parking field? 2116 North Roan Street. You can't miss the big red and white bull's-eye. Then we'll decide where and what we're going to eat. All right?"

There was a hesitation in Denise's voice. "All right."

"Meanwhile, I'll call Mario of Monte Rio Caterers and tell him I've just lined up the best damn manager in the tri-state area. How's that?"

"Manager? But I thought you said—"

"Hostess? Your days of servitude are over, darlin'."

"What do you mean? I thought this was a temporary gig."

"It is if you want it to be. I know about your problem. Or should I say your husband's problem. It's all over the news down here. I'd like to help. Aside from that, when the boys from the Bohemian Club get a gander at you, well, you'll write your own ticket."

"Bohemian Club?"

"I'll tell you all about it when we meet. Last three women I introduced to Mario, well, one of them just opened her own place, one already has a chain of restaurants, and the other makes six figures part time and is willing to teach you the ropes."

"Ropes? I thought there were no strings attached," she kidded, assuming an air of composure while feigning fear for Justin's benefit.

Sep Cramer laughed good-naturedly. "No strings. Promise. You can go as far as you want in this business with hard but rewarding work. You'll decide. Wish to remain waitressing at the diner? Fine. Wish to relocate in one of more than a hundred cities across the United States? The choice is yours. And let me again assure you that Mario is on the up-and-up. Me? I'm a happily married man."

Justin almost laughed into the mouthpiece.

"Friday the twenty-fifth, twelve o'clock, the parking field of Target, 2116 North Roan Street, Tennessee," Denise confirmed.

"The Volunteer State. You in?"

"Not for nothing, so let me hear those numbers once again. Not the ones in the address, but the ones that add up to dollars and cents," she asked boldly. "Please."

"It was four to six thousand for two weeks work last we spoke."

"Was?"

"As a manager, and speaking for Mario, we'll make it ten. After that, you'll decide how far you want to go up the corporate ladder. All right?"

"I'm in."

"Smart girl. Listen, let's make that twelve thirty just in case I'm running a little late. I don't want you hanging around a parking lot."

"How will I find you?"

"Don't worry. I'll find you. Just wait in your car."

Sep Cramer terminated the conversation and did a silly little dance alongside his flower garden. "Y'all come on down, hear?" he waved and summoned forward no one, stepping rhythmically to the music playing in his head. "Yeah, y'all come real soon, Justin Barnes. And bring along a female decoy cop. Right? Am I on target or what? Ten-four?" he trumpeted insanely, do-si-doing a scuffle hoe for a partner. "And don't forget to bring along that fucking dog."

226

Chapter Fifty-One

In Yaphank, bright and early the following morning, Justin Barnes stood in Lieutenant Powell's office and was given a set of specific instructions.

"You are to rendezvous with Sergeant Doreen Michaels at Tri-Cities Airport in Blountville, Tennessee on Thursday afternoon of the twenty-fourth. One day before Denise Holloway's scheduled meeting. I believe you two already met. From there you will coordinate with a Captain Powers and his SWAT team from Special Services who have been fully apprised of the situation. Sergeant Michaels is already in possession of Holloway's car and clothing. From a distance of a few yards, except for her hair, Michaels *is* Holloway. But they'll certainly fix that. Holloway will remain here until this is over," Powell went on. "Sep Cramer is under surveillance as we speak. If and when he moves into, shall we say, an engaging position at Target in Johnson City, he will be accosted and detained, his person and vehicle thoroughly searched. If in fact he is there, serving as a good Samaritan to lend comfort and support to Holloway, especially in her time of need, whether expressed under the name of Ace Reaper, Mother Theresa, or Father Fucking Flanagan, for all I or anyone else gives a flyin' good fuck, that's his business and we back off. Are we clear?"

"I thought this was *my* operation, Lieutenant."

"Insofar as it does not conflict with the authorities of another state and jurisdiction, Barnes. Is that so unreasonable or hard for you to understand? Do you know the area in question? The layout? The lot? Do you have backup other than what Johnson City police and other jurisdictions are willing to provide? Chief Wilcox and Lieutenant Garvey didn't want you within a hundred miles of Virginia. The police in Kingsport, Tennessee feel you're a royal pain in the butt but are more than cooperating, not to mention the state troopers in Kentucky who want to stomp your ass for the shit you pulled in Cramer's driveway. I had to pull a white rabbit out of a black hat in order for you to even appear at the staging area. You don't have one friend down there."

"That's not true. I have Sergeant Baker who I bribed with a box of doughnuts. He'd swear to anything for another plain or cream-filled dozen."

"Yeah, I also heard about the episode with Garvey and Baker at police headquarters as well as the incident on the plane with Holloway. And you wonder why they confiscated your weapon and ammo. You're a loose cannon, Barnes. Know that?"

"Then why are you even bothering to send me back down there?"

"Because if all else fails and their operation turns to shit because Cramer outsmarts them, you'll find a way to stick it up his ass for good. That's why. If Cramer is our serial killer, and he somehow escapes their clutches, which quite frankly I can't see how, then and only then will you find him and put him down. If he is arrested and/or brought in for questioning, or wounded or fatally shot because he draws down on their decoy, that's where it ends and you come home. If on the other hand, he shows his hand, resists arrest and somehow manages to escape, you locate him and put one or more of these in his head for a keepsake. Those are the only conditions *you'll* draw down on him."

Ethan Powell stood and spilled a handful of bullets onto the desk.

"What are these for?"

"Consider it an even exchange for the ammo the boys at LaGuardia confiscated and shitcanned."

Justin nodded and swept up the ammunition.

"No heroics. Hear me?"

"I hear you."

"If this were on our turf, things would be a lot different, I'd promise you."

"Moot."

"True."

"Anything else?"

"Leave your canine partner home this time. Edna will be glad to baby-sit both Holloway and the pup."

"How do you know that?"

"I asked her."

"What else do you know?"

Powell grinned. "That a stewardess on the plane gave you some sound advice. Ring a bell?"

"Belle?"

"The one and only."

Justin smiled broadly. "Just who is she exactly?"

"Daughter of Belle of Belle's cafe at the airport in Westhampton Beach. We use her every now and again. Quite capable. She knows Doreen personally and promises me you're in very good hands."

"Jesus."

"Only watching your back, good buddy."

Justin turned about and walked from the lieutenant's office in a trance.

Chapter Fifty-Two

Several miles northeast of Johnson City, Sep Cramer sat engaged in a business meeting. The man opposite him was a friend and longtime member of the Bohemian Club, a heavyweight behind-the-scenes organizer on George W. Bush's campaign for reelection. Within a private room, the two men were enjoying breakfast in Elizabethton. The elder former statesman and Washington lobbyist optimistically tapped the backs of Cramer's hands with a pair of ancient, arthritic, liver-spotted, lobster-like claws, assuring his supporter that 'Georgie's' win would be a landslide victory. They spoke quietly and swore allegiance to the incumbent, toasting to another four-year term in spite of rising oil prices and burgeoning terrorism.

"Reform or conform. And quite frankly, Sep, the majority of American voters—not to mention the electorate—are too worried to change horses in mid-stream. Reform is in progress, so the process will carry Georgie boy across still waters, which in the eyes of the public *always* run deep. Listen, if gas goes to five dollars a gallon, they'll all saddle up and let their buggies come to roost and rust in their yards and garages. Hell, he'll be a hero overnight for helping to clear the air," the frail figure joked, chuckled and coughed to excess. "At least on the highways and byways, and we'll all breathe easier again. Sure as shootin', Sep, they'll conform and love it. Quite frankly, they're scared. What this country needed was a good kick in the hind quarters. Gives them something to really gripe about. Like fuel shortages, power outages and prolonged blackouts. Folks love it when they're in the dark and running on empty as they pool and pull together for the common good. Even New Yorkers banded together during the blackout of sixty-five. Fuck 'em and confuse 'em and they love it."

"Good for the soul. Granted," Sep agreed. "But on a grand scale, are they ready for and can they handle another Vietnam? Horse-and-buggies and gas-gouging prices are one thing."

"It's all in the packaging, Sep. You know that. Even the clergy can't keep turning the other cheek because on the face of things there won't be any flesh left to go around. Pick it up from the day that Jew was wheeled off the deck of the Achille Lauro in eighty-five. The bombing of the USS Cole in 2000. But the real and palpable fear was literally brought to our own shores and soil over eastern Long Island with the downing of Flight 800 in ninety-six, followed by the WTC Disaster of 2001. Now that's real terror that strikes within their very hearts and souls. And a horse of quite a different color. So, we've jumped from the occasional fistfight and shooting at the gas pump on odd-and-even days of yesteryear to the infernal and towering infernos of today. But a big boost to our economy in the long run, Sep. And a sorely needed push to once again regain American pride and patriotism."

"At the cost of many American lives."

The aging ex-senator smiled. "Business is definitely business."

Sep Cramer smiled back in agreement. "Business is definitely business."

"So. How are you coming along with your speech?"

"Hawkish as hell."

"Hell is where you've got to take them, Sep. To hell and back home again."

"Yes, sir."

"You're a damn good man and one helluva American."

"And you're one hell of a statesman, Senator."

"Was. Today, I'm just an old hack."

"Not in my eyes or in the eyes of the Republican Party."

"You're forgetting that I was once a Democrat."

"And I but a lowly soldier and scholar."

"And so we both became learned and wise in the ways of the world. You, a good deal earlier. Me, pretty late in the game, I'm afraid."

"But for the betterment of the many who must be ruled by the few."

"Some who dare call us elitists."

"I vant their names, rank, serial numbers and the immediate reopening of stalags in all fifty states," Sep half-joked.

"No, I can do that!" the senator emeritus swore, chortling and wheezing quite gleefully. "I can definitely do that."

The two men were about to terminate their weekly meeting with a second cup of fresh-roasted Arabica coffee, setting their Bloody Marys aside.

"So, where are you off to, Sep?"

"Johnson City, to help a friend. And you, Senator? Back to Knoxville?"

"Knoxville, Nashville, Brownsville. You know how I love to drive."

"I know. How far is it from Knoxville to Nashville anyhow?"

"A hundred seventy-nine point seven miles. A three hour and twenty-nine minute drive. Why do you ask?"

"Because I love the way you always answer those sorts of questions. Never rounded off, but rather right to the tenth of a mile and minute. How do you keep all those figures in your head?"

The old man smiled and shrugged but didn't answer. "I'd like to see a draft of that speech, Sep. Maybe next week?"

Sep Cramer reached into his jacket pocket and produced a copy of his keynote address along with the stub of a red lead pencil. "It's not a draft but the finished product, Senator." Sep handed over both items.

"What's this?" the old man asked, holding up the one-inch section of wood.

"Not *too* many corrections and changes if you please, sir."

The Senator guffawed and choked, waving a hand to indicate that he was really quite all right, leaning back comfortably in the booth and putting on his glasses. He read the pages most carefully, slowly sipping his coffee, occasionally nodding impressively before finally setting the papers down upon the table.

"This is dynamite, Sep. Pure dynamite. I'll make sure Dick, Don and Colin have a front row seat," he concluded most seriously.

"Thank you, sir."

"No, no. Thank you, my boy. We're all on the same page, I'm delighted to see." The old man picked up his cup. "Ah, best coffee in the county if not the entire state of Tennessee."

Chapter Fifty-Three

A turquoise blue Mercedes Sprinter entered the parking lot of Target in Johnson City, ten miles southwest from where Sep Cramer and the semi-retired politician had enjoyed a late breakfast an hour earlier. At five miles an hour, the panel van approached the line of vehicles parked directly across from the front of the department store. The driver suddenly slowed to a crawl, scoping the immediate area, searching for a dark gray Ford Escort.

The dark-haired woman sitting behind the wheel of Denise Holloway's compact was alerted that the van was now seventy yards to her left and closing steadily. Sergeant Doreen Michaels wrapped a hand confidently around the pistol grip of the handgun on her lap.

Two marksmen positioned on a rooftop toward the front of the store held high-powered rifles at the ready. Standing beside a window in an adjacent building, the captain of the SWAT unit confirmed the Sprinter's license plate as being registered to Sep Cramer, shifting the focus of attention to a figure leaving the store. Captain Scalla locked his binoculars on the foreigner, cautioning both Michaels and his team.

The Asian walked briskly toward Michaels, both hands hanging at his sides while holding a white, weighty plastic bag in each. Transferring a bundle to his left hand as he reached the rear of the car parked next to the policewoman's, the middle-aged man fumbled for his keys, finally unlocking the trunk and depositing both packages.

A third marksman in a distant construction trailer, set high on a hillside, ran the cross hairs of his optics along the Korean's temple as the man opened the driver's side door and slid behind the wheel of his Honda Civic.

The panel van pulled in behind the Honda as the car pulled out through the empty space ahead.

The figure behind the wheel of the blue Mercedes parked alongside the Ford Escort, inadvertently locking then unlocking the van's doors before pressing another button and sending down the passenger side window.

Michaels' window was already down; her door unlocked; her forefinger on the trigger.

"Hi there, Denise," the man greeted as instructed, reaching for a concealed gun on the seat next to him, raising it toward the window in the instant the left side of his head exploded into a halo of crimson. In a nanosecond, a second shot was fired, and the upper front portion of the man's skull flew off altogether.

Michaels was out of the car, the sergeant's arms fully extended into Cramer's van, the barrel of her weapon sweeping the interior of the vehicle before lowering the magnum to her side, her eyes fixed upon the bloody body slumped between the driver's door and the dash.

Men in flak jackets and uniforms and suits were running toward her as she walked around and opened the passenger door then climbed inside, staring down blankly at the black plastic pistol lying on the floor. Withdrawing a handkerchief from a pants pocket, she carefully lifted and examined the toy.

"A fucking water gun!" she exclaimed, squeezing its trigger and shooting a stream against the inside windshield. "A fucking water pistol," she blew.

"Fuck it, Doreen. He drew down on you," one of the detectives fumed. "Fuck it, and fuck him. You did good, girl."

"Who's him?" Sergeant Doreen Michaels questioned.

"Huh?" the detective responded in bewilderment.

"That's not Cramer," she said flatly.

"How the fuck can you tell *who* he is?" a member of the SWAT team questioned, opening the driver's side door and allowing the body to topple out backwards.

"I saw him. He said hello to me before he grabbed the gun. That's not Cramer," the undercover cop insisted.

"What in hell is the problem here?" a lieutenant from the Johnson City Police Department demanded to know. "What are you doing going through his wallet, man?" he shouted at Lieutenant Garvey. "Are you fucking crazy?"

"I wanna know who this dude is. That's what I'm doin', Lieutenant."

"I told you beforehand who's running this show. We are! Now back the hell off."

"Show's over. So calm the hell down," Garvey insisted, handing over the wallet opened to the man's expired driver's license. "Peter Griffing of 105 Millway Street, Elizabethton. Anybody here know him?"

A dozen heads responded in the negative. One of Johnson City's senior uniformed officers went over to an approaching radio car.

Justin Barnes edged his way through the group to the body. "Sure as shit ain't Cramer. But he sure as shit is—was—Cramer's patsy."

"What are you talking about, Barnes?"

"Just what I said. Cramer set this poor bastard up to take the fall. The fair-haired sicko you're protecting knew all about this stakeout. Had to have."

"How?"

"I don't know how. But you can bet your boots I'm going to find out."

"Wrong, Barnes," Captain Scalla said, coming up on Justin's heels. "You've got your orders and your walking papers, and unless you're out of here by tonight—"

"Is that anything like, 'I want you out of town by sundown, cowboy,' Cappy? Because if that's the case, I'm gonna use my last hours to plead mine to the press by asking what Sep Cramer's vehicle is doing here less Cramer's body, and why he put this scapegoat in the driver's seat. And then I'm going to give them the answers."

The uniformed officer returned from the police car with information that he quietly shared with Lieutenant Garvey. Garvey simpered and simply shook his head.

"Well, the answer to your questions are now pretty straightforward, Mr. Barnes," Garvey began. "It seems that Mr. Cramer's vehicle, this vehicle, was reported stolen just outside The Coffee Company and Eatery in Elizabethton, not more than twenty minutes ago by Sep Cramer himself, and verified by one of our former state senators, with whom he was having breakfast. I just hate to break your bubble, Barnes. But once again it appears that you're barking up the wrong tree. Care to comment?"

"'It *seems* and *appears*,' you said. Your words. I'd say it seems and appears that there might be hope for you yet, Lieutenant. Care to respond?"

"No, he wouldn't." Captain Scalla stepped forward. "As senior man of this operation, Barnes, I'm asking you politely to leave this scene, now!" he commanded.

"As second in command, I second that mandate quite strongly," Scalla's lieutenant stated firmly.

"And you, Louie?" Barnes taunted. "I guess you gotta go along with this other Louie, here. Although he's a first-rate asshole second only to the captain."

The member of the SWAT team who had fired one of the fatal shots came through the crowd of spectators and cordoned-off area before viewing his handiwork.

"That was some shot there, buster," Justin remarked. "Between you and Sergeant Michaels, here, I wonder which one of you could duplicate *that* shot." He turned and pointed to Target's logo at the entranceway off U.S. Route 11 and West Mountain Drive. "That there your piece of work also, Mister Marksman? How about yours, Doreen, darlin'?" In the center of the red and white bull's-eye was a discernible hole; that is, if anyone cared to notice. "That wasn't there yesterday because I looked. Probably hit last night. Care to take a guess who really fired that shot? Another of his little games. He's sending y'all a message."

"Sure, sure, Barnes. Just some wise-ass kid," the Johnson City police lieutenant answered up. "Same thing happened at a Target in Asheville last year."

But Justin was firmly shaking his head, turning about to face Captain Scalla. "Put your binocs on that target, Captain. Tell us what you see. Go ahead. Humor me."

The leader of the SWAT unit raised his field glasses.

"Well?" Justin asked.

"Clean clear through the middle," the captain remarked.

The SWAT shooter brought his weapon smartly up to his shoulder and adjusted the variable sight, scanning the center of the bull's-eye as several people in the distant crowd uttered in awe. "Dead center," was the marksman's clear and concise observance.

"So what?" a Big Stone Gap detective snapped.

"Cramer was under constant surveillance for the last seventy-two hours," Garvey declared.

Looking disdainfully down at the body, Justin laughed. "Yeah, like you really had him and his vehicle under a watchful eye in Elizabethton, I can see."

"Well, we're not going to stand around here and argue this any longer, Barnes. You're out of here. Doreen."

Sergeant Doreen Michaels stepped forward.

"See to it that our observer here finds his way back to the airport; and once again, personally escort him aboard the plane," Garvey ordered. "His observations are noted null and void."

"Yes, sir."

"Bye, y'all," were the maverick's final words.

It was as Michaels and Barnes were walking away that a figure behind a distant berm sighted in his Thompson/Center Encore 209x50 magnum muzzleloader with variable scope of wide-angle focal plane, aligning its fine filament fibers down the backbone and across the breadth of the man's broad shoulders.

"Here's looking at you, kid," Sep Cramer remarked, touching off the trigger and sending a single Sabot Shock Wave bullet through the humid mid-day air, shattering Barnes' spinal column.

Customers, cops and culprit hit the ground, the latter running for all he was worth.

The smell from the powder charge still lingered in the air as the serial killer made his way to Christian Lane, where he was picked up by a woman in a white Ford Bronco.

"Easy now, lady. We don't want to make it seem as though we're running from the law," Sep Cramer directed then tittered. "Say, is this not somewhat reminiscent of a famous '94 so-called chase scene or what? White Ford Bronco, tooling down the highway at thirty-five miles per hour. Come on, girl. Think back. O. J. Simpson, Denise. Recall? His good friend Al Cowlings was driving and O. J. was in the passenger seat. Only *that* black bastard is lying back there with a shattered spine. Not exactly what I'd call being in the driver's seat either." Sep was doubled over in a fit of laughter.

"Where to?" Denise Holloway barked, keeping her speed to thirty miles per hour, her heart pounding away at a hundred miles a minute.

"Elizabethton. Nine point seven three miles; sixteen minutes," the madman positively roared. "That is, if you take this horse-and-buggy up a notch," he added when he finally caught his breath.

Chapter Fifty-Four

Detective Brian Archer revisited the holding cell at Riverhead jail. Barret Dexter was already seated at a small table, his wrists secured in manacles at his back, the teenagers left ankle shackled to an iron ring in the steel floor. The fettered prisoner grinned up at the imposing figure.

"Well, well, well. What have we here? A vis·i·tor. When they told me I had company comin', the last person in the world I expected to see was you. How the fuck ya been, Brian?"

"Detective, to you."

"Oooo, dat's right. You da man. An' an angry lookin' one at dat. So, you here to cheer me up, or jus' slummin', De·tec·tive?"

"You know, you remind me of someone I knew and hated, but he grew up real fast," Archer shared.

"Dat a fact? Let's see, now. Yo daddy, right? He give you a good ass-whippin' some time ago and you come back fo mo 'cause you one o' dem mas·o·chists," Barret said decidedly, smiled and nodded satisfactorily.

"No, I came here to make the deal," Brian said bluntly.

"The deal?" Barret questioned, staring up at the ceiling in puzzlement.

"Make, model, color, year, partial license plate number, and any other information you can give me on the shooter who drove off from Shelly's Deli that morning back in mid-March."

"Oh, dat deal. Well, it seems to me, Detective, dat dat deal had a time limit attached to it. Seventy-two hours as I recall. You recall that conversation, Detective?"

"Yeah, well it took some time and convincing to bring a few

people around."

"Around what?"

"Around to my way of thinking."

"That a fact? And who exactly are these people, and what are they thinkin' and doin' about all your convincin'?"

"You want out of here or not?"

"What I want is the facts, my man."

"The fact is the D.A. is talking to your lawyer as we speak."

"No shit?"

"No bullshit."

"Coming from a cop, dat ain't worth dick."

"You wanna deal, or you wanna rot? Your choice."

"I ain't gonna give you jack-shit unless my lawyer says it's the real deal. And as you well exceeded my seventy-two hour offer, flunky, I'm gonna up the ante."

"You wanna play poker and sit in the poky? Fine." Brian got up to leave.

"Not so fast, honky. Sit the fuck back down and lay it out for me."

Brian sat. "You give me the information, and if—"

"And *if* nothing. If it leads to an arrest and a conviction, or if it leads down a dead end because the guy's too smart for you is your fuckin' problem. Not mine. I give you the information, I walk the hell out of here with what I came in with plus a grand. Penalty for exceeding my time limit. Take it or leave it. I ain't fuckin' 'round wif ya. I got somethin' you want badly or you wouldn't be back here. And you got something I want. My freedom. And to tell you the truth, it ain't no picnic here, but it ain't no holiday out there either without any bread. I'd use the dough for a fresh start in the Carolinas. Got some kin folk down there."

Brian sized up the youth and the situation. "Five hundred greenbacks out of my own pocket, which you keep your mouth shut about. I'll send your lawyer in here to talk to you shortly. I'm sure you'll find everything to your satisfaction. As you walk out the gate, I'll have someone pick you up and hand you the money. She'll give you a ride back home to your stepsister's apartment."

"Who'll give me a ride?"

"The woman you called a black bitch. The woman I wanted to

kill you over. My wife. Deal?"

Barret Dexter smiled and nodded. "Done. I guess I gotta trust you on the money end. But like I said, I'll blow the whistle on this guy if and when my attorney tells me this is the real deal. Not before."

"Right." Brian got up and walked from the claustrophobic space.

"Hey, Detective."

Brian turned around.

"You actually trust me with your woman?"

"I think you know that if you harmed a hair on her head, I'd hunt you down and kill you."

"You know, I really think you would *try*, Detective Archer. I really and truly do." Barret Dexter grinned the width of the table or so it seemed.

It also appeared to the detective that the smart-ass grin he was minding, pearly whites and all, was a smile akin to a trusted friend lying on an operating room table who might never again see the light of day.

Chapter Fifty-Five

Detective Archer drove into the driveway of Robert Redler's and Liza Downs' home on Riverside Drive in Riverhead. Liza was busy gardening in the backyard, and Robert was edging the property along the Belgium block surrounding a giant red leaf maple tree. Archer pulled the car to the end of the apron and parked as the couple looked up.

Liza immediately sensed that something was not quite right. Robert hadn't a clue. The pair put down their tools and walked up to the tall figure stepping from the car.

"May I help you?" Robert asked.

Liza studied the way in which the man scrutinized the two of them. She, in turn, observed his body language and stern cast; the plain, partially pressed dark gray cotton suit and polished but semi-scuffed black shoes; the clean, nondescript late model Plymouth sedan.

Robert was getting the picture, too. The depiction unquestionably spelled cop.

"My husband asked if he could help you."

Brian held a thick, clipped packet of papers in one hand; the other he extended to Liza. "He's really not your husband, Ms. Downs. But after thirty-two years together, that's got to count for something," he said with a smile. "A lot of marriages today don't last thirty-two months. Then again, I know someone whose marriages lasted better than a hundred years when you add them all up. Problem being, the guy's a scumbag polygamist as well as a serial killer to boot."

"What are you talking about?" Robert asked, hesitantly accepting the man's handshake after Brian took, clasped and shook Liza's.

"Oh, way more than you could possibly imagine at this point, Mr. Redler. Perhaps we can all go inside to talk, please," he suggested. "I pulled around back here so your neighbors wouldn't get a sense of what's going on."

"*I* don't have a sense of what's going on," Robert hedged anxiously.

"Ah, but I think you do. And I know that Liza certainly does by now. Isn't that right, Liza?"

"I don't know what you're talking about, and I want you off our property unless you tell us who you are and what you're doing here."

Brian produced his shield. "Detective Archer. Suffolk County Homicide."

Liza was shaking her head in disillusionment.

"Now, can we go inside and talk, please?" Brian repeated the request politely. "And yes, I'd love a glass of something cold because it's hot as hell out here, and I *will* be staying for a while. We have lots to discuss."

Liza now shook her head in anger.

"Well, we can do this here or back in Yaphank, Ms. Downs. I came alone so as not to create a scene by having to make an unnecessary arrest. You may consider this an unofficial visit at this point in time. Now, please. For the third and final time." Brian tapped the packet. "I'll be doing most of the talking. I just want you both to listen. All right?"

Robert and Liza looked at one another before she led the way to the back door and through the narrow vestibule off the kitchen, then into their modest home set along the Peconic River.

Liza turned abruptly about, stopping the detective cold. "Just tell us what this is all about in a single breath before you take another step," she insisted.

"In a single breath, Ms. Downs, it's about the shootings that happened several months ago at the deli down the block from you. But long-windedly, the things I'm first going to talk about go back several years to when Robert, here, shot and killed Richard Geist and his associate."

"There was a trial, and Robert was acquitted on *all* counts," she growled.

"And believe me when I tell you, I'm very happy for both of you. I had a lengthy conversation with a former associate of Riverhead P.D. and know a good deal of the story. I also know about your nephew's murder at the behest of Angelica Manns and the Barbara Giordano cartel, Liza; as well as the contract put out on you and Robert. I know, too, your dealings with The Triumvirate, your bravery in taking them on against all odds. I know very little about your extraordinary *gift*, except to say, in the words of a certain police chief, it is surely God-given."

"I don't have—we don't have this gift any longer," Liza snapped. "It's gone, and quite frankly, I'm glad of it."

"Well, perhaps it's just lying dormant," Archer suggested. "Like both of you," he added coyly.

"And just what the hell is that supposed to mean?" Robert barked.

"All in good time, Rob. All in good time," the detective said, switching to the familiar and once again tapping the packet of papers. "Let's move ahead in time to the Howard Mills serial killer trial, which you attended every day as a spectator for a period of better than fifteen months; that is, pretrial, trial, penalty and sentencing phases. Fodder for your book, *Trace Evidence*. And in the course of your research, you conducted your own investigation, which led you to the conclusion of his brother Jeffrey's guilt; guilt as a serial killer along with their half-sister, Beth Tracy, who he probably murdered, too.

"We may have rushed to judgment in arresting Howard for the murder of those prostitutes," the homicide cop continued. "As you both know, it was the first death penalty case on Long Island in practically a quarter of a century back then. We strongly believed we had the right guy from the get-go. However, you suspected Jeffrey committed those murders early on. There's no doubt that Howard dismembered their bodies and that both of them are culpable. There's no question that Jeffrey helped his brother dispose of the bodies. At least a couple of them. But as to who actually murdered the women for whom Howard Mills was sentenced to death, well, let's just say that we now certainly have our doubts. And I know you know how the dirty politics played out in the end between state and federal governments concerning Jeffrey's freedom, dirtbag that he surely was.

"So, you shot and killed Jeffrey Mills in Bogotá, just outside a small village called Villavicencio. Can't prove it. Don't even want to. The rub today is that the D.A. is pushing hard on this triple deli homicide," he lied. "I'm the case detective. I can investigate this thing from now till doomsday if I have to, or I can make it go away—for good. The problem is I have a witness," which was true enough, indeed. "The evidence the shooter left behind that fatal morning leads right to this doorstep," the detective put forth plainly. "I've got far more than a circumstantial case at this point in time. I believe I can prove beyond any doubt that you shot those three men, Mr. Redler . . . one of them in cold blood. Again, I don't want to have to move in that direction."

"Exactly what *is it* that you want?" Liza demanded.

"Help," was the single, succinct remark.

"What kind of help?" Robert questioned cautiously.

Uninvited, Detective Brian Archer took three steps from the kitchen into the adjacent cozy dining room and placed the set of papers down upon the oval table. "I'd like you both to read these files very carefully. Take your time and digest each and every word. Then tell me what you think."

"Think about what exactly?" Liza pressed.

"About helping us to nail a serial killer who took the lives of seven people that we know about to date. One of them was my partner. Another man that we work closely with was shot in the back, we believe, by our prime suspect. Now, how about that cold drink, guys?"

"And if we say no?" Liza asked directly.

"Let's not get ahead of ourselves, all right? Just go over those files for now."

"And if we say take your files and scram this minute?" Robert tested.

"Then I'll ask you both to come with me voluntarily to answer questions back in Yaphank. Like I said before, if you decline, I'll return with a warrant for Robert's arrest. Then I'll be doing all the reading; that is, the reading of his rights."

"Is that a threat or a fact?" Redler challenged.

"Written in stone as clearly as the inscription being engraved in granite on my partner's marker as we speak," Archer swore. "Any other questions?"

Liza glowered. "Lemonade or soda?"

"Lemonade, thank you."

"Ice?"

"Please."

"Have a seat," Robert offered with a gesture.

Detective Brian Archer unclipped the stack of papers and pushed them toward the writer. "Why don't you get started and Liza can catch up?"

Robert nodded glumly.

"Incidentally. How would you two like a month's all-expenses-paid vacation to the center of wine-producing country this July? Sonoma, California. I know you love and know wine, Rob."

Robert sneered. "What else do you know?"

"That you could use fresh fodder for your new novel. How about I get you both an undercover assignment at the Bohemian Club? Ever hear of it?"

"Yes, and you can't get near the place from what I understand."

"My team can set it up."

"How?" he asked. "You know what security must be like?"

"Willing to work a bit before you play?"

"Work at what?"

"Food services."

"As a waiter?"

"Something like that."

"And Liza? Aren't women excluded? Food services or any other kind?"

"Not true any longer. Court rulings changed all that. They now have female employees. Along the same lines, blacks were excluded from joining the club. That, too, has changed. There are now token African-American members, mostly from the field of entertainment. The fellow I told you who was shot in the back is black and was about to go undercover for us."

"Swell." Robert couldn't help but smile.

"What's so amusing?"

"You said, 'mostly from the field of entertainment.' And I was thinking, field—straight from the fields for certain, but not from the cooperate world of business or high finance, I'm sure. And when they finally are accepted into certain levels of society, it's usually for someone else's entertainment, like from the days of vaudeville, then through early television, and finally into modern day movies. But nothing *really* ever changes."

"Well, there's the writer in you, picking apart and weighing every word. But I can't very well send you off to a conservative encampment sounding like a liberal, now can I?" Archer questioned with a smile.

"You're not sending me off anywhere."

"We'll see. Read."

Liza stepped into the dining room with a tall mug of lemonade filled with ice. "Here you go."

"Are you a liberal, too, Liza?"

"Neither Rob or I can be labeled liberal or conservative, democrat or republican. Our views crisscross and sometimes even transcend party lines. Personally, what this country needs is a benign dictator, the death penalty enforced instead of the farce it truly is, and a good two dollar bottle of wine."

"*Salute.*" Archer raised his glass. "An intellectual with a sense of humor. Very rare to find these days."

"You'll see what kind of sense of humor I have if I hear any more threats. We'll read what you ask, and then you're out of here."

"And like I just said to your other half, we'll see," he repeated, toasting a thanks to his most ungracious hosts.

Chapter Fifty-Six

L iza Downs put down the final page in utmost protest, balling her fingers into clenched fists. Robert Redler smiled and ran a palm across a stubbly growth of day-old beard.

"A hostess at a house of prostitution!?" she blurted.

"It's a refurbished inn," the detective elaborated, "located on the border of Bohemian Grove. Sep Cramer helped finance it and has been going there every year for the past four years. Prostitution is not listed on their program of events," he further explained with a wide grin. "But certain members 'jump the river,' or used to anyhow. Problem being that there were criminal charges brought against several owners and operators of various establishments. Namely, a tavern and a hotel. But Quaker's Inn is and isn't on the line of demarcation. Meaning 'the game room,' as it's been dubbed, and is a safe haven for their extracurricular activities. The inn is not on Grove property and therefore fair game. But you've got to go through the inn and along an underground tunnel in order to get to the playrooms. Some top level guys who are inclined to indulge in this . . . shall we say, indoor sporting event—which is how it was actually posted and channeled through madams working in nearby towns and cities—now patronize prostitutes without fear of persecution or prosecution. It's rumored that Sep Cramer and the innkeeper set the whole thing up. Law enforcement out there has it on their taboo list. It's understood that they don't go near the place in exchange for hefty contributions made to certain organizations."

"Where exactly is this in-house/house of ill repute?" Robert asked. "Show me."

Archer opened and pointed to a section on the map. "Just

upstream from the Grove, along the river here. You'll be bringing in gourmet food prepared in Monte Rio and Bodega Bay, in addition to selecting very expensive wines for the gala. See why you're so perfect for the part? You know fine food and wine."

"Yeah, but the people don't know me."

"You let me worry about that. Their gourmand/sommelier is suddenly going to be taken ill. You're going to step in and save the day. You're also going to take Sep Cramer's life sometime after he delivers his keynote address and heads for holiday. And Liza, here, is going to put Denise Holloway down."

Liza looked at Detective Brian Archer as though the man had lost his mind. "You can't be serious."

"I'm quite serious. Those two are to be exterminated like bugs before the celebration ever ends. The finer details are being worked out as we speak. I'm just cluing you in early on."

"I can't believe we're having this conversation, Detective," Robert stated both warily and wearily.

"Better believe it."

"You're actually standing before us and asking us to commit murder?" Lisa asked incredulously.

"Before you and before God. Yes."

"And if we say no to you, which is what we're saying to your face," Robert declared, "I suppose you're going to threaten me with a trumped up murder charge concerning that deli homicide."

"Homicides. Plural." Archer held up three fingers.

"Like I'm really going to cave. Is that what you think?"

"Look. Let's stop playing games. I know you did that deli scene. All right? I even had this sneaking suspicion it was you before I found a witness."

"Is that so?"

"That's so. Riverhead. Proximity from the deli to your home. Past history. Physical evidence as well. The scarf you left behind, which I'm sure Steve Quick clued you in on. And I now have a witness who can place you at the scene along with a full description of your vehicle: the make, model, year, and color of your car; even a partial license plate number. All I'd have to do is pull Steve Quick out of his shop for forty-eight hours—doubt that he'd even make it to twenty-four—grill him in that eight-by-eight cell that you love to write about in your articles and novels, and he'd roll over on you faster than he can put together a hero sandwich. Doubt that for a second, Rob?"

Neither Robert nor Liza uttered a solitary sound.

"Didn't think so. I leaned on you guys so at least you'd hear me out. I don't need to threaten you with charges. You're going to do what we ask in the final analysis anyhow. Know why? It's just like you taught your students in composition writing classes, Rob; always save your best for last. Here's mine." The cop laid down a final file along with two photographs he was holding back. One was a picture of Sep Cramer; the other, a recent photograph of Denise Holloway. "Holloway is not the unassuming housewife/waitress we thought she was. She was, in fact, one of Angelica Manns' lower echelon soldiers under the Giordano regime. Sep Cramer is second in command of a powerful underground organization that carries on the directives of Giordano's quondam, meaning former, cartel."

"Who's heading this show?" Robert Redler practically demanded.

"We don't know. What we surmise is that it's someone very high up in rank in the Bohemian Club."

"Rob," Liza said, directing his attention.

Robert turned toward Liza and the picture she was holding. "What?"

"I recognize her. Older now. But she was one of them."

"You sure?"

Liza nodded most assuredly.

Robert faced the detective. "Let's just suppose that we went along with this lunacy. Hypothetically speaking, of course. You're talking high-level corrupt government officials: federal, state and local. You're talking Mafia. You're talking security within the walls of the 'Greatest Men's Party on Earth,' held annually in sunny California. You're talking about security that will be protecting the president of the United States himself as well as members of his cabinet and club, be it at Bohemian Grove or Quaker's Inn. How in the world would you take down such a powerful figure as Cramer, not to mention an underling, who may one day soon be made a captain, too, from what I gather in those files?"

"A better question is how the hell do we pull something like that off and get out of there with our lives intact?" Liza queried. "Or maybe that part of the equation isn't of interest to your team, Detective," she tabled, distrust written across her pretty features.

Brian Archer consulted his watch. "We've been at this for almost two hours. Got another hour or so to spare? Or do you want to continue this tomorrow?"

Liza looked back and down at the picture of a young Denise Holloway. "Shoot."

Robert simply rolled his eyes. "Listen, before we continue, I have an unrelated question."

"I'm listening," Brian said.

"How do you know how I taught a class? What did you do, interview a former student?"

"As a matter of fact, that's exactly what I did."

"Who? Or for that matter, why?"

"A nephew of mine who had you at Queensborough Community College some years back. Why? Insight into your character, I suppose. He's a psychologist today. He thought the world of you. Said you were the best teacher he ever had." Archer consulted his notes, turning over several pages. "And I quote. 'Three-step model: thesis, support your proposition with a good argument, conclusion. Five-step model: thesis, good argument, better argument, best argument, conclusion. Five-step sophisticated model: thesis, good argument, rip the opposition—presenting a weak argument to show your reading audience that you understand the flip side of an issue, but at the same time bolstering your own opinion—followed by best argument, and conclusion.' He said he writes nearly every scholarly paper today by simply adding and expanding arguments in ascending order. Says you taught him that, too."

"I'm impressed," Robert said sincerely.

"You should be. He's tops in his field and claims you turned his life around."

"What's his name? I'd probably recall him."

"Donald Effer."

"Your nephew, you said? Donald Effer is black."

"Last I looked, he still is." Brian said and beamed mischievously. "Besides talking to my nephew Don and Chief Grear of Riverhead P.D., I also spoke with several other retired law enforcement officials who either love you or hate your guts. Seems there's no middle ground."

"I wouldn't have it any other way."

"And speaking of retirement, Liza, how are you enjoying yours?"

"I was enjoying it just fine until you came into our lives two hours ago."

"That was some commute you had. Riverhead to Harlem. How many years?"

"Eight out of thirty-two."

"From classroom teacher to staff developer. Quite an impressive record, too."

"You're racking up Brownie points as clear as the nose on your face," Liza relented. "So, you staying for dinner?"

"The thought did occur to me. All right with you, Rob?"

"Suit yourself."

"We'll go over the general plan step-by-step. No more threats or game-playing. Everything on the up and up. Promise. The assignment is doable but admittedly somewhat dangerous."

"Somewhat," Robert stated flatly.

"You'll have good people putting this together, I can assure you."

"You like Italian dishes, Detective Archer?"

"Call me Brian. And, yes, I love Italian food, Liza."

"Good, because that's what we serve-up here along with a side order of revenge," she stated evenly, still staring down intently at the photograph of Denise Holloway. "Yes. Revenge is a dish best served up cold."

Chapter Fifty-Seven

Immobilized in a prone position, the patient stared blankly at a white wall, dropping his dark eyes to the thin cushion the nurse was carefully positioning beneath Justin's chin for comfort and support, about to sponge bathe the back of the big man's body. A doctor appeared in the unit and pushed aside the curtain. Smiling pleasantly, he politely shooed the woman away.

"I want to know exactly how I stand, Doc," Justin said weakly, not realizing the profundity of the pun, not knowing that he'd never walk again.

"For openers, Mr. Barnes, I want you to know that you're very lucky to be alive," the neurosurgeon said quite frankly, words far removed from any form of cliché. "If you want it straight from the shoulder, you're a living miracle. And I perform them every week. But I can't do very much more for you from what I see here," he stated evenly.

Justin barely had the strength to speak. "And what exactly do you see, Doc? I want the truth. I want it now. Not a week or month from now. No hopes or promises. Just the short and long-term clinical prognosis. Please."

"Your spinal cord has been severed. I performed a laminectomy. The lesions—"

"I didn't know I had breasts. You take them both? Is that why I'm lying on my belly? To hide your handiwork? Or am I mixing that up with a vasectomy? Uh-oh. You didn't slip, did you, Doc? I know you know I only got one of those."

"A good sense of humor along with a strong constitution is what's going to get you through this, Mr. Barnes."

"Through what?"

"The lesions are severe. What we call complete."

"So were the beatings my so-called stepfathers gave me as a boy, but I beat the odds. This body of mine never ever let me down, Doc. Know why? Because I work hard at it. That's why I'm a living miracle. Not yours but mine. I'm my own miracle man, my man. I can beat down whatever curve you throw at me. Believe me I can."

"I had to remove segments of the posterior arch of vertebrae in order to access the spinal canal and remove the bullet. With low-velocity missiles, the success rate of laminectomies performed on patients with complete lesions can range from fair to middling, with partial to measurable improvement. However, you were hit by a small cannon: a Sabot slug fired from a .50 caliber muzzleloader. The damage is, I'm afraid, most severe. The projectile transected the spinal cord."

"How long will it be before I walk again? Best and worst case scenario."

"You won't."

"And if I beat those odds?"

"There aren't any."

"Where am I right now?"

"In ICU at the moment. We're going to monitor you carefully before we move you to the floor. But you may and do have visitors. More like a parade waiting in the wings," the man remarked.

"Doc, I want you to wheel me back into surgery. Forget weighing any risk-benefit factors. I'll sign any papers you want relieving the hospital of any and all responsibility. You do what you have to do to get me back on my feet again. I'll take care of the rest through rehabilitation. I'll even renew my contract with God, not that the old one actually expired. All right, I admit I never really had one. I'll even sign His, too. Unconditionally. Please, Doc. I'm begging you. The last time I begged anyone was for my mother not to let another stranger into our tenement flat. Please."

But the surgeon was shaking his head. "I already consulted with a Doctor Frederick Waters in Downy, California. A top man in the field. There's nothing anyone can do. When I tell you that you're lucky to be alive, consider it an understatement. And you're not out of the woods yet. You went into renal shock and there were and are other complications. You asked for it straight, and I'm giving it to you. You'll be confined to a wheelchair for the rest of your life. But that doesn't mean you can't or won't lead a productive one. After your company leaves, or should I say battalion, I want you to meet and talk with someone."

Justin tried to bat a tear from an eye but couldn't. "Do they know?" he demanded.

"Your fiancée, Edna, knows."

"You had no right telling her, Doc."

"I didn't."

"Then how?"

"She got ahold of and read the reports, along with the MRIs."

"Yeah, that sounds like something she would do. She in trouble?" The patient forced a smile.

The doctor smiled back. "Only if you want her to be."

"I'd like to see her first before the rest of those clowns come in."

The neurosurgeon nodded, touched Justin's hand gently, turned and started to walk from the room.

"One more thing, Doc."

The man faced about. "Name it."

"I'll even spell it: m-o-r-p-h-i-n-e. More, pleeease?"

Dr. Baskin smiled rather sadly. "I'll put you on a cloud."

"Just put it on my bill, Doc."

Chapter Fifty-Eight

Liza Downs stood in the kitchen washing the dinner dishes while Robert Redler dried and put them away. With paper towels, each plate and utensil had first been wiped clean of sauce or gravy, the salad bowls of oily dressing, the pots and pans of any grease. A cylindrical two and a half quart clear container filled with hot soapy water and a thick dishrag sat in a corner of the sink as Liza took a moment to dry her hands and tune in the six o'clock news. *How many more American troops were going to die on foreign soil in this bloody war*, she wondered.

Robert dumped the empty topneck shells, removed and discarded the crumpled heavy-duty aluminum foil from a baking sheet on which a dozen clams casino had cooked. He put away the pan in a shallow space above the refrigerator-freezer. Next, he cleared the dining room table of three remaining cups and saucers and placed them on the counter for Liza to wash and rinse. Taking a flour sack cloth from his waist, which served as an apron/dishtowel, he finished drying and putting away the items in a corner cabinet by the stove.

The two of them listened in a trance as it was reported that three more American soldiers had been killed in a roadside bombing in Baghdad.

Liza turned off the radio.

Robert opened the back door for some air.

"So?" Liza questioned.

"So?" he echoed.

"Besides having little choice in the matter, are we going to do this thing?"

"I guess your mind is already made up."

"I guess I'm trying to get into yours."

"Did you ask yourself why the police don't do this thing themselves?"

"Archer told us why. It would never fly. Cramer and his troops would smell a trap a mile off. He knew that a trap was being hatched in New York while laughing up his sleeve at them from Tennessee."

"Sure. He had Denise Holloway in his corner the whole time."

"Captain Denise Holloway if what Archer says is true."

"Correction. Captain Denise Cramer/Reaper," Robert said with a smirk. "Or soon to be anyways, according to the file."

"Whatever. She's going down. Besides those serial murders of innocent civilians, the authorities know that she and Cramer are responsible for the death and serious injury of two law enforcement people: Archer's own partner as well as a man who acted in the capacity we once did."

"Who is getting paid for what he was doing. We weren't."

"So tell Archer to put us on the payroll," she suggested with laughing eyes.

"I just don't want you to do this because you think he's got me over a barrel with this deli thing."

"Oh, he does have *us* over a barrel, but I'll do it because of who Denise Holloway is and what she did to us years ago. She could have just walked away from that Giordano/Manns mess when it was over. But she chose to do otherwise by following in their footsteps. She's not a naive kid anymore. She chose to be recruited by an evildoer because she's evil incarnate."

"You trust Archer?"

"I trust him."

"Fine. But there are others in authority who could make trouble for us just the same."

"I'd say we have very little choice in the matter."

"Once again, I don't want us to do this for the wrong reasons. I want *us* to want to put Sep Cramer down because he's pure evil and a top player in this sick cult of theirs. We can accomplish what the police can't do alone simply because we're anonymous."

"Maybe once upon a time we were. I'm not so sure about that anymore."

"We've been out of the loop for years, Liza. They're not going to know us from Adam. Archer and Team Three are going to assure our anonymity."

"After this, we hang up our guns for good. Yes?"

But Robert was shaking his head. "One more."

"Who?"

"*Número uno*. The head of Cramer's group who I have a strong feeling is going to bring this country to the brink of disaster."

"I thought we're already there."

"Almost, but not quite."

"Well, we're in the midst of a serious war whether you know it or not."

"I feel we ain't seen nothin' yet, Liza."

"How did things ever get this far?"

"You know damn well how. A two-party system, poor policy decisions, and lofty liberals."

"And the fix?" she questioned dismally.

"There isn't any. Unless . . . ."

"Unless what?"

"Unless we back off or drop the bomb, like in nuclear. That's what Cramer's speech at the Bohemian Club is going to be about."

"How do you know that?"

Robert didn't answer but just stared knowingly.

"You got that old feeling back," she said in sudden realization.

Robert nodded.

"Jesus."

"The United States is going to be hit again. Only it's going to be a disaster far greater than the World Trade Center bombing of ninety-three. Mark my words. Sep Cramer and his followers would love to see an incident with the hope of engaging this country in all-out war with the Middle East."

"Are you suggesting taking out Cramer before he delivers his keynote speech?"

"Can't. Not at the Grove. According to Archer, the play's already in motion. Besides, you can't tell the police how to run their show."

"Do you believe that Cramer's speech could really have that much of an impact? Don't you think that Bush, Cheney, Rice and Powell will decide a course of action? Not Sep Cramer. He's highly respected, but he doesn't spout or dictate policy."

"What I get from Archer's wife is that Cramer has charisma and the power of persuasion to set a certain mood and tone and plant a deadly seed. He's a masterful and dynamic speaker. If we experience another attack, who knows where that will lead and what may happen?"

"*You* seem to," she remarked.

"Look at me. You knew early on that our fight in Vietnam was wrong. And we paid a dear price. We both know the Mideast situation is another story. It's not just al-Qaida, Liza. It's practically a dozen countries we have to worry about. We've gotten too damn big for our britches. Made lots of enemies. Some of them we think are our friends."

"Silly us."

"It's no joke. People like Cramer want ultimate power. Bush and his people wouldn't want to drop the bomb, but they will if our liberties are compromised. Cramer and his group will exacerbate matters if given the opportunity. That's why he and his group of fanatics must be stopped. The police aren't telling us everything, nor should they. But I guarantee you this business goes way beyond serial murders."

"I can't believe the Tennessee police swallowed his story about the stolen car."

"Hook, line and sinker. And why not? They practically got the case wrapped up, they figure. They shot to death the perfect scapegoat and found all those Thompson/Center handguns, scopes and ammunition in Peter Griffing's house."

"They've got to be asking themselves who shot that Barnes fellow in the back."

"They probably figure a copycat or an accomplice."

"Yeah, one with a black powder muzzleloader this time out."

"How very clever of and convenient for Cramer."

"Who of course has a perfect alibi."

"From a former senator of the state of Tennessee."

"You think he might be involved in this cult?"

"I don't know, but I'm going to make it my business to find out."

"How?"

Robert shrugged. "I promise you'll be the first to know when I do."

"Lucky me."

"So we're absolutely committed then."

"Certifiably so."

Chapter Fifty-Nine

There was no question in anyone's mind that Sep Cramer was the man of the hour. The applause was stupendous. Even his detractors were impressed, though absolutely aghast. His supporters ran between the poles of nervousness to outright fright. One would have to be inhuman not to run the gamut of emotions, for Sep Cramer had calmly managed to metamorphose a benign face upon his mortal message, his intendment couched in a single word. Survival. Survival of the United States of America. Near the end of his delivery, the speechmaker held up a single sheet of paper with a picture of a cat.

"A pussycat at that," he told the assembled group of seventy select men, inquiring as to how many times a piece of ordinary paper, of any size, could be folded in half.

Several guesses were battered about, but only one correct answer was immediately given by two long-time members of the Bohemian Club, while others in the audience were busy tearing out blank pages from their pocket planners or notepads.

A question was raised by a young senator as to whether or not it mattered if the paper were square or rectangular.

"You wouldn't know a square from a rectangle from an asshole," a member of the lower house joked playfully.

"Why, sure I would, Dan. Am I not sitting next to one?"

An ambassador-at-large sitting directly behind the pair leaned forward and put an arm around each man. "I think one of you should just blow the other the fuck off and leave it at that. Either that or kiss and make up. Now, how's that for diplomacy?"

"Not until I see and learn the correct answer for myself," the congressmen decided, intrigued by the junior senator's antics of mightily trying to fold in half, for a final time, the piece of rigid paper.

"Five!" an arthritic industrialist announced, painfully doubling the tiny wad until he could fold it no further.

"No, no. We said six!" a former president along with a Wall Street banker positively noted.

"Six," two Texas state lobbyists nodded in confirmation.

"Watch very carefully, gentlemen," Sep said before his colleagues, friends and acquaintances, folding the sheet of paper seven times.

"That's impossible!" one man shouted.

"Keep watching," Sep insisted. "Eyes front and center, please."

Sep slowly unfolded the same sheet seven times before their unbelieving but fascinated eyes, reopening it to a page of history: a full-length, large print newspaper headline referencing the bombing of Hiroshima, August 6th, 1945. Next, he refolded the page, this time forming an origami tiger, complete with tail. The metaphor was not lost on a single soul gathered in the amphitheater.

"We appear to be, in the eyes of many, weak and weak-minded. But we are *not* a paper tiger," Sep continued. "We must do one of two things. Fold . . ." he let the word hang there for emphasis, ". . . or strike back with a vengeance that will literally shake the uncivilized world. We must decide to go nuclear. We must, in order to survive. We must move first and foremost. We must obliterate a nation of murderers in one masterstroke. Diplomacy has run its course, gentlemen." In one fantastic motion, the paper tiger went up in flames. In the next instant, a flag of the United States of America was being waved from Cramer's hand.

The assembled group went positively wild.

"Surprise and timing are everything," Sep Cramer assured everyone. He smiled most modestly. "Survival or surrender, gentlemen. There is no middle ground. We annihilate the middle of the Middle East. Its very core. Swiftly and without mercy."

"What about their cells throughout the world, Sep?" the second in command asked bluntly.

"It'll be like putting out little fires, Dick. Once the body is broken, the cells die off rather rapidly. The kind of cancer we'll give them will be diagnosed incurable," Cramer concluded firmly.

Chapter Sixty

On the border of Bohemian Grove, at an inn connected to an underground tunnel leading to a spacious *game room* framed in wall-to-wall, floor to ceiling leather, were twenty-one half-clad courtesans of unparalleled beauty. On leather courting chairs and sectional sofas, most of the women were engaged in sexual acts with a male partner—or several—selected from the ranks of the country's elite. No one from President Bush's cabinet was present. The men were people of wealth and power, mainly from the corporate world of business and finance who had served past administrations and/or the present one.

A banker from Milwaukee licked caviar off the back of a twenty-three-year-old up-and-coming actress who was performing fellatio on a legislator from the Boston area.

A lobbyist for the NRA sat atop a winged leather club chair and ejaculated onto the exquisite faces of two barely legal teenagers who laughed with delight while fondling one another.

A would-be senatorial candidate from Illinois sat glumly off to a corner, fully clothed, and accepted a small plate of lobster salad ringed with clams casino/Rockefeller from Liza Downs. Robert came over with a glass of champagne, setting it down before the forty-four-year-old.

"Krug Grande Cuvée, 1975," Redler offered and smiled pleasantly. "One of the very best available on the face of the planet."

"Get bent," was the Republican's remark.

"Pretty hard to do in these surroundings, sir," Redler retorted, stepping aside as a topless buxom blonde brushed by between them.

"Ah, I see you met Mister Charm," Sep Cramer said, moving

into the corner and placing a reassuring hand on Robert's shoulder. "The man has his problems at the moment and has to be excused. Jack, you behave yourself, here?" he directed before turning back to the steward. "I only brought him along for cheer, but I think I should have left him home alone to cry in his beer. Hey, I'm a poet!" Sep smiled disarmingly, a little drunk but still sober enough to adjust his own bow tie as well as Robert's cummerbund. "Spiffy. Where you from?"

"Bridgeport, sir."

"Call me Sep. Everybody does. So, Bridgeport. Tell me what you think of that fine fox on the floor behind you. Like some of that? Not exactly what I'd call sloppy seconds—yet."

Robert glanced over at the young woman engaged in *handling* two politicians simultaneously.

"I think I'd better keep my eyes and mind on my work, Sep. These party people are not only hungry for sex, they went through a hundred and fifty pounds of lobster, sixty pounds of shrimp and assorted shellfish so far, and we're only getting started," he enumerated rather boyishly. "I've got to send up to the inn for several more cases of claret."

"You tell Joe that Sep said to send down a case of Lafite-Rothchild that he's hiding up there. He'll know."

"All right."

"A bottle goes on my table over there," he decided, pointing a finger with authority. "See that pretty lady in the far corner with no top? A claret for Denise. Show her the bottle and pour label up. She's into pomp and ceremony," he instructed and winked. "And no spillsies because I know you'd love to lap it up. But that woman's off limits to everyone. At least for now. When the *real* show starts a little later, you're not going to believe your eyes. She's going to take on twelve guys. You know, I *am* a fucking poet!" he swore. "I'll be one of the dirty dozen. A little initiation rite. Oh, excuse me."

Sep went up to an elderly gentleman entering a private door.

The smell of new leather momentarily pervaded the room, overwhelming the scent of fresh bouquets, perfumes and colognes—even the odor of Scotch trailing Sep's mint mouthwash breath, Robert discerned.

"I bet you never hosted a celebration party quite like this," a tall, upper middle-aged man stripped down to his waist and wearing white suspenders said to Liza as she handed him his third Jack Daniel's.

"How would you possibly know where I hosted or even *hooked* for that matter?" she questioned, catching the man off guard.

"Wow! You don't mince words, do you?"

Liza smiled and started to turn away.

"Wait a second."

"May I get you something else?"

"Maybe later. But right now I'd like to voice an observation. If you hooked instead of hosting here tonight, you'd diminish the likes and looks of *all* these lovely ladies by a landslide," he crooned.

"And I suppose you can surmise all that with *all* my clothes on."

"That and a whole lot more."

"Really?"

"And truly."

"Well, you certainly are a flatterer."

"I mean every single word."

"I'm old enough to be their mother and young enough to be your daughter. Think about that. Still, I thank you for the compliment." Again, Liza started to take her leave.

"Before you go and leave me with a broken heart, enlighten me as to your preference of age in a man," he practically pleaded. "Please. I want to know exactly how I stand."

"I'm surprised you can stand at all," she put forth directly. "It must be those suspenders".

"Tell me what age," he persisted.

"The Age of Reason. How's that?"

"Then if that be the case, tell me what either of us is doing here this evening."

"Well, let's see." Liza pondered, putting a pinky to a dimple in her cheek. "You're here to get your rocks off, I suppose. And I'm here to make a living," she clarified, about to take her leave.

"Wait, wait, wait. Please don't go. There's something I must know. If you had your pick of any man in this room to be with for an intimate hour, who would it be? Point that person out to me. I just have to know."

Amused but focused, Liza scanned the room then pointed a

finger at the elderly gent who had spent the past fifteen minutes talking with Sep Cramer. "Him."

"Sep Cramer?"

"The other one."

"But he's as old as the dinosaurs. You've got to be putting me on. Right?"

"You asked me and I told you."

"I thought I was too old for you. That you were young enough to be my daughter, you said. Why, you could be his great-granddaughter for crying out loud."

"Who is he?"

"Who is he? I thought you said you hosted and hooked," he whispered. "Why, he's the greatest whoremaster who ever lived. That's who. That and one of the finest senators the state of Tennessee ever had."

"That a fact?"

"That's a fact. Want to meet him?"

"No, not really. I better go."

"Please stay."

"I'm sorry, but there's a rule about fraternizing."

The man laughed vigorously.

"What's so funny?"

"I make the rules."

"Really?"

"And truly. You don't know who I am, do you?"

"Should I?"

"Oh, I think, indeed, you should."

"So tell me."

"I'm Joe," he said, extending his hand formally. "I run the inn," he nodded in the direction of the tunnel door. "Everything funnels through me. Quite literally. It's Sep's set-up and party, but if I want to fraternize with the prettiest lady of the lot, I'll fraternize."

Liza turned her attention back to the two men. "Pretty chummy, those two."

"Sep and the senator? Thick as thieves," he nodded soberly. "He's a strange one though."

"Which one?"

"Both actually, but especially Sep. Lot of rumors going

around."

"Like what?"

"Like he marries the women he takes up with."

"What's so strange about that?"

"The fact that he takes up with several at the same time."

"And marries them?" she whispered in mock surprise.

Joe nodded.

"Isn't there a law against that?"

"There is and there isn't."

"Meaning?"

"Allegedly, he marries them all legal-like and everything. Only, it's anything but legal, of course, because he's already married."

"Polygamy?"

"Right. But from what I understand, the way he gets around it, there's this gray area."

"Between his ears."

The innkeeper grinned and laughed appreciatively. "He's a member of a secret cult," Joe whispered an inch away from her ear. "A double ceremony is performed within the confines of the church. Their church. By their law, he can have as many as seven wives. So long as the women consent and sign certain documents, there's little that can be done to stop it, unless the state governments want to drag the business through the courts for decades, which apparently they don't. None of the women are complaining from what I gather. And why should they? Supposedly, they all know about one another, and they're all provided for quite nicely."

"Do they all live together in a commune or something?"

"Hardly. They live private and respectable lives spread through several states."

"That's wild, Joe!"

"Want to know another little secret?"

Liza nodded.

"There's one woman here tonight he's going to marry in the very near future. But first there's going to be an initiation rite."

"Here?"

"Right before your pretty green eyes, which will probably fall out of your head when you see what he has in store for her." Joe flashed ten then two fingers.

"You're kidding."

"Not," he said and hiccupped.

"Does the senator know about this business?"

This time Joe's lips were pressed firmly against Liza's ear. "He's their high priest."

"They don't offer up sacrifices or anything like that, do they?"

"Of course not. But you'll soon see what they offer up instead. The senator will introduce her to the group as a form of this evening's entertainment. He'll then, as you so crudely put it, get his rocks off, figuratively, as an honor to be bestowed upon the old fart. Kind of like throwing out the first pitch at a ballgame. And then the games begin. That's why they call this the game room or playroom. I'm not talking pool or ping-pong," he assured her.

"Free-for-all? No rules?"

"Something like that. Like I showed you." Ten and two fingers flashed before her eyes anew. "Handpicked by Sep himself. He'll be one of them. It's more or less choreographed at the beginning. After that, natural, or should I say, unnatural and primal urges take over." Joe smiled and winked.

"Sounds like you were around for the rehearsals, Joe."

"Well, I did take a little peek at the program."

"You're not one of the twelve, are you?"

"No, Sep and I keep business and pleasure pretty much separate; his pleasure, my business."

"I see."

"I'd like very much to see you after the show. Stacy, is it?"

"It is, indeed," Liza fibbed.

"I'll even sport a cane and run a gray color-comb through my crop if that's what turns you on."

"Sounds hot," Liza said seductively. "But let's take it a step at a time."

"Meaning?"

"Meaning that there are many beautiful women out there, Joe. You may not want to meet me afterwards. The show could turn out even hotter than you might imagine."

Joe inserted a pair of thumbs beneath his suspenders, stretching the supporting straps forward to their limits. "No contest, Stacy. I'll look forward to seeing you at the inn tonight."

"Just out of curiosity, Joe. How did the place get its new name?"

"Quaker's Inn?" Joe smiled proudly. "I refurbished and named it in honor and memory of my favorite president. Richard Millhouse Nixon. He was a Quaker, you know."

"Oh, I know."

"But we're not going to talk politics tonight, Stacy."

"No, we're certainly not," Liza assured the man.

Chapter Sixty-One

Ten muscular men clad in pagan costume held center stage . . . held their audience spellbound . . . held Denise Holloway firmly to the floor by her slender shoulders and ankles as one well-endowed male after the other stripped completely then took the seductive woman in uncompromising positions before they came at her in pairs, performing double penetration upon her lithesome body made beautifully bronze by the California sun.

The dim lighting was momentarily reduced to a mass of mere shadows before being brought up keenly to expose three figures sandwiching the woman's torso: one man squarely beneath the form, two more taking turns mounting her buttocks, her long, shapely legs and inner thighs stroked by pairs of powerful hands. Several anonymous souls intermittently massaged her breasts and belly while another applied a fragrant yellow oil, poured from a green cut-glass flask.

Several impatient spectators went positively wild, performing their own acrobatics with paid-in-full female partners of their choosing, reclined in low, thick-cushioned leather chairs or lying upon upholstered Holly benches set at eye level before the periphery of the stage. One overzealous gentleman was being pried away from a trio of scantily clad ladies. He was invited and encouraged instead to join the main attraction.

The well-endowed captain of industry finally acquiesced and straddled the face of the female performer holding center stage, ramming his turgid, lengthy rod down the back of Denise's throat.

Sep Cramer suddenly stepped in and brushed away the buggerers at her backside as well as retiring the industrialist and the one employed beneath her slithery body. Bringing the woman to her knees, he spread wide the woman's legs, driving home his manhood to the sound of outrageous applause. Denise heaved her hips and gave a deep-throated, guttural, foamy muffled sigh while furiously pounding fistfuls of steel-like flesh for the presumed finale.

Not until the industrialist and every performer ejaculated within or upon Denise's silky coppery body did the clapping and frenetic whistling come to a close.

Sep had returned to his table, seated in a soft beige terry robe between four fully clothed and attractive women.

One by one, the male performers stepped from the stage.

Denise remained behind, gently massaging her privates while waving a foot-long dildo grabbed from beneath a robe as three ladies-in-waiting cleaned her up with sponges dipped in crystal bowls filled with colored, perfumed water.

"*Quim* pro quo," Captain Karen Carper quipped, realizing the show wasn't quite over.

"I mean, what the fuck is she going to do for an encore?" Captain Sharon Espe raved.

"Oh, my God!" Captain Rebecca Pace cried when she saw the four-legged animal being drawn forward across the stage.

"Is she going to screw it with that rubber cock, or is it going to screw her with his donkey dong?" Captain Brenda Reece giggled in delight. "Because they sure as hell can't get it on together."

"Not by any stretch of the imagination," Karen agreed.

"Wait and see," Sep responded enigmatically. "That cock of his can stretch from here to doomsday . . . wrap around corners if need be," he added for good measure while spacing his hands the full length of the table. "El burro, there, can put any animal here to shame, I'm so sorry to say," he elaborated.

"What are you going to do for entertainment by the time you reach bride number seven, Sep?" Rebecca reproached. "Thank God the four of us didn't have to go through a ritual like this."

"I think she's absolutely going to love it," Brenda interjected, swallowing the last of her champagne.

Liza immediately approached their table and withdrew the magnum from a sterling silver stand, pouring two glasses of the bubbly before setting the chilled cuvée back into the sweaty, icy bucket.

Robert followed on her heels with an unopened bottle of Bordeaux, displaying its label up before setting the wine down upon the table. He watched as Liza headed in the direction of the stage. Reaching behind his back beneath the broad black band, he withdrew the implement, slitting open the neck of foil, partially screwing in its tiny, shiny, snaky spiral before locking the hinge atop the lip of the bottle, drawing the cork out with a sudden pop.

"May I pour a glass for anyone?" he asked politely and as calmly as he could.

Everyone except Sep declined.

Robert put down the tool and poured the man his vin.

"Hey, Bridgeport."

"Yes, sir?"

"Sep," Sep insisted.

"Yes, Sep?"

"The show everything I said it was so far?"

"Absolutely."

"Wait. You haven't seen anything yet. I caught the act you're about to witness both in Central and South America some years ago. You won't believe your eyes."

Robert Redler smiled.

"Look, they're getting them ready now. Did you ever see such a dick on a donkey in your life, Bridgeport? Bet you never knew it could grow in size like that. Did you?"

Robert watched as Liza made her way across the room.

"Look!" Karen pointed toward the stage. "I think one of the hostesses wants in on the act," she said mischievously.

Liza was loosening an article of clothing as she neared the bench on which Denise lay. Denise looked over invitingly at the woman, summoning her closer. Liza unbuttoned and removed her blouse, dropping it casually to the floor, moving toward center stage in a powder-blue bra.

Denise sat up and massaged herself amorously. It wasn't in the script, but what the hell, she figured. Sep was always full of surprises. A little female foreplay before the concluding act.

Joe stood in a trance, propped up against one of the doors, pulling on his suspenders. "Wow! Is she something else or what."

Behind and beneath her hostess apron, Liza reached as if to

unzip the back of her skirt. She smiled down lovingly at Denise Holloway.

Robert picked up and put away the wine opener at the back of the cummerbund, withdrawing a coal-blue steel revolver leveled at Sep's temple as the man was taking his first and final sip before the flash of gunfire.

There in the subdued light, it was difficult to tell what ran and stained the front of Sep's robe. Was it the rich, full-bodied wine or the blood that spilled from Cramer's skull, Robert wondered, placing a second shot in the center of the man's chest.

The muzzle of Liza's pistol discharged a 35-grain hollow point into the middle of Holloway's forehead. Another round caught the corner of her cleavage, surely bursting open wide the woman's heart.

As the two assassins quickly made their way unimpeded toward the tunnel door, Liza detected the essence of gunpowder overpowering the balmy sweet smell of incense, fresh flowers and new leather. The pair reached one of the two exits at the exact moment.

"Out of our way, Joe," Liza ordered, "or you're fucking history," she swore, aligning the sights of her weapon between the innkeeper's eyes.

Joe swallowed hard and stepped aside. "You won't walk off this property," he promised.

"Oh, I don't intend to, Joe. Hey, we have a date with destiny. Remember?" she said with a bright smile. "Now, step aside."

The brazen old man with whom Sep Cramer had spoken earlier, approached the doorway. "The door's locked like the other one. I'm afraid you're not going anywhere," he stated with conviction, locking his ancient eyes upon the couple.

"It's good to be afraid, Senator," Liza stated before sending a bullet through the man's right eye, blind to a female in the audience punching out a set of numbers on her cell phone.

"It's locked!" Robert panicked, struggling with the doorknob.

"The keys, Joe," Lisa threatened solemnly, holding the cowering figure in her sights as the man's trembling hands rose vainly to protect his frightened pale-white face. Liza grinned. "We're talking fire hazard here, Joey," she tormented, cocking back the hammer of the handgun for the full effect.

Joe fumbled for then produced a set of keys from a pants

pocket.

"Open it," Robert demanded.

As Joe unlocked the door, he suddenly bolted into the tunnel while Liza and Robert held the group at bay, crossing the threshold with barely enough time and space to slam and lock the door behind them as four of Cramer's wives charged forward.

Robert Redler was on the heels of Joe the innkeeper when the man suddenly turned and thrust a knife blade past the assassin's cheek, which went sailing from the assailant's grip in the instant the former Marine parried and straightaway snapped the innkeeper's neck.

Chapter Sixty-Two

L iza and Robert helped each other gather and don dry suits, hoods, weight belts, masks, Aqua-lungs and respirators hidden behind the 6 x 6 x 4 foot display tank set off in a dark and musty corner of the tunnel. The pair stepped up and onto its pallet. Robert boosted Liza up and into the watery glass enclosure filled with hundreds of large, live three- to five-pound lobsters, their claws held firmly in place with small, coded yellow or orange rubber bands. Pulling upward with all his might, Robert barely managed to make it over the top of the tank if not for Liza's aid.

As no handguns had been permitted to be carried through the tunnel or into the lounge area, Captains Carper, Espe, Pace and Reece first had to retrieve their weapons from the head of security. The grounds, inn, tunnel and playroom were sealed and secure. Karen safeguarded the lounge and both doors leading to and from the tunnel. Sharon stood sentry at its other end. Rebecca and Brenda quickly turned Quaker's Inn into a fortress. A private security team posted along the perimeter of the property assured the four women that the two assassins were still ensconced somewhere in the tunnel between the lounge and the wine cellar, for no one had entered or left the building or grounds as security had been alerted seconds after the former senior senator was shot.

"They're here and we'll find them," the team's leader stated emphatically.

"Those two go down, Geoffrey," Sharon made clear. Got it?"

"Got it."

"Make damn well sure your team's got it, too. I want them dead at any cost."

"I understand." The head of the security lowered his chin to his shoulder and immediately transmitted the order into a microphone clipped to a Kevlar vest. "Alpha One to Omni. The duo goes down and dirty. No exceptions. I repeat. Down and dirty. No exceptions. Copy?"

"Copy that," a dozen voices answered up smartly.

"Alpha One, standing by," Geoffrey replied, turning back to Sharon. "They've got to be sandwiched somewhere in the tunnel, Captain. Several of my men will do a sweep of the passageway; the rest of us will hold down the fort as well as the outer perimeter. They'll never leave the property."

But Sharon was shaking her head in the negative. "We'll handle the tunnel. Just be sure not even a breeze passes by out there."

"Suit yourself. You still want to contain all members and guests, or would you like me—"

"They stay right where they are until those two are found and terminated."

"Yes, Captain."

"You'll cover every square inch past the tunnel to the inn. If they somehow made it to the main building, I'll need your help, and we'll rendezvous there. But like you, I believe they're trapped within the passageway. They have to be. I called you the instant the senator was murdered. If you secured the inn and property like you said, they could not have made it to the cellar, elevator or stairs."

"We had the building locked down tight sixty seconds after your call. Even if they hauled ass from the get-go, it would take them several minutes to get to the wine cellar. And if Joe stalled them for a moment as you said, no way did they make it to the inn. They're in that tunnel."

Sharon called Karen on her cell. "You got that group under control?"

"Do now. Practically had a panic on my hands, but everything is cool for the moment."

"Good. Lock them down tight. Start moving yourself back through the tunnel. I'll meet you somewhere in the middle. Rebecca and Brenda will be right behind me. Over."

"You're breaking up. I'm to head out and meet you in the middle of the tunnel. What about Rebecca and Brenda?"

"They're coming in right behind me. Over."

"That's a copy. C3 moving out. Over."

"Leave no stone unturned, Karen. Be sure both doors are locked behind you. Roger that?"

"Affirmative; C3 standing by."

"C2, C4. You with the program?"

"Read you loud and clear, C1," Rebecca replied.

"Ditto," Brenda echoed.

"All right then. I'm on my way back to the tunnel."

Twenty minutes passed before a call came through to Quaker's Inn from the president's own party located three miles downriver, arranging for the exchange of lobster tanks, as there had been an apparent mix-up and the Bohemian Club was running dangerously low.

"No can do," was the response given by the second in command of security at the inn. "We have a situation."

"No, you don't understand," bellowed the caller. "*We* have a situation. We're almost out of fucking lobsters over here. You got our tank. We got yours. We have over two hundred members and guests who are shrimped and oystered out and *demanding* lobsters. A truck is on its way over to you to load that pallet and tank pronto."

"I told you. No can do."

"Put Geoffrey on immediately."

"We're busy here, buster." The man terminated the conversation.

Several minutes later, Geoffrey's cell phone sounded.

"Yeah?"

"Yeah, you there, asshole? This is former Secretary of Defense Casper Weinberger calling on behalf of the president of the United States. I mention his title just in case I'm speaking to a fucking ignorant foreigner. Have I got your attention, lamebrain?"

"Yes, sir," Geoffrey choked.

"Good. We're nearly out of lobsters over here, which is big time on the fucking menu. Three and five pounders. We got your tank by mistake for seventy people. We've got two hundred members and guests. They're practically all gone. The lobsters, not the people. Got the picture? A truck is on its way over for you to make the switch. A Mr. Kibber will load that pallet without anyone giving him a song or a dance. Are we clear, Geoffrey?"

"Yes, sir."

"How tall are you, Geoffrey?"

"I beg your pardon?"

"Pardon? George W. will never ever grant you one if you fuck this up. Understand? Now, how tall are you?"

"Six-three, sir."

"Fine because I'll find me a six-by-six foot tank, have it filled with horseshit, and have you standing tall in the center of it before our commander and chief if those lobsters are not here pronto. Are we fucking clear?"

"Yes, sir. They'll be there."

"They damn well better be."

Chapter Sixty-Three

Captains Karen Carper and Sharon Espe met somewhere in the middle of the tunnel. Captains Rebecca Pace and Brenda Reece brought up the rear. Not a trace of the two assassins was to be found anywhere.

"I can't believe they ever made it to the inn or beyond the building," Sharon steamed.

"Maybe they had help on the inside," Brenda exploded.

"But where could they go?" Rebecca brooded. "They couldn't have gotten into the main building or the grounds."

"Not through Geoffrey's team," Karen agreed.

Sharon went over the blueprints in her hands. "There's got to be something here we're missing. Some escape hatch in the ceiling, floor or wall. Or maybe they had outside help."

"Like who?" Rebecca snapped. "Geoffrey and the team immediately rounded up the entire staff and put them in the Nixon Room for their own safety. Everyone's accounted for and hasn't moved from that spot."

"And there's not a customer or guest at the inn because of the private parties both here and at the Grove," Brenda amplified. "The place is secure. The grounds were guarded from the moment the team got word. No way in hell did they make it past the wine cellar," she confirmed.

"Then we start over," Sharon suggested. "We work in pairs. Karen can come with me to the wine cellar. You and Rebecca work from the lounge on back this time. Every inch of flooring, ceiling and walls. They're hiding in this tunnel. Look for an opening . . . a crease, a wrinkle, a loose brick or board. We owe it to Sep. The senator and

Denise, too. None of us here really knew the extent of power those two men wielded until today. A mighty sect, we all believed. True enough, indeed. But never did we ever imagine the magnitude or majesty to shape man's destiny within the very ranks of military might. We all read Sep's speech delivered at the club this afternoon. Too bad we couldn't have been there. But you heard the powers that be buzzing before our party began.

"Each of us was to have, and still has, the obligation and honor of serving Sep," Sharon droned. "Our own cells to operate so as to undermine the current regime and help pave the way for an all-out attack. We must be as fearless as our enemies. We must not be afraid to meet but to also greet death with welcome arms if need be. We will live on forever through our children and their children's children until we all pass through the gates of eternity to be united once again. We are truly the chosen." Sharon bowed her head and clasped their hands in unification.

"Amen," Karen said in supplication.

"Amen," Rebecca and Brenda echoed solemnly within the tunnel's walls.

Suddenly, the foursome heard the elevator descend and its doors draw open. At breakneck speed, the group went running in the direction of the wine cellar. Weapons drawn. As they reached the east end of the tunnel, a piece of machinery was moving into position before the prodigious watery tank.

The women immediately raised their handguns. Four barrels were pointed at the operator's upper body and head.

The driver of the forklift immediately braked and raised his hands high.

"George Bush's orders, ladies. Check with Geoffrey," the man began to explain. "There's been a screwup with the lobster tanks. The club's got yours; you got ours. My truck's in the driveway, and I've been instructed to get these crawly creatures back. Your tank is already unloaded topside. And what's with those guns, girls?"

Sharon smiled at Karen. "Rebecca, Brenda. Check the elevator. Then go over his truck with a fine-tooth comb. If dust so much as rises, blow it back to kingdom come." Brenda and Rebecca quickly headed toward the elevator. "What's your name, fella?"

"Kibber."

"Well, Mr. Kibber. I'd like you to climb down off that forklift and step over there," Sharon commanded.

"I have orders—"

"COUNTERMANDED! I give the orders. Check with Geoffrey," she instructed. "Now, move."

Rebecca and Brenda reported back that the truck was secure. Karen and Sharon had checked the forklift from top to bottom, finally allowing Kibber to operate the machine, watching as the man maneuvered the two power-driven prongs between the slats at the base of the pallet, raising the nine thousand pound gallon tank several inches off a solid stone floor, then back about a foot. Hundreds of the crustaceans began moving about as the heavy load rocked unevenly.

Robert and Liza clung tenaciously to the inner rung running horizontally across the blue-black back wall, its Delphic umbrae providing protective cover that matched the inky color of their dry suits.

Robert's suit fit snugly around the collar, wrists and ankles, damning and sealing off the flow of water along his body.

Liza's dry suit did not, allowing the passage of forty-degree water to circulate about her limbs and torso for the past forty-five minutes. She dared not move a muscle except for her infernal shivering there in the corner of the tank, encased within the column of air bubbles created to keep the lobsters fresh and alive, bubbles mixed among her own air supply, which had approximately fifteen minutes of precious compressed air left in their single cylinders.

Karen checked behind the tank then pressed her forehead firmly against the cold dark glass, surveying the mass of mottled black-brown, dull-green, stalk-eyed crustaceans.

"Who are you looking for in there? Jacques Cousteau?" Sharon joked.

Kibber got down from the forklift and disconnected the electrical cord leading to the aerator pump at the rear of the tank.

Robert and Liza held their breath, lest a single bubble break the surface.

"I guess nobody was gonna pull that tank or line out accidentally," Kibber swore. "Thing weighs better than four tons."

One large lobster that had lost its yellow band found Liza's ankle, gripping the 5mm neoprene material like a pair of Channel-

Grips. Liza cursed silently as the claw clamped down firmly against her ankle bone.

Karen backed away from the tank. "Somebody has got to have them hidden somewhere," she steamed angrily.

"Now tell me something I don't know. Like where?"

"We'll find them, Sharon. Believe me we'll find them."

Sharon walked over to Kibber. "All right. Get this monstrosity the hell out of here. And don't steal any lobsters on the way back to the club."

"Very funny. Like I'm really gonna steal government property. You want me to bring back the other tank? It's less than half this size and practically empty."

"No point. Party's over. Put it in the storage shed for the time being."

"Yes, ma'am. You want me to plug it in or bring the remaining lot down here?"

"How many we talking?"

"Not many. Maybe a dozen."

"Tell you what. This area is secured. You tell Geoffrey I said you can have them."

"You serious?"

"You like lobster, Kibber?"

"Yes, ma'am."

"So take them and scram."

Kibber climbed back aboard the forklift and carefully drove the heavy load into the dimly lit service elevator.

Liza and Robert took several breaths beneath the noise of the machine and the closing elevator doors.

Chapter Sixty-Four

Twenty gallons of water had to have sloshed out of the lobster tank as Kibber raised and tilted the load further rearward for greater stability. He feared that the wooden pallet might crack from the massive weight as he slowly rounded the curb on his approach to the flatbed truck, gingerly raising then lowering the pallet upon the steel deck at the rear of the cab.

Robert and Liza didn't dare release another breath for fear the next one might be their very last as there was no pump to commingle and cloak their column of air.

Geoffrey went over to Kibber and had him sign a manifest the moment the man finished strapping down and securing the towering tank. Kibber signed, backed out the forklift, pivoted around smartly while lowering the prongs to the pallet on the ground on which the smaller tank sat.

"What do you think you're doing now?" the head of security questioned irritably.

"Gonna put this one in the shed over there."

"I'll take care of it," Geoffrey said impatiently.

"Fine with me. Listen, one of the women in charge down there said I could have the remaining lobsters from this tank."

"Well, I'm in charge up here, and I'm telling you to take a hike."

"Hike?"

"Take your truck and beat it. You can come back tomorrow for the lobsters; that is, if they're still here."

Kibber nodded sourly, climbed down from the machine and up into his truck. "I'm gonna tell George W. you treated me badly,"

Kibber threatened with disappointment written across his face.

"You tell 'im for me I'm a Democrat. He'll understand," Geoffrey responded with a scowl.

A mile and a half from the inn, Kibber pulled off the road and into a clearing, stepped out and up to the platform, slapping the side of the tank three times.

Robert surfaced almost immediately.

Liza did not.

Robert purged his face mask and went back for his partner, unfastening the metal buckle at her weight belt, allowing it to fall freely. Releasing a firm grip from around the rung to which Liza clung, he brought her to the surface, removing the mouthpiece, regulator and single tank as Kibber lay flat on his stomach on the roof of the cab, supporting the woman by her shoulder.

"It's all right," Robert told her, opening the waterproof zipper across the front of her body followed by the second closure, struggling to remove the garment.

The right side of Liza's leg was in spasm. The large lobster still clung to her ankle, clamped across the Achilles tendon. Robert broke the claw off in a single twist of its body then pried open the pincer.

"Christ, why didn't you signal me?" Robert said breathlessly.

Liza shivered and shook. "I tr-tried. But you were t-too goddamn busy ho-holding breath l-like me."

"All right, let's get you both out of here before they figure out what happened," Kibber insisted, pulling Liza up as Robert helped push her body clear of the tank.

"She's trembling like a leaf," Robert said with sheer concern.

"She'll be fine. Look at this fucking fit," Kibber complained. "That's why she's shivering to beat the band. These gasket seals did little to prevent the water from entering her suit. Instead of keeping water out, it kept it in like a wet suit. No joke at forty-five to fifty degrees. And the fact that the lobster did a number on her ankle just added to the problem. Look at that rip in the suit."

Robert opened the waterproof zipper across the front of her body followed by the second closure, struggling to get her out of the garment. Her undergarments were soaked.

"Those garments come off now, Liza. I've got blankets inside,"

Kibber ordered.

Robert finally got out of his own suit.

Inside the cab, Liza shuddered and cringed while Robert examined her bruised and bleeding ankle.

"You'll be fine," Kibber promised. "You two did great. When we get moving, I'll tell you about real cold. Arctic cold. Where a wet suit would buy you forty seconds and a sea ceremony in less than two minutes. Where our regulators would freeze up regularly—"

"All right. Enough," Liza snapped.

"Yes, ma'am."

"What's your name," Robert asked while rubbing and massaging Liza's body through the blanket.

"Doctor Cormick, M.D., but call me Brett."

"What do you do, Brett? Police dive team? Instructor? What?"

"These days, mostly impersonations. Want to hear a Casper Weinberger? I also do a mean George W. Bush," he jabbered, turning on the heat before putting the vehicle in gear. "And I do mean *mean*. Especially if there was going to be any trouble swapping tanks. Meaning the lobster tanks, not the dive tanks. But that's a whole other story."

"Never m-mind the story," Liza cried. "Where is my change of clothes?" she demanded, running a hand beneath the seat between them, opening and slamming closed the glove compartment, passing another hand along the shelf above the windshield.

"There isn't any. I couldn't very well keep a set of clothes in here without them catching on, now could I?" the doctor explained.

Liza leaned forward and slid the heater lever and fan to full blast, directing all the vents within reach directly toward her. Clutching the corners of the cotton blanket at her bosom, she stewed quietly for several moments. "Could have at l-least brought a wool blanket," she griped.

"During the third week of July in sunny California? We'll have you both safe and sound, clothed and fed in no time," Brett promised and smiled. "Meanwhile, in memory of a great communicator, would you like to hear me do Ronald Reagan?" the UK team-leader/doctor/diver prompted.

"Where are we going?" Liza insisted.

"Blanket party," Doctor Brett Cormick kibitzed, noting that

Liza's voice and body signs were returning to normal.

"Not funny, fella," Liza puled.

"At least be nice and give me credit for the rung, which I epoxied on the wall with Marine-tex at the last moment so as to help keep you both near the pump. Buoyancy can sometimes be a bitch," he trifled frivolously.

"I just wish you would have epoxied the claw shut on that big guy instead of relying on rubber bands," Liza complained while massaging her wounded ankle.

"I'll put you in for a medal, Liza Downs," Cormick wisecracked. "Robert, be thankful that this is over for the two of you. The two of you did great. Team Three and the others are very grateful. Believe me. As a matter of fact, you'll see a familiar face or two aboard the vessel we'll be running, followed by a deep sea expedition for game fish. I hear Liza's quite the fisherperson. First fish, biggest fish, and high-hook on her last trip out, I heard. That's why there's no pool being offered on this trip," he teased. "Guys would go positively nuts. We should be boarding in less than ten minutes. So before I fall asleep at the wheel or simply pass out altogether, would you mind turning down the heat a notch, Liza? And wait till you two see what's on the menu for tonight. I hope you both like lobster Thermidor. That ought to warm the cockles of your hearts. Seconds upon request. No problem."

"Can you do an impersonation of Julia Child?" Liza half-kidded while turning down the heat.

"Julia Child?" Cormick mimicked in a throaty rich tenor. "Not only can I do her, I can cook just as well. Perhaps even a tad better, you'll soon see," he said unabashedly, launching into a full rendition regarding the preparation of Napoleon's favorite shellfish dish, allegedly named by the Little Corporal himself in the month it was first served to him. That is, Thermidor or Fervidor: the eleventh month in the French Revolutionary calendar; a period running from July 19th to August 17th. "And I'm sure you'll note the coincidental timing of *our* celebration," the impersonator, doctor, diver, driver, pedantic historian and supposed chef pointed out with the widest grin imaginable.

Chapter Sixty-Five

Aboard *Special Interest*, Detectives Brian and Kim Archer greeted Liza and Robert with a hardy welcome accompanied by a series of heartfelt hugs. After examining the couple, Doctor Cormick served up cups of hot fish broth from the galley before excusing himself, heading for the aft compartment to take a nap.

"That'll hold you till after I get my beauty rest," he called out.

"The man's been up for the past seventy-two hours planning and preparing that tank," Brian explained. "Getting the dive equipment into the inn took a bit of doing."

"You mean a heap of ingenuity," Kim amended the understatement.

"How did he manage it?" Liza asked through a sharp cough.

"Well, as you both know, on Saturday afternoon, Quaker's Inn *mistakenly* received the larger of the two lobster tanks meant for the Bohemian Club, along with boxes of fresh shrimp and oysters; the same fare they were serving up at the Grove, but for well over two hundred members and guests—not Sep Cramer's licentious group. It was Brett's brother who made the delivery to the inn. Two additional *tanks*," Kim set forth with a wink, "or in this case Aqua-Lungs along with the other paraphernalia that were listed on a separate invoice as if shipped from a dive shop in the area so as to avert suspicion in case security found and questioned the cylinders and such. When the load was finally cleared and directed to the elevator by forklift, your gear was already hidden within the larger tank. Once inside the basement off the wine cellar, Brett's brother, our sea captain up there," she gestured toward the wheelhouse, "set the lobster tank close to the tunnel wall with your equipment concealed behind it as we said it would be."

"How did he manage that without anyone seeing him?" Robert asked over the large cup of steaming broth.

"Very clever of that cagy Englishman," Brian picked up the story. "What he did first was place the lobster tank smack against the wall of the tunnel, blocking access to the electrical outlet before driving the forklift back toward the elevator, later realizing, or rather pretending to realize, that he couldn't plug in the aerator pump in order to keep those crawly creatures alive and kicking till Monday evening," the detective explained, "which meant, of course, he'd have to go back to the unit, return to the tunnel, reposition the lobster tank, plug it in and set up the pump. Security couldn't be bothered waiting around."

"Especially after receiving a call around the same time that someone suspicious was seen roaming the grounds," Kim elaborated. "Anyhow, he managed to get your gear out of the tank and behind it without raising so much as an eyebrow."

"What if things didn't go so smoothly? What if they stood over him until he finished with the pump and then made him leave?" Liza asked with irritation, massaging her bandaged ankle.

"Yeah, what if they found the scuba gear?" Robert interjected. "What then? There was no way to call off the mission, was there? We'd be as dead as Joe, Denise, Sep and the senator."

But Brian was shaking his head. "We'd have gone to Plan B, Rob."

"Which was?"

"Joe's birthday was right around the corner," Brian continued.

"I don't understand," Robert said, sternly inviting an explanation.

Kim calmly and patiently expounded. "The cover story was that the cylinders and accessories were to be secreted on premises as a surprise gift from his daughter, since both of them scuba-dived and kayaked together on a regular basis and would on his birthday."

"And if that story leaked like my fucking dry suit?" Liza whined. "What then? What if they put two and two together at the last moment? *Our* last moment. Tank, tank, tank, tank," she enumerated on the tips of her fingers. "What if Cramer's followers had examined the tank more closely and found us in there? What was your cover story going to be then? Huh? 'Oh, those two. They're just minding the fucking fish farm,'" she fumed.

"But they *didn't* find you," Kim said sympathetically, tenderly touching the back of Liza's hand.

"We covered all bases as best we could," Brian reassured the couple. "That's why Brett's brother carried a second invoice with a note as a backup, to show that the equipment was purchased as a gift from the dive shop, with special written instructions by Joe's daughter herself as to where to stash the stuff. Even their dry suit sizes were precisely the same as the ones we placed in case anyone with a discerning eye questioned them, like Joe's wife who works the bar. Or their younger daughter who makes up the rooms."

"That's why yours fit fine, Rob. Liza's a little loose," Kim clarified.

"And where's this diving daughter who supposedly sent these gifts and set of instructions?" Liza inquired suspiciously. "Wouldn't she have blown our cover if she suddenly turned up? I really don't understand what you're saying here. And why would she want to help us?"

"She wouldn't," Kim put forth plainly. "We had to twist her arm," she added candidly. "We have her under wraps for the time being. Brett called her mother and impersonated the daughter, leaving a message explaining that she had business in Seattle, and a surprise waiting for her father on her return. I'm not saying nothing could have gone wrong, Liza. You knew that going in. But we took every possible precaution we could to guarantee your safety, including a hostage that Joe would give up his life for if push ever came to shove. But that's all behind us now. In a little while, you're going to be debriefed, have a victory celebration dinner here tonight that your taste buds won't believe, a little R and R tomorrow before we head on home, and then we're going to make you both an offer that you either can or can't refuse," Detective Kim Archer said most solemnly.

"Oh, and by the way, Rob. Don't feel too bad about Joe the innkeeper. When we show you the list of people he's wasted in order to get where he is—or rather was—you'll have no regrets. Besides, it was a do or die situation back there. And as for the senator, Liza, well, that evil bastard's number was just about up anyhow. Terminal cancer; very late stages," Detective Brian Archer swore. "Your targets were Sep Cramer and Denise Holloway. Those other two? Collateral damage."

Chapter Sixty-Six

While underway, Kim Archer laid out four glossy photographs across a chart table. One photo was of Sep Cramer. Brian drew a grease pencil diagonally across the face of the serial killer. Kim took the pencil from her husband's hand and did likewise to the features of Denise Holloway and Joseph (the innkeeper) Matuco.

"Joe is the brother of Sergio Matuco, a Long Island resident whose son was shot in the back in Manorville by Sep Cramer, orchestrated by Joe in retaliation for some internecine feud going on between the two brothers for years," Kim expanded. "We believe at this point that all of Sep's murders have a direct connection to his victims, that none were random as first thought. There's that blind woman from Virginia he murdered, Carla Banks, who we think he approached as a possible recruit but turned him down. Carla Banks and Denise Holloway were once good friends. We think that when Carla said no to Cramer, he killed her and befriended Denise."

"We can draw connections between Cramer and some of his other victims. Not all. Not yet. But it's all moot at this point," Brian said, taking the pencil back from his wife and unwinding the spiral paper strip at its tip before striking a line through the face of the senator. "Former Senator Brandon Ashly of Tennessee. An advisor and personal friend of presidents going back to the days of Lyndon Johnson. As Joe himself told you, Liza, the senator was the high priest of the clan. Powerful. Super rich. Most dangerous. Terminating that man was a bonus we didn't count on. We have it on good authority that he was directly responsible for the mass murder via the bombings in Indochina during the late sixties and early seventies, set squarely on the shoulders of Henry Kissinger—not that he wasn't responsible, too, but something of a scapegoat in terms of recorded history."

Kim unwound a thin red cord at the top of a Manila envelope, opening the flap and withdrawing four additional black and white photographs, spreading the tetrad of attractive women beneath Robert and Liza's gaze.

"Recognize these lovely ladies?" the female detective asked.

"They were sitting with Cramer at his table in the lounge," Robert responded immediately.

"Yeah, the only four who had all their clothes on," Liza remarked.

"They're four of Sep Cramer's brides and trusted captains," Kim elaborated, rearranging the photographs in an array with Senator Ashly's photo at the top of the chart table. Beneath the statesman's picture were Sep Cramer's and Denise Holloway's faces. "Denise was to have been Sep's homeland gal while the other four did his bidding in the Mideast, we're informed. West Coast mafia chieftain, Joey Matuco, underscores the trio." Below the set, Kim placed the remaining four faces in a row. "Meet Captain Karen Carper of East Marion, housewife with two children, refined or ruthless, depending on which side of the bed she wakes up. Political analyst. Brilliant. Captain Sharon Espe of Millinocket, Maine, homemaker with an infant. Although equal in rank to the others, she is the undisputed authority. An expert with a knife and garrote. Up close and personal is how she settled her scores, it's rumored."

"So what you're saying is that if we were discovered in that fish tank, we'd be drawn and quartered," Liza posited through a grimace.

"More like filleted and then served up as some sort of bogus sushi would be my guess," Doctor Brett Cormick offered good-naturedly, returning from his nap. "A fleshy morsel served up as a canapé before indulging in the Real McCoy. Which reminds me, I better get cracking," he decided, stretching and smiling quite happily, dropping three steps down to the galley before withdrawing half a dozen three-pound lobsters from an Igloo cooler, hunting through a drawer for his stainless steel cleaver and red-winged claw-crusher.

Liza smiled. "He's really a bit eccentric," she whispered, returning her attention to the photo array. "Who's this?"

"Captain Rebecca Pace of Denton, Maryland, wife with two

degrees in political science. One grown son living in Asia. She worked in Washington as an intern for the senator before she met Cramer. And there's Captain Brenda Reece, missing for a decade before turning up in Quantico and McLean, Virginia. A real honest-to-goodness captain in the United States Marine Corps, we learned most recently. Not under the name of Reece, of course. Ties to the FBI and the CIA. Fluent in seven languages and believed to have spent the last nine years in the Middle East. One daughter in Baghdad. For reasons we won't go into right now, if at all, we want these four terminated. Succinctly put, they pose a grave danger to our national security," Kim concluded, running a fingernail across all four faces.

Liza nodded knowingly. "And you want to enlist our help."

"We'll talk some more about that after dinner," Brian answered.

"No, we'll talk about it right now," Robert Redler stated firmly. "The answer is no!"

Liza placed a palm over Robert's right hand. "Let's just relax and enjoy dinner, dear," she said demurely. "There are things we have to hear and think about," the retired schoolteacher said, gently rocking her head to the rhythm of the boat upon the waves.

Detective Kim Archer smiled appreciatively, reaching down into a boat bag and removing a checkered gray-black silk scarf encased within a clear plastic evidence bag, sliding it across the table toward Robert.

Brian went into his Lands' End canvas attaché case and produced a small transparent envelope containing several dirty-blond hairs. Likewise, he passed the item toward Robert. "Whatever you two decide," he nodded solemnly. "Whatever."

Robert Banfelder holds a BA degree in English (Cum Laude) and MA, genre Creative Writing from Queens College. He is an award-winning mystery/thriller novelist and outdoors writer. His psychological thrillers include *No Stranger Than I, The Author, The Teacher, Knots* and *Trace Evidence. The Author and The Teacher*, the first and second books in the Justin Barnes series, both received "Best Suspense Novel" accolades from NewBookReviews. *The Good Samaritans* is the final book in the Justin Barnes series.

In addition to his novels, Robert writes outdoors articles, which have appeared in numerous publications: *Nor'east Saltwater, The Fisherman, On The Water, Big Game Fishing Journal, Hana Hou! The Magazine for Hawaiian Airlines, Deer & Deer Hunting, New York Game & Fish*, to name but a few. He presently maintains a monthly online report titled North Fork Bays for *Nor'east Saltwater*. He is a member of the Long Island Outdoor Communicators Network and the New York State Outdoor Writer's Association.

Robert also co-hosts (with Donna Derasmo) Cablevision TV's *Special Interests with Bob & Donna*. They have interviewed a number of artists, entertainers, writers and consummate outdoors enthusiasts.

www.RobertBanfelder.com
Facebook @Robert Banfelder
Twitter @RBanfelder

www.ingramcontent.com/pod-product-compliance
Lightning Source LLC
Chambersburg PA
CBHW070836280626
47161CB00015B/683